"WE'RE BREAKING FREE . . ."

Geordi said, breaking off as the *Enterprise* abruptly shuddered beneath them, nearly as violently as it had when they had first encountered the energy field.

"Captain!" Geordi said tersely, "the field is strengthening. The more power we put into resisting, the stronger the field becomes. If we keep this up, we'll blow the warp engines."

"Cut power," Picard ordered. He eyed the floating hulks of dozens of derelict spacecraft of all shapes and sizes. *They might be thousands of years old,* Picard thought, *or millions.*

"They're trapped," Geordi whispered. "And we're going to be too . . ."

Look for STAR TREK Fiction from Pocket Books

#13

STAR TREK®
THE NEXT GENERATION

THE EYES OF THE BEHOLDERS

A.C. CRISPIN

POCKET BOOKS

New York   London   Toronto   Sydney   Tokyo   Singapore

An *Original* Publication of POCKET BOOKS

POCKET BOOKS, a division of Simon & Schuster Inc.
1230 Avenue of the Americas, New York, NY 10020

This book is published by Pocket Books, a division of
Simon & Schuster Inc., under exclusive license from
Paramount Pictures.

ISBN: 0-671-70010-3

First Pocket Books printing September 1990

10 9 8 7 6 5 4 3 2 1

POCKET and colophon are registered trademarks of
Simon & Schuster Inc.

Printed in the U.S.A.

This book is dedicated to my friend Irene Kress
with love and thanks
for all her understanding and help.

ACKNOWLEDGMENTS

I would like to thank all the other writers whose inspiration, encouragement and friendship proved so helpful to me while I wrote this novel, as well as during the writing of my two other Star Trek books, *Yesterday's Son* and its sequel, *Time for Yesterday*.

Special thanks go to:

Carmen Carter, who read and critiqued the first draft, and provided many invaluable insights and suggestions . . .

Howard Weinstein, who suggested that Data use the transporter to emulate Ernest Hemingway . . .

Vonda N. McIntyre, because she's always an inspiration, as well as a friend . . . and who shares with me fond memories of marmots and the RoVaCon '89 banquet . . .

Margaret Bonanno, for her insights into Vulcan maternal instincts . . .

Diane Carey, who provided me with a good laugh when I desperately needed one . . .

Peter David, for his vivid portrayal of Worf in *Strike Zone* . . .

Diane Duane (accept no substitutes!), for her Next Generation episode featuring the Traveller, which I referenced in these pages . . .

Melinda Snodgrass, for her excellent *Next Generation* episode "Measure of Man," which gave me a tremendous insight into Data's character . . .

AND, last, but assuredly not least, my editor, Kevin Ryan, for advice and encouragement.

THE EYES OF THE BEHOLDERS

Chapter One

LIEUTENANT COMMANDER Geordi La Forge, chief engineer of the starship *Enterprise,* awoke in his shipboard cabin from a sweating, heart-pounding dream of absolute blackness to the real darkness of his unassisted vision. For long moments he lay blinking and gasping, wondering whether he was, indeed, awake. As full awareness returned, he sat up in his bunk, right hand reaching unerringly for his nightstand, where his VISOR lay.

Slipping it over his eyes, he centered its sides over the bioelectronic sensing leads implanted in each temple, then pressed them quickly into place, automatically suppressing a wince of pain. It hurt to activate his vision.

Geordi was accustomed to the constant discomfort that "seeing" caused him; most of the time he was barely aware of it. He'd trained for years in biofeedback techniques that allowed him to live with the pain, master it. It was the price he paid for having a normal existence, and he paid it gladly.

But acceptance of the pain did not eliminate it,

though it was the first step in living with it. La Forge sighed as the ache took up its usual place in his temples. His darkened cabin sprang into view as the VISOR illuminated the infrared portion of the spectrum. Objects showed as wavering, varicolored shapes, depending on how they retained or reflected heat.

The engineer swung his legs out of the bunk and sat up. Then he asked the room, in a voice roughened from sleep, what time it was.

Obediently, it replied. It was still the middle of the "night" according to La Forge's duty roster.

"What day of what month?" he asked, seized by a sudden intuition about what had sparked his fear-filled dream. "Earth calendar, not stardate."

"It is September sixteenth."

On some level I must've been aware of that, La Forge thought. *Even if it wasn't consciously. Twenty-seven years ago on this date, at this time, I was experiencing my last hour of true blindness.*

Geordi vividly remembered the smells and noises of the hospital where he had awakened the morning of his surgery, a small, frightened child—frightened but nevertheless determined to undergo this new treatment the doctors said would enable him to "see."

"See?" he remembered himself asking when his parents and the doctor had first told him about the new techniques medicine had developed. He'd been holding his favorite toy, he recalled, a model of a starship. As he'd listened, his sensitive fingers had caressed its familiar sleekness, tracing every millimeter, every faint irregularity and crevice on its graceful shape. "Will I be able to see as well as everyone else?"

"In many ways," Doctor Lenske had told him solemnly, "you will be able to see *better* than everyone else."

"Well enough to go to Starfleet Academy?" Geordi

had asked, his small, sturdy body tense with sudden, unexpected hope.

"I believe so," the doctor had replied. "But . . . Geordi, I must be honest with you. There will be a price attached to your new vision. The VISOR is new, and using it will be painful for you."

The little boy's jaw had tightened. He knew what pain was—pain was when you stubbed your toe, or tripped and fell if you weren't wearing your sensory-net clothing. His fingers had tightened on his sleek little replica. "I don't care," he said quietly. "I want to go to the Academy more than anything. I want to be a Starfleet officer. I want to see."

Caught up in memory, La Forge recalled how it had felt to lie on the antigrav gurney and take that long journey down echoing halls to the operating theater. The scent of Mama's perfume had warred with the muted but still nasty smells of the hospital. Her hand, and Daddy's hand, had been clasped warm and tight around his fingers. Their touch was the last thing he recalled—that and the warmth against his eyelids that told him there was a bright light overhead.

When he'd awakened, and they'd first slipped on the VISOR, he'd screamed—partly from the pain but mostly from the disorienting shock of images that had flooded his mind, coiling and wavering and shifting. Color—to see *color!*

I wonder, Geordi thought as he stood up and padded over to his closet to pull on an off-duty pair of pants and a short-sleeved shirt, *whether what I call 'red' looks anything like what people with normal sight call 'red.'*

La Forge suspected his disturbing dream of blindness had been triggered not only by the anniversary of receiving his VISOR but also by his visit to sickbay the previous morning. Doctor Crusher had examined him, assured him that he was in the best of health, then gently asked if Geordi had made a decision about whether to keep his VISOR or to allow her and Doctor Selar to attempt to regenerate his optic nerve.

If I had normal vision, La Forge thought as he washed his face and ran a pick through his short hair, *I wouldn't feel self-conscious about the way my eyes must appear to others—especially women—when I remove my VISOR.* He felt his face grow hot when he remembered the way ill-mannered strangers had reacted to him when he was small. "Oh, the poor little thing!" one woman had gasped. And, "He can't see out of those eyes, can he?" a man had boomed, as though Geordi couldn't hear, either.

On the other hand, if he gave up his VISOR to gain normal vision, he'd lose his unique ability to "see" what "normal" people could not. Also, being blind and wearing the prosthetic device was part of who he, Geordi La Forge, *was*—as much a part of how he defined himself as his Starfleet career. Did he want to become somebody different?

La Forge knew that it would take him at least a year to have the regeneration treatments and learn to see as normal people did. He'd recently been promoted to chief engineer, and Captain Picard had commended him on his performance. Did he want anything to jeopardize that?

Geordi sighed aloud, tired of wrestling with questions that seemed to have no satisfactory answers. For a moment he considered going down to engineering, but the almost imperceptible vibration of the *Enterprise's* impulse engines assured him that they were functioning perfectly. Impulse power was all that was needed on their current assignment, while the big ship mapped and explored this relatively unknown sector.

Yeah, and don't forget that Sonya Gomez is on duty, Geordi reminded himself. *The poor kid's nervous enough already. You don't want her to think you don't trust her to stand her watch competently—that you feel the need to check up on her.*

Besides . . . he wasn't in the mood for work. He wanted to talk to someone. Not officially, it wasn't serious enough to seek out the ship's counselor, but . . . talking would help him exorcise the terror of the dream where he'd been truly *blind* again.

Pulling on a pair of soft shoes, La Forge left his cabin and turned left down the corridor. He had a hazy idea of going down to Ten-Forward and talking to Guinan. The enigmatic hostess was a good listener, and a drink would relax him.

Guinan intrigued Geordi. He'd been told that her skin color was almost the same as his, and he knew that outwardly she appeared equally human, but La Forge's unique vision let him see more than most people. He knew that Guinan was an alien—humanoid but not human. Her basal temperature and metabolic rates gave her away, along with certain other differences he could detect.

Halfway to the turbolift, though, the chief engineer halted, frowning. There were bound to be friends of his in Ten-Forward, and Geordi really wasn't in the mood for socializing with a crowd. Most of his closest friends were assigned to the same duty shift as he was, so they were undoubtedly sound asleep . . .

. . . with one exception, of course.

Smiling, La Forge turned around and walked back up the corridor to the door of a cabin and signaled it.

"Come," a voice said. The door opened and Geordi entered.

"Data, it's me," La Forge called as he walked through the bedroom to the small living area. It contained the usual furniture, with the addition of an easel. A bank of computer displays winked on the walls. On the desk there was a violin case, now pushed to one side.

Lieutenant Commander Data sat at his desk, holding some kind of short, slender instrument La Forge didn't recognize in his hand. The android was surrounded by a white-gold halo of energy, and his body shimmered orange, yellow, lime green. The colors spread out evenly over his form, instead of brightest in the trunk area, as humans appeared when he used the infrared portion of his vision. Geordi knew that the artificially created officer appeared quite human to his normally sighted crewmates, except for his pale gold complexion and glittery golden eyes, but the VISOR recorded his image quite differently.

Data glanced up as his friend entered, and he placed some sort of cap over the thing he held. "Hello, Geordi," he said in his precise, unaccented tones.

"Hi, Data. What have you got there?"

"An exact replica of an old-fashioned fountain pen," the android officer replied, holding it up.

"A *what?*"

"A fountain pen." Evidently recognizing La Forge's continued bewilderment, he added helpfully, "An instrument for writing by hand."

"You mean producing hard copy by *writing* on paper? Why would you want to do that?" La Forge asked. Inwardly, he sighed. He'd already had considerable experience with Data's sudden enthusiasms, and something told him he was about to gain more.

"To awaken my muse," Data said. "A famous twentieth-century author whose works I have been reading has stated categorically that it is impossible to produce true literature by electronic means."

This time La Forge sighed aloud. It was on the tip of his tongue to point out that not only did Data function by electronic means, but so, in the final

6

analysis, did human beings. But he restrained himself. "Uh, you mean that you're producing literature by writing it out manually?"

"I believe I said that," Data replied.

"What kind of literature?"

Something akin to pride tinged the android's voice. "I am writing a novel."

"Oh," La Forge managed, after a surprised pause. "Uh . . . that's . . . great, Data. What is it about?"

"It is a fictionalized retelling of the first days of interstellar travel. A work of epic scope, full of passion and nobility, but stylistically rendered to be accessible to a popular audience," Data explained.

"What's it called?"

"The work is as yet untitled. I am confident that inspiration regarding an appropriate title will strike before it is published."

"Published?" Geordi was nonplussed. "You've *sold* this book?"

"No, it is not complete, so I have not yet submitted it. However, when the time comes, I am certain that it will be deemed worthy of publication," Data said evenly. "After all, I have analyzed more than five hundred years of human literature down to its most basic themes and components. I am confident that I can match—if not exceed—the quality of the fiction appearing currently."

"Uh . . . yeah," La Forge said without much conviction. He'd had a friend in the Academy once, Laura Wu, who'd tried to publish several of her short stories, only to meet with rejection. Crushed, she'd abandoned her aspirations.

"Would you like me to read you the scene I am currently polishing?" Data asked.

Geordi groaned silently at the idea, remembering as he did the times that he'd tried to read and comment on Laura's efforts. Hurt feelings and mutual resentment had been the only result. "Sure," he said aloud, managing a credible amount of enthusiasm.

"Very well." Data picked up a piece of paper with a proud flourish. "Ahem," he said, attempting to theatrically clear his throat but managing only a sort of artificial gargle. "This scene takes place between Fritz and Penelope, my two protagonists. They are at Luna Starbase, beneath one of the observation domes—a most romantic setting for a love scene, do you not agree? Penelope is upset because Fritz is departing the next day aboard his ship, and she is afraid that she will never see him again." He began to read:

> "The jagged lunar mountains stabbed the blackness of the star-studded sky like tuning forks vibrating to the music of the celestial spheres. Penelope turned to Fritz with tears streaking her makeup and reddening her otherwise exquisite sapphire eyes.
>
> "'We only have tonight,' she whispered. 'Tomorrow you will be gone, and we will never see each other again.'
>
> "He took her into his arms with a strength that made her breath rush from her lungs as her diaphragm was forcibly compressed.
>
> "'I will come back,' he promised. 'Our journey may take years, but I swear that I will return to you. Will you wait, my darling?'
>
> "'I have no choice,' she said. 'When I am with you I feel transformed. My legs grow weak, my blood rushes madly through my veins, my entire body tingles from your nearness. Why is it that only you can make me feel this way?'
>
> "'Those reactions are not unique, Penelope. They are simply physiological indications of sexual arousal in the human female,' Fritz murmured as he bent

8

to possess—to plunder—her waiting lips with his own.

"She moaned as he—"

"Uh, Data," Geordi broke in, waving a hand to gain his friend's attention. "Hold on a second. I'm no writer, but something about Fritz's speech to . . . uh, Penelope, did you say her name was? Well, a human male wouldn't catalogue all those physical symptoms of . . . passion. Instead he'd just kiss her."

"But she asked him a question," Data pointed out. "When a question is posed, a reply is expected."

"Well, that's usually true, but in a case like this, old Fritz—or any man—wouldn't take the time to make a speech correcting the lady. He'd kiss her and go on from there."

Data regarded his critic with growing dismay. "He would? Are you certain?"

"Well, I don't claim to be the universe's greatest authority on lunar love scenes, but yeah, I'm sure." La Forge grinned wryly. "If you want somebody who no doubt *is* an expert, you ought to ask Commander Riker."

"I will correct that portion," Data promised solemnly. "But otherwise, what did you think of it?"

Geordi hesitated. Frankly, he'd thought it was pretty terrible. But he couldn't be truthful; he didn't want to hurt Data's feelings—assuming the android had feelings that could be injured. He certainly seemed to be almost humanly proud of his literary effort.

"Well . . ." he began, "I would definitely say it was . . . interesting. Definitely very interesting."

"Can you be more specific regarding what you liked or disliked? What emotions did it arouse in you?"

The chief engineer groaned inwardly. "Well, I—"

La Forge was rescued by a beep from the intercom

in Data's cabin. "Lieutenant Commander Data?" the voice of bridge officer, Ensign Whitedeer, followed.

"Data here," the android said.

"We are receiving a message from Starfleet Command, sir."

"Where is the captain?"

"In his quarters, sir."

"And Commander Riker?"

"On Holodeck Three, sir."

The android stood, tugging his uniform into place, and quickly capped his pen. "I am on my way to the bridge now, Ensign."

"Yes, sir."

Geordi was already halfway to the door, profoundly grateful to be relieved of the role of literary critic. "I'll go get into uniform and mosey on up to see what's cooking."

"Cooking?" Data echoed, then he nodded. "Ah, yes. You mean 'what is cooking' as in what is up, what is going down, what is shaking, what is the story, what is happening, man, what is—"

"You've got the idea, Data," La Forge called back as the door to the android officer's cabin slid open. "See you on the bridge."

When La Forge, once more clad in his dark gold and black uniform, reached the bridge, he found Commander William Riker there ahead of him. If Data had summoned Riker, it meant that the message was more than a routine communication. Geordi went over to check the displays on the engineering station on the bridge, keeping one ear cocked for any hint of what was going on.

Moments later, Captain Jean-Luc Picard himself appeared, impeccably dressed and groomed as always, but Geordi had the impression that the *Enterprise*'s commander had been sound asleep. The engineer only hoped that this mysterious message would be worth the disruption in everyone's duty schedule. Starfleet Command sometimes generated mountains from molehills.

Picard silently scanned the message, then straightened up. "Commander Riker, Mr. La Forge, Mr. Data please join me in the conference lounge room," he said, his diction impeccable as always, his tones dispassionate. "Mr. Crusher, you have the conn."

Geordi relaxed slightly as he walked toward the conference lounge. The captain seldom showed any trace of his native Gallic accent—usually only when he was deeply worried or upset. Which plainly wasn't the case now. *Obviously not a full-scale Romulan invasion,* the chief engineer concluded. *New orders, maybe. But we haven't yet finished our mapping assignment in this sector . . . which means that, whatever it is, it's pretty important to pull us away with our mission half done.*

Once seated around the table in the conference lounge located behind the main bridge, a comfortable room whose neutral furnishings were eclipsed by its stunning view of the stars, the senior bridge crew expectantly regarded their commanding officer.

"We have been ordered to investigate trouble along a newly established trade route that passes through Sector 3SR-5-42, linking Federation territory and the Klingon Empire," Picard began. "The only inhabited nearby planet is Thonolan Four, a recently settled Andorian colony. Starfleet Command has advised me that several Federation freighters have disappeared as they traversed this sector—vanished without a trace, apparently. There have been three vessels missing in the past six months."

Uh-oh, La Forge thought. *I smell trouble. This sounds like one of those "Go stick your head in the noose, guys, and find out what happens" missions.*

11

"Yesterday, the Klingon High Command lost contact with one of their ships, the Klingon cruiser *PaKathen*. We have been ordered to investigate its disappearance and, if possible, rescue the *PaKathen*."

Picard turned to Data. "Mister Data, from our present position, how long to reach Sector 3SR-5-42 at maximum cruising speed?"

"Four days and seven hours, Captain," the android replied almost instantaneously.

"We will leave by thirteen hundred hours, as soon as we have terminated operations here." Picard glanced around the room, his expression somber. "Questions or comments, anyone?"

Commander Riker nodded. "I gather that some ships have made it through this area without incident?"

"Correct, Number One."

"Then I suggest that we access the public record logs of any of those ships. Perhaps one of them noticed something that would give us a clue about what has happened to the missing ships."

"I concur, Number One. Have Commander Data implement such a search once we are under way." Picard regarded his second-in-command thoughtfully. "Commander Riker, what is the current status of our mapping mission?"

"We are"—Riker smiled ruefully—"*were* about halfway through, sir."

"Instruct your scientific teams to halt their efforts and transmit all currently completed data to Starfleet Command. Remember, we depart within the hour." Picard inclined his head at his senior staff. "Dismissed."

Lieutenant Selar watched the small, blue-skinned child wearing the shimmering black mesh over her short tabard walk hesitantly toward a bulkhead, then suddenly halt. "Distance from the wall?" Selar demanded.

"One point three meters, just as you said," the little girl reported.

"Excellent," Selar said. "You are gaining confidence."

"It's getting easier each time to combine what my sensor net reports with what I sense with my antennae. This sensory net is much better than my old one." The child turned to face the Vulcan doctor, her pale eyes staring fixedly over Selar's head. "Thank you for teaching me to use it, Doctor Selar."

The Vulcan shook her head, momentarily forgetting that the Andorian child couldn't see her gesture. "It is my job, Thala. One does not thank another for the simple performance of one's duty."

The child grinned suddenly, impishly. "You've spent extra time with me, and I know it. I heard Doctor Crusher say so during my last examination. She thought I wasn't listening, but I was."

Selar raised an eyebrow in surprise. "I shall have to caution Doctor Crusher about the acuity of your hearing."

The little girl's blue-skinned features crumpled suddenly beneath her cottony white hair and antennae. "Oh, no, I've done it again, haven't I? What Wesley calls letting my mouth move in warp drive while my mind is still in impulse."

The Vulcan woman thought privately that the image was particularly apt, but her amusement did not show on her well-schooled countenance. "The more you are able to practice using the sensory net before we dock at the nearest Starbase and you take transport for your home world, the better you will be able to manage."

Thala nodded silently, tight-lipped as any Vulcan. Momentarily, Selar regretted mentioning the child's approaching departure, but she steeled herself. Thala had to become accustomed to the idea that she would be leaving soon, to grow up on a planet she had never seen.

The Andorian child had been born in space. Her father, Thev, had been an Andorian diplomat on an extended goodwill voyage. Thala's mother, a linguistics expert, had died six years ago when her baby was only a year old, of a virus the linguist had contracted. The child's father had died five weeks ago, one of eighteen people to perish during the Borg attack.

Now Thala was alone, and regulations decreed that she must be sent back to her family at the earliest opportunity.

Ever since Thev's death, Lieutenant Selar had tried to tell herself that Thala would be better off with her relatives, but she was concerned about the child's future. Life aboard a starship was far different from life on a planet—especially a place like the Andorian homeworld.

Andorians were a passionate race, not as technologically or as socially advanced as Vulcans or even Terrans. They clung to ancient traditions that were steeped in their barbaric, bloody past. Weaknesses or disabilities were regarded not with toleration but as personal and familial shame. Some Andorian clans, it was whispered, still exposed children who were born less than perfect. It was certainly true that Selar, in her fifteen years of medical practice with Starfleet, had never seen an Andorian who was in any way handicapped.

How would Thala be regarded by her people? Within the past year, Selar, working first with Doctor Pulaski and then with the returned Doctor Crusher, had been testing and evaluating Thala to receive a VISOR much like the one Lieutenant Commander La Forge wore. The implantation of the sensors and calibrations of a VISOR had never been done for an

Andorian. Selar had been doing much of the work herself, with assistance and advice from La Forge.

If Thala left, Selar wondered, would her clan make sure the child was given the best of medical care so she would one day "see" as the chief engineer could? Privately, the Vulcan doubted it.

And there was something else . . . something Selar had worked closely with Doctor Pulaski on developing: bioelectronic replacements for body parts. They had already come up with a way to give Lieutenant Commander La Forge bioelectronic eyes that would give him a normal appearance—assuming he did not wish to have the optic nerve regeneration. But so far the chief engineer had declined, because giving up his VISOR would mean losing a significant percentage of the range of his unique vision.

But for Thala, who had never grown up with the expanded vision provided by a VISOR, might not the bioelectronic eyes be ideal? They would look and function more like normal vision, although allowing her to "see" more spectra. And with them the little Andorian girl would not have to live with the constant pain that La Forge experienced.

Selar sighed aloud, and Thala's head turned toward her in surprise. "Are you tired, Doctor? We can end the lesson if you wish."

"No, not at all," the Vulcan said. "But at the moment it is time for lunch." She stood up gracefully, a tall, slender woman who wore her dark hair cropped short, bangs nearly touching her slanting eyebrows, revealing her elegantly pointed ears. The doctor was forty, still young as her people reckoned age, and her clean-cut features were attractive despite their lack of mobility.

"Yes, I'm hungry," Thala said. She hesitated, then asked quietly, "Will I see you for another lesson tomorrow, Doctor?"

Selar hesitated, noting the admirably restrained eagerness in the child's expression. "I believe so," she said. "Unless we experience some kind of unexpected emergency in sickbay." Something in the child's wistful expression made her ask, "Would you like to accompany me to Ten-Forward for lunch? I have no other plans."

"Could I?" Thala breathed, then she smiled broadly, her antennae twitching with excitement. "That would be wonderful! Thank you so much, Doctor!"

"There is no need to thank me," Selar said. "We both must eat, and pleasant companionship at meals promotes good digestion." The child started toward her, her steps still rather uncertain. *She has not yet become comfortable in the use of her new net,* the Vulcan thought. *It would not do to have her progress set back by a stumble or fall at this stage.*

So when Thala reached her, the doctor held out her hand. "Come, we'll go up together, then."

Small blue fingers closed around sallow green-tinged ones, and they left the child's cabin together and started down the wide corridor, with Selar unobtrusively steering her small charge. Through the physical contact, the doctor could telepathically sense her companion's pleasure and excitement at the prospect of spending more time together.

"After lunch, you can bring me up to date on how your studies have been progressing," the Vulcan said as they walked.

Thala nodded. "I've been studying hard, and this new net is going to make it even easier to work with the computer, Doctor."

"We have known each other for one point four years now," Selar observed, looking down at the little girl's earnest features. "Haven't we?"

"That's true," Thala agreed gravely. "Ever since

you began working with Doctor Pulaski to help me see better. I was just a little kid then," she said, drawing herself up to her full height.

Selar's mouth twitched slightly. "And now you are of a vast age, correct?" Thala nodded. "In that case, since we are now nearly contemporaries, perhaps it is time for you to begin calling me by my name. Could you call me Selar, do you think?"

The child inclined her head formally, and her grasp on her teacher's hand tightened. "I would be honored, Selar," she said softly.

Lieutenant Commander Data sat before the computer console in his cabin, going over the logs of all ships that had traversed Sector 3SR-5-42 within the past five years. The trade route between Thonolan Four and the Federation had not existed until last year, nor had this new one between the Federation and the Klingon Empire, but some ships had entered that sector, mostly small cruisers and independent freighters.

And, as Data had just discovered, 15.4 percent of those ships had not been heard from again.

Space travel was, by its nature, still a risky occupation, but that percentage was still higher than could be accounted for by the ordinary perils of interstellar travel, Data knew. But none of the logs of the ships that *had* made it through safely reported anything out of the ordinary.

The android scanned the log files one more time, searching for any scrap of information that he could present to Picard, but there was nothing. *Renegade Gatherers?* he speculated, then dismissed the idea. That far from the established space lanes, their presence was unlikely. Any cargo they could steal would not be worth the fuel or travel time necessary to resell it on a receptive world—such as Arcturus Six—where the planetary government turned a blind eye to underworld fencing and credit-laundering activities.

Data's pale features remained serene as he got up from his chair and paced slowly around his cabin. Many humans claimed that movement helped them to think more clearly. The android was skeptical but willing to allow the notion an empirical test. Perhaps he should get out his meerschaum pipe and his deerstalker hat from his Sherlock Holmes adventures on the holodeck.

As he strode past his desk, Data saw the fountain pen and pages covered with his own copybook-perfect script. A sudden memory of his talk with La Forge flashed through the android's mind. Geordi had not seemed as enthusiastic about Data's book as the aspiring author had hoped he'd be. Perhaps the engineer was not a connoisseur of fiction.

Or perhaps the writing was not good. Perhaps, as in so many other things, Data had failed to grasp some intangible *something* that would make his work understandable and appealing to a human audience. It was possible that he had failed yet again.

The android decided that he needed another opinion—or perhaps two or three.

Resolutely he returned his attention back to reviewing all the records he had accessed in his search, verifying that he had missed nothing, overlooked nothing. His positronic brain was extremely thorough and accurate, but Data was not a computer, and it was remotely possible for him to make an error.

But not this time, he concluded a minute or so later. He had missed nothing, and there was not enough information to permit a hypothesis, even a tentative one.

Data left his cabin and headed resolutely for the bridge to make his report to the captain. Picard would not be pleased, he knew, though he would not blame his android officer. Jean-Luc Picard expected results when results were possible, and he brooked no excuses, but he was a fair man who could recognize a genuine mystery when he was confronted with one.

Which is what they were faced with now. Something was out there, but there was no way to speculate on what that something might be. The *Enterprise* and her crew would have to find out by experience.

Chapter Two

LIEUTENANT SELAR sat alone in her cabin, rereading the personal communication that had come in on the subspace channel before the *Enterprise* had gone into warp drive, heading for their new priority assignment. The message read:

> In recognition of commendable research publications and extensive experience in development of bioelectronic prostheses, most particularly in the field of xenobiology, the Directors of the Vulcan Science Academy extend to Selar, current rank Starfleet Lieutenant, Medical Corps, current assignment U.S.S. *Enterprise,* NCC-1701-D, an invitation to become Head of Bioelectronic Research at Vulcan Science Academy.

The Vulcan doctor had to firmly repress a surge of pure egotistical pride as she finished the communiqué for the third time. Opportunities such as this came to most people but once in a lifetime, if that. Logically, she should accept the post with alacrity.

Selar thought of what it would be like to go back to Vulcan after fifteen years away. She'd been contented and satisfied with her life aboard the starship—the lieutenant knew she was doing essential work, she was needed, and being useful was a goal most Vulcans had aspired to since the days of Surak, who had said: "Life without a beneficial purpose is empty existence. You ask me what is a beneficial purpose? It is one that counters the progression of entropy in the universe."

But as head of bioelectronic research at the Vulcan Science Academy, she would be able to do much more. She could help develop procedures for implanting bioelectronic prostheses in different species, so there would be established methods for physicians to refer to throughout Starfleet and the Federation. Children such as Thala could be helped, whether or not they were fortunate enough to live on board a starship.

Selar rose from her seat and moved slowly around her cabin, glancing over the art objects and curiosities she had gathered during her fifteen years in Starfleet. She had joined only a few days after completing her residency at medical school—and she hadn't been back since.

Her fingers tightened on a polished piece of petrified wood from Komeera Seven. What would it be like to return to her native soil? See her family again? Would they finally be able to put the past behind them? Would *she?*

Selar's mouth tightened as she envisioned the faces of her father, mother, grandparents, cousins. Holo images were limited in what they revealed. Would they all have changed as greatly as she had?

The lieutenant came from a family that was very traditional; her clan was an old one, proud of its lineage. They looked with disapproval on many of the changes that had come to Vulcan since their world had

joined the Federation. As with most Vulcan tradition-
alist families, Selar had been betrothed at age seven,
mind-linked to a boy who would one day become her
husband. The girl's betrothal to Sukat had been
regarded by her family as a most promising match.
Sukat's family, while not as old as theirs, was far more
wealthy and influential.

As the two children grew, they saw each other
occasionally, but, aside from the tenuous, easily ignored mental bonding they shared, she knew little of
the boy she would one day marry in the *Koon-ut
kal-if-fee*. Sukat was simply part of the distant future,
far removed from her day-to-day existence.

From her earliest days Selar had wanted to be a
healer. Saving lives and relieving suffering seemed to
her to be the noblest of life missions. She studied
hard, proving to be an exceptional student, even for a
Vulcan. When she was seventeen, she was accepted by
a good school and began her medical studies.

Within a year, Sukat also began courses at her
school. She saw him frequently, for they shared a
number of classes and lab periods, and they ate either
the noon meal or the evening one together nearly
every day. For the first time, Selar grew to know her
betrothed . . .

. . . and found that she did not *like* Sukat. The
thought of spending fifteen or sixteen decades as his
wife was intolerable.

Their natures were simply not compatible. Selar
had a lively curiosity about other species, including
humans, and an appreciation for the differences between cultures. Xenobiology fascinated her. She re-
spected and adhered to the tenets of IDIC, the Vulcan
credo that urged reverence for Infinite Diversity in
Infinite Combinations.

Sukat, on the other hand, regarded beings who were
not Vulcans as automatically inferior, intellectually,

physically, and ethically. In many instances he was correct in his belief, Selar acknowledged, but that did not rescue him from being what humans hundreds of years ago would have called a bigot.

Selar wanted to see faraway planets and the wonders between the stars, while Sukat regarded travel as an infrequent but sometimes necessary unpleasantness.

The only trait they shared was their ambition. Selar envisioned herself as a leader in her field someday, and so did Sukat. But Selar had a slight edge as a student, and, once both began their residencies, she achieved higher praise from her mentors. Sukat reacted to his wife-to-be's success as if she had deliberately set out to make him look bad by comparison. He never, by word or deed, revealed that this was how he felt, but Selar knew.

During the final year of their betrothal, Sukat confided to his intended his desire for a large family and that he felt delays in childbearing in order to further the wife's career were ill advised. After all, he pointed out, it was much more logical for females to pursue their careers once children were grown to the age of independence, rather than have to interrupt them at a crucial point for the increased responsibility of child rearing.

Selar did not agree. It seemed to her that it would be preferable for her to establish a foothold in her own career first, then for both parents to share in the child-rearing responsibilities. But she did not voice her opinion. By now she knew without asking how Sukat reacted to people who did not agree with him.

Ultimately, as their final graduation to the title of "Healer" loomed ahead, and with it their scheduled wedding, Selar knew that she could not go through with the marriage.

Dispassionately, she informed her family of her

decision. They were as disappointed as she had fore-
seen. Her marriage to Sukat was eminently logical,
they reminded her. They were a perfect match in
every way—socially, educationally, genetically. Selar
was told that she was being foolish—all her work with
those humans must have contaminated her.

The young Vulcan was obdurate, however. She
would not marry Sukat. She went to his family and
told them so. They reacted, not with disappointment,
but with scorn and ill-concealed relief that Sukat had
not married such an illogical, immature person.

Tight-lipped and stony-eyed, Selar left their
beautifully appointed home and went to Sukat's
apartment to speak with him. Memories of that visit
were still vivid in her mind, not one whit dimmed by
the passage of years . . .

*Sukat stared at her blankly, but through their bond
she could feel his incredulous disappointment. "There
must be some misunderstanding," he said flatly, his
handsome features darkening. "One does not sever a
bonding for no reason."*

"I have a reason," she replied steadily.

*"But you have just said that I am fully acceptable,
physically and mentally, and that I should not regard
this decision as reflecting upon my desirability as a
prospective mate," he said, sounding both irritated and
slightly shaken. "If that is true, then what possible
reason for your rejection could there be?"*

"I have a reason," Selar repeated softly.

*"May I know this reason?" he inquired, cold arro-
gance in his voice. Through the bond she could feel his
disapproval.*

*"It is nothing to do with you, only with me, so I did
not think it relevant to relate why I do not wish to
marry you," she said after a moment.*

"Nevertheless, I wish to know. It is my right," he insisted.

"Very well," she said. For the first time she hesitated, her eyes falling before his intent stare. *"I do not believe we would be . . . compatible,"* she murmured.

"Compatible?" Sukat raised an eyebrow. *"What has compatibility to do with anything? You sound like a human, with all their prating about love! What an illogical . . ."* He groped for words. *"Utterly . . . ridiculous . . . notion!"*

"I do not believe it is ridiculous or illogical for a husband and wife to be comfortable and content in each other's company," she maintained. *"I believe it is essential for their well-being, and for the welfare of their offspring."*

"I am comfortable with you."

The moment had come. She'd hoped he wouldn't push her to this extent; but he had, there was no remedy save the truth. *"But I am not comfortable in your presence,"* she announced bluntly. *"When we are together I wish only to be apart from you. The idea of . . . physical intimacy . . . between us is not one I wish to contemplate."* As she finished, Selar longed for this interview to be over, to be outside, under the clear sky, tinged redder than ever with the rising of Vulcan's companion planet.

"How can you say such things?" he demanded. *"You told me yourself that I am one whom most females would regard as extremely desirable. Your reaction is totally illogical."*

"Perhaps my reaction is illogical, Sukat," she admitted. *"If so, so be it. I cannot marry you. Let us leave it at that."*

"You are a fool, T'Para," he said coldly. *"I am well rid of you."*

"That is not my name anymore," she replied,

scarcely noticing the insult, so relieved was she that this interview was almost concluded. "The 't' prefix is only suitable for a bonded woman, and I am no longer one. I have selected a new name, to take with me on my new career in the Starfleet Medical Corps. As of tomorrow I will be Ensign Selar. I am going to break the bond now. I request that you do likewise."

Without another word, she reached inside her own mind, knowing that Sukat was angered enough to obey, and severed the mental linkage. Then, feeling oddly naked, but intoxicatingly free, she turned and walked away . . .

Selar came out of her reverie with a start at the sound of her intercom. Mentally chastising herself for giving in to old memories, she pressed the switch to activate it. "Lieutenant Selar here."

Doctor Beverly Crusher's beautiful features, crowned with hair the color of Vulcan's sky, filled her screen. "Selar, I've just received some bad news concerning Thala," she began without preamble.

The Vulcan fought down a surge of anxiety, habit born of years of control keeping her features serene. "Has she been hurt?"

"Oh, no, nothing of the sort," Crusher reassured her. "I'm sorry, I expressed it badly. Physically Thala is fine. But I just received a message from her family concerning her."

"Yes?"

"Her clan doesn't want her. They said they had no facilities for the care of a disabled child." Beverly Crusher's mouth tightened bitterly. "They were very blunt about it. They don't want Thala, and they don't give a damn about what happens to her."

"What do regulations dictate in a case such as this?"

The auburn-haired doctor sighed. "I'm afraid

they're quite specific. If there is no family to return the child to, she is to be taken to the nearest world containing a majority population of her people and handed over to the planetary authorities as an orphan." She shook her head. "In Thala's case, that would be Thonolan Four, I suppose."

Selar experienced a pang of distress at the thought that within days she might never see the little girl again. "But the people on Thonolan Four are hardly likely to welcome her, either," she pointed out.

"But they would have to take her. I suppose she'd wind up in some kind of foster care."

"Or an institution," Selar said bluntly.

"I hope not." Crusher shuddered at the thought. "Oh, God, I hope not. Thala's such a bright little thing!"

"Is there any legal alternative?" Selar asked. "If someone were willing to pay her passage to Earth—or Vulcan, for that matter, would that be permitted? Even though Thala has no family there, I can assure you that institutional facilities on Vulcan would be far preferable to any found on Thonolan Four—or any Andorian world. Vulcans value children, and Thala would be no exception. The child's mind would be challenged on my world. She would receive good care and excellent schooling."

"I don't know whether sending her elsewhere would be permitted or not," Crusher said wearily. "I can ask Lieutenant Greenstein. He's the regulations expert."

"Please do so," Selar said. "In the meantime, I suggest we say nothing of this to Thala. There is no need to frighten her with our concerns for her future."

"I quite agree."

Long after Beverly Crusher's image had faded from her viewer, Selar stood staring at the blank screen. *It is not fair,* she thought, her mind filled with Thala's image as she remembered it from yesterday, laughing as she ate her dessert. A smudge of orange sherbet beside her mouth had contrasted ridiculously with her blue skin. *You have so much to offer, if only they would give you a chance* . . .

The Vulcan doctor sighed, reminding herself that the universe was not, and never had been, known for its fairness.

"Commander Riker . . . excuse me?" Data's voice reached the preoccupied first officer just as the turbolift's doors began to close.

The tall man, whose handsome features were enhanced, not obscured, by the beard he wore, turned at the hail. "Lift hold," he ordered. "Doors open." The lift obeyed. "Sorry, Data," William Riker said as the android joined him in the turbolift. "I was . . . thinking. Resume," he added, to the lift.

"I quite understand," Data said as they whizzed along. "I, too, have been puzzling over what may await us at our destination."

"It's the wrong quadrant for Gatherers and too far from the neutral zone to be Romulans. Renegade Klingons?" Riker guessed. "Maybe they dispatched more of those sleeper ships, in addition to the one Worf and K'ehleyr were able to head off at the pass."

"Perhaps," Data said. "But if so, why have they not left that sector? Why simply prey on a few merchant ships? Klingon honor of a century ago would demand an assault on Federation space and Federation vessels."

Riker shrugged. "You're right." The turbolift stopped. "I'm heading to engineering for an inspection," Riker said. "Where are you going?"

"At the moment, nowhere in particular," Data replied. Will Riker noticed that he was carrying something folded in one hand. "I suppose that I will go up to the bridge, since I will be on watch in an hour.

But, Commander . . ." The android trailed off with an almost human hesitation.

Riker regarded him curiously. "Something on your mind, Data? I mean, besides our mission?"

"Frankly, yes, sir." The android seemed to brace himself. "I would like your opinion on a piece of fiction."

"I'm not the best-versed person in literature, Data," Riker cautioned. "The captain is much better read than I am."

Riker and Data left the turbolift and started slowly up the corridor together. "I do not need advice on selecting reading material, sir," Data said. "The writing in question is my own."

"Oh," Will said. Hearing the lack of enthusiasm in his own voice, he amended heartily, "Well, it's an honor to have a budding author in our midst. What did you want me to do?"

The android handed Riker a piece of paper. "Simply read this and render me your truthful opinion."

The *Enterprise's* second-in-command leaned against the bulkhead as he slowly read the handwritten scene. He rubbed thoughtfully at his jaw as he searched for words, then said finally, "Well, without having read the entire thing, I can't be too definitive . . ."

"I would be pleased to give you as much as I have written so far," offered Data quickly.

Riker cleared his throat, searching for words. "Uh . . . Data . . . I'm extremely flattered, of course. But things are a little busy right now, with this unknown menace in Sector 3SR-5-42. You understand . . ."

"Of course, Commander," the android said equably. "However, you still have not given me your initial reaction to my scene."

"Oh . . . well. Yes, of course. I found it very interesting, Data. Your use of language was extremely . . .

distinctive." With a surge of honesty, Riker added, "But that kind of love scene . . . well, that's not really the style of thing I usually select for my own reading. I enjoy a more . . . overtly masculine style of storytelling, I guess you'd say."

"Such as?"

"Well, Riverton is one of my favorites. And of course Hemingway. *A Farewell to Arms* and *For Whom the Bell Tolls*—he was definitely a master. Great stuff."

"I . . . see," Data said. "Thank you, Commander. You have given me much to consider. Perhaps some rewriting . . ."

Riker clapped the android on the shoulder. "Keep at it, Data," he said in a hearty man-to-man voice. "All great authors learn the value of rewriting, I'm sure."

The commander headed down the corridor toward engineering, feeling a nagging prickle of guilt and a surge of pity. *I couldn't say it was bad,* he told himself. *That would have crushed him.* Riker sighed, remembering the first time he'd ever met Data. *Poor Pinocchio . . .*

"Message coming in from Starfleet Command, Captain Picard," said Ensign Whitedeer.

"Thank you, Ensign," Picard said. "I will receive it in my ready room."

Rising to his feet, he strode across the bridge and entered his own private sanctum. Picard stood before his ready room window for a second, his slim, elegant body outlined against the blackness and the starstreaks. The captain was bald, with a prominent, high-bridged nose and penetrating hazel eyes. He had a rather imperious face, one that would not have looked out of place on a Roman emperor, but the haughtiness was softened by a suggestion of humor around the eyes and mouth.

But at the moment, the captain was feeling anything but humorous. Seating himself at his computer link, he instructed Whitedeer to relay the message.

The captain's mouth tightened as he scanned. The *Marco Polo,* a Federation-registered trading vessel, had entered Sector 3SR-5-42 yesterday and had been expected to dock at Thonolan Four's space station six hours ago.

But now the ship was definitely overdue, and the subspace transmitters at Thonolan Four reported that they had lost contact with the freighter—apparently contact had simply ceased. There had been no previous indication from the trader that anything was out of the ordinary.

Now the *Enterprise* was ordered to search for and rescue the *Marco Polo* as well. Jean-Luc Picard gazed across his private sanctum and allowed himself a deep sigh. In his years in space he'd developed certain . . . instincts . . . that he seldom acknowledged openly. Generally, he made all his decisions by reasoned thought, but there was that one-in-a-hundred situation where reason proved inadequate and one had to rely on human intuition.

Picard experienced a sudden sense of foreboding that sent a chill tiptoeing down his spine. *Could this prove to be our last mission?* he wondered uneasily, glancing around him at this magnificent vessel that had been entrusted to him. He watched his colorful exotic fish swim in the circular aquarium, then his gaze wandered to the model of the *Stargazer. After losing the* Stargazer, *I cannot ever again lose my ship. To do so would be to lose myself.*

He sighed, then heard the door chime. Picard looked up. "Come!" he called. When he saw the identity of his visitor, he smiled. "I've been expecting you."

Ship's Counselor Deanna Troi smiled gently at the captain, her exotically black Betazed eyes sympathetic. "You know, when you are this troubled, that I cannot help but be aware of your feelings," she reminded him in her gentle, musically accented voice. She was a stunning woman with a perfect figure and masses of black hair held back from her face by a jeweled band.

"I know," he agreed. "Counselor, another ship has gone missing. A freighter this time. Federation registry. The *Marco Polo*."

"Disturbing news," she said, regarding him intently with her ebony eyes. "But your unease does not stem solely from that. You are puzzled by something . . ."

Picard nodded. "The *Marco Polo* was carrying a shipment of seed grain on its way to Thonolan Four. *Feleen* seed that had been especially modified to grow in Thonolan's soil, which is higher in potassium than other Andorian worlds."

"And?" she prompted when the captain hesitated and then lapsed into silence, scowling at his steepled fingers, deep in thought.

He started, as though only now remembering that she was there. "What—oh, yes, sorry, Counselor. I'm puzzled by what anyone would want with that particular ship. They couldn't sell its stolen cargo anywhere else—that *feleen* seed would be worthless on another world. It wouldn't grow. And if the thief attempted to sell it to the Thonolans, they would know then who had made off with the *Marco Polo*."

"You are operating under the assumption that these disappearances are caused by pirates or similar foul play?"

"I *was* operating under that theory, yes. But now all

that's changed," Picard said heavily. "I've been forced to scrap the most plausible theory, because it has now become not only implausible but impractical. And thieves, whatever their moral failings, are usually practical to a fault."

"So that leaves you with what?"

"I don't know. I cannot imagine Romulans straying that far out of their space and preying openly on Federation vessels. That would be an act of war, and they have given no indication that they are ready for open conflict at this time."

"Ferengi?" Troi guessed doubtfully.

Picard shook his head. "They would never capture a vessel whose cargo was worthless to them. It would go against their deepest convictions and desire for profit."

"So what does that leave us with?" asked the counselor, as if she already knew the answer.

The captain nodded confirmation. "If it's not someone or something we know, then it must, by definition, be alien. Quite possibly something never encountered before. Something possibly hostile . . . and, it seems, deadly."

"A force of nature?"

"Some kind of previously unknown space phenomenon, you mean?" Picard drummed his fingertips on the polished surface before him. "Perhaps . . ."

"But you think not," Troi said, reading his hesitation with the experience of a trained observer.

"I don't know!" Picard betrayed his frustration momentarily, then his customary calm descended again. "But I think not, Deanna. Instead my . . . instincts, I suppose you would call them, tell me we should prepare to fulfill this ship's primary purpose."

"Alien contact."

"Yes. Except that in this case this particular alien has eight strikes—or lost ships—against it. I don't intend to allow the *Enterprise* to become the ninth."

The counselor nodded sympathetically. "It is a mystery, Captain. One worthy of your Dixon Hill, it seems to me."

One corner of the captain's mouth went up in a reminiscent half-smile. "Ah, yes. Perhaps I would do better investigating the problem if I assumed my hat and trenchcoat."

Troi smiled impishly, her black eyes sparkling. "In that case, sir, it would be only fair to allow Commander Data to get out that ridiculous hat he calls a deerstalker and that smelly pipe."

Picard's smile widened, and he waved the air before his face, his nose wrinkling at the memory. "The hat I could perhaps countenance," he said. "But that pipe constitutes a menace to the environmental systems. Scratch Dixon Hill, as well. I will have to solve this one as Jean-Luc Picard."

The captain's expression sobered, hardened. "And solve it I will, Counselor," he finished softly.

Chapter Three

"ENTERING SECTOR 3SR-5-42, Captain," Acting Ensign Wesley Crusher announced. The bridge crew glanced up from their tasks at the stars streaking by in rainbow-hued trails.

"Reduce speed to warp one, Mister Crusher."

"Aye, sir." The young helmsman touched the huge starship's control panel, and obediently, the mammoth vessel slowed her headlong rush. "Warp one, Captain."

Jean-Luc Picard sat back in his contoured command seat in the center of the bridge, Ship's Counselor Deanna Troi in her usual position to his left. "Very good, Mister Crusher." Picard turned his gaze to his android officer, who sat in his accustomed position at the Ops console beside Wesley. "Mister Data, at our present speed, how long before we reach the last recorded position of the *Marco Polo?*"

"One hour and seventeen minutes, Captain," Data said. His abnormally pale features appeared even more inhuman in the bright lights of the bridge. "I am conducting long-range sensor scans as ordered, sir."

"Thank you, Mister Data. And how long before we will reach the vicinity of the *PaKathen?*"

"That ship's last recorded position was relatively close to the coordinates where the *Marco Polo* lost contact, sir. About half a light-year. I cannot be more precise than that, because the *PaKathen* was not transmitting when it vanished, so the Klingon vessel's precise location remains unknown."

"I see . . ." The captain thought for a moment, then straightened in his command seat. "Mister Crusher, prepare a sublight search pattern that encompasses both sets of coordinates with a point-five light-year overlap as a margin for error. Ensure that it allows for both minimum search time and maximum fuel economy."

"Yes, Captain!" Wesley responded eagerly. Immediately the teenager began communing with the computer, his thin, handsome young features taking on the faraway expression he customarily wore while working to solve some abstract problem, be it homework or the piloting of the great ship. *He's so much like his father,* Picard thought. *Jack used to get that same intent expression whenever he was faced with a challenge—and the more difficult that challenge was, the better he liked it.*

A small, fond smile touched the captain's mouth as he regarded the brown head bent so earnestly over the computer console. Then he realized that Troi was watching him with a faint, knowing smile of her own, so he hastily adjusted his features.

"Mister Data," he said briskly, "do you have that information on the *Marco Polo* that I requested?"

"Yes, Captain, I do." The android officer swiveled to face his commanding officer. "Shall I put it on the main viewer, sir?"

"Please do so, Mister Data."

Data pressed a button on his Ops console, and a

36

schematic of a ship took the place of the starfield on the main viewscreen. The ship was a bulky freight carrier, lacking the *Enterprise's* sleek lines. Below its small saucer section, the vessel's cargo holds bulged gravidly. "The *Marco Polo* is a class-one freighter, Captain," Data said, his voice falling into his "lecture mode." "Designed to ship agricultural products and luxury items, it has a crew complement of forty-three. Its cargo holds can carry a payload of—"

"I am familiar with the cargo capacity of class-one freighters, Mister Data," the captain interrupted. "How old is this particular ship?"

"It was originally launched ninety-three years ago, sir, but it was completely refitted thirty-one years ago."

"Still rather an antique," the captain said, more to himself than to anyone on the bridge. He rubbed his chin thoughtfully. "With a ship that old, there should be a fair amount of ion leakage from her engines."

"I would surmise that you are correct, Captain."

"We may be able to pick up an ion trail, then. Scan for it, Mister Data."

"Yes, Captain."

"Selar, am I going to have to leave you and Doctor Crusher and my friends soon?" Thala asked hesitantly. "Are my relatives going to come and take me away from here?"

The Vulcan doctor raised an eyebrow at the little girl's questions. She and the Andorian child were sitting together in the doctor's quarters, listening to one of Selar's favorite human composers, Johann Sebastian Bach. In the Vulcan's opinion, Bach was the human genius who had best understood the value of understatement, of order, of emotion controlled and channeled into the production of beauty. Listening to Bach often helped her sort through her problems, as even the music played by Vulcan composers on Vulcan harps could not.

Thala also enjoyed human classical music, but of a very different character. *Her* favorite Earth composer was Elvis Presley.

Reaching over to the computer link, Selar muted the music to a background murmur. "Why do you ask, Thala?"

"Because you and Doctor Crusher told me that my relatives on my homeworld had to decide what to do with me, and that I wouldn't be able to live on the starship anymore. But that was days and days and *days* ago, and neither of you has said anything since." The child's unseeing eyes stared over Selar's left shoulder, but the healer had a sudden disconcerting feeling that the little girl could read her in ways a sighted person could not.

Her suspicion was confirmed a moment later when Thala added, "And I can tell that you've been worried about me lately."

"You have been . . . often . . . in my thoughts lately," Selar affirmed slowly. "It is true that I have been concerned about your fate."

"Why?"

The Vulcan stood up and paced slowly across her quarters, thinking, *Thala is an imaginative child, for all her practicality. Her imaginings by now may well be worse than the actual situation. And I cannot lie to her. I am a Vulcan.* She halted before the small, scarlet-curtained niche with its traditional firepot and chose her words carefully. "When you first learned that you would have to leave the *Enterprise* and possibly travel to your homeworld, to live with relatives that you have never seen, do you remember what you said, Thala?"

"Yes," the little girl replied steadily. "I said that I didn't want to go and live with strangers, even if they were people who are related to me."

"Yes. Well, when Doctor Crusher contacted your clan, apparently your relatives expressed much the same reaction." Selar swung around to face the child, waiting to see whether disappointment would fill her features. But they remained as blank as any adult Vulcan's.

"Well, I don't blame them for not wanting me. I don't want them, either," Thala said. "It's not as though I *know* them or anything."

"That is true," Selar agreed.

The child considered for a moment more, then her expression brightened. "If they don't want me, then does that mean I can stay with you on the starship, Selar?"

"I do not know at this point what will happen, Thala," the Vulcan said carefully. "I may not be remaining on the *Enterprise* myself."

"What do you mean?" Thala asked blankly.

"I have been offered a position on my homeworld with the Vulcan Science Academy, as a head of research. It is a very good position, and I am considering accepting it."

For the first time in weeks, the child showed real dismay. "You'll be *leaving?* Oh, no! If you leave, I'd never see you again!" She began rocking back and forth on her seat, huddling into herself. Andorians did not weep—they had no tear ducts—but a thin, keening sound came from deep in her throat.

Selar's mouth tightened, and she hesitated, wondering whether she should summon Beverly to deal with this. Emotional upsets were not something she felt competent to treat. Thala's grief at the thought of parting from her was obvious. The entire episode disquieted the Vulcan more than she would admit, even to herself.

After a long minute's hesitation, though, she realized that she could not just stand by and do nothing. Walking back to the child, she hesitantly put a hand on her head, between the little antennae, feeling the fluffy down of the white hair, the small, round, warm skull beneath it. Something twisted inside her when she felt the child's grief. "Thala," she said softly, projecting calm and comfort as strongly as she could. "Please, do not go on like this. You will find new friends, wherever you go . . ."

"But they won't be *you,*" the child gasped between those small keening wails.

"Thala, listen to me." Selar kept her voice soft but allowed a note of authority to enter it. "Are you listening?"

"Yes . . ."

"I swear to you on my honor that I will not leave the *Enterprise* before I see you settled. Do you understand? I will not accept this position until arrangements have been made to safely deliver you to your new home, wherever that may be." She thought of what a lengthy delay might mean to her chances of taking the position and resolutely squelched the thought. *Someone* had to take the responsibility for seeing that Thala was properly cared for, and she was the child's physician and teacher. It was her duty.

"You . . . promise?"

"I have just said so."

Small blue fingers reached up and tightened around her own. "Thank you, Selar."

"Now, try not to worry. Doctor Crusher and I are doing everything possible to ensure your well-being."

"I know."

Selar heard the tremor in the small voice, but, seeing that Thala was trying to regain her composure, she overlooked it. The Vulcan also ignored her own small surge of relief that the decision brought—relief that she could now delay even further the day of

reckoning when she would have to face her family—
and Sukat and his family—back on Vulcan.

"I don't know, Sonya," Geordi La Forge said to the
young olive-skinned woman who was checking
readouts on the *Enterprise*'s warp engines under his
supervision. "This entire assignment gives me the
creeps. Ships that are there one moment, gone the
next—I don't like the sound of it."

Ensign Gomez pushed back a lock of her shoulder-
length dark hair, then made a notation in the engineering log. "It's probably just some renegade Ferengi
or pirates or something. Maybe outlawed Klingons.
You watch, the moment they see the *Enterprise* on
their screens, they're going to be scared spitless and
run like hell."

"Maybe . . . ," La Forge said. "I'd agree completely
if only that Klingon ship hadn't disappeared. Tackling
a ship full of Klingons is not something most pirates
would contemplate in their wildest dreams. And you
know the contempt the Klingons feel for the Ferengi.
They'd fight to the death to avoid the dishonor of
losing to those greedy little trolls."

"Well, maybe it was another ship full of Klingons."

"The last thing Klingon renegades would want is to
attract the attention of an official Klingon vessel. The
empire would send out an entire squadron to avenge a
cruiser, if necessary."

Gomez glanced up, thought a moment, then
shrugged. "You're right. This *is* kind of a weird
assignment, isn't it?"

"Yeah. It reminds me of stories I read about Old
Earth, when they had sailing ships."

Gomez, who had never seen Earth, being from a
colony world, was intrigued. "What kinds of stories?"

"Hundreds of years ago they had legends about

41

places that were deathtraps for hapless sailors. You could get becalmed in the Horse Latitudes—"

"I didn't know that horses lived in the ocean," Gomez interrupted. "I thought they were herbivorous land mammals."

"They didn't—don't—" Geordi said. "Only seahorses live in the ocean."

"Seahorses? Those aren't horses that live in the sea?"

"No, seahorses aren't equines. They're . . . damn, I don't know what they are. Mollusks, maybe, or crustaceans . . ."

"Whales? The humpback ones in that repopulation project they keep publishing articles about?"

Geordi was beginning to feel the way he often did when he talked to Data—as though he'd fallen down a rabbit hole. "No, Sonya, those are *cetaceans.* Intelligent marine mammals. Seahorses are little critters about yea big"—he made a space with his thumb and forefinger—"and they've got nothing to do with four-legged horses."

"Okay, I'm with you. Go on. These sailors got lost . . ."

"Yeah, ships used to disappear, and they had all these legends about why. Everything from sea dragons eating them to them sailing right off the edge of the ocean. They used to mark the unexplored areas on their navigational charts with the warning 'Here Abide Monsters.'"

Gomez giggled. "And the real truth about those mysterious disappearances was that the crews just decided to mutiny and live blissful lives of leisure on a tropical isle with beautiful, scantily clad women, right?"

"Sure, lots of times. But there were places out there that were really deadly for ships. One of the deadliest was the Sargasso Sea."

"Sargasso?"

"Sargasso is a type of thick seaweed that grows all the way up from the seabed. A ship would be sailing along, free as a bird one minute, and then the next it would get caught in a sargasso bed and come to a grinding halt. The seaweed would wrap its tendrils around the ships' keels, and they'd be caught—trapped, so they could never break free."

"They couldn't cut themselves loose?"

"Those unfortunate sailors would try everything to break free—towing the ship out with longboats, cutting the weed, anything they could think of. I suppose sometimes they got out, but all too often they were caught past all hope of escape. The ships and their crews would stay there, helpless, stranded, until there was no more fresh water and food ran out. Sometimes the men would manage to survive for months on rainwater and fish they caught, but . . ." He shook his head, imagining what it must have been like. "Eventually, they must have gone mad and turned to can—"

He broke off abruptly, realizing how gruesome a picture he'd been painting. "Anyway, it was pretty grim. Ships would come back to port and tell tales about discovering these rotting wooden hulks with skeletons sprawled across the decks . . ."

Geordi saw Sonya shiver suddenly, watched her body color alter with her mood, and realized contritely that he'd really scared her. "Hey, enough spooky stories," he said, giving himself a mental shake and her shoulder a comradely pat.

"We'd better get busy on that fuel consumption report," he said briskly, changing the subject, "before Wesley calls again. Wes is so gung ho to impress the captain with the efficiency of his search pattern that he's going to be down here himself, wanting to count every individual atom used for power."

"Right, chief," Gomez agreed, and she gave her

superior officer a shaky grin. "And by the way," she said thoughtfully as they walked over to the other side of the engineering deck, "if you ever decide you're bored with serving on a starship, you could probably have a career as a horror writer."

Geordi chuckled. "I'll leave the writing to Data."

Doctor Beverly Crusher sat before the communications screen in her office, struggling not to reveal the anger she was feeling. Her call to Thonolan Four was not going well.

"Let me get this straight, Administrator Thuvat," she said. "You agree to accept the little girl at your facility, but only if we contact *every* possible relative of hers on *every* Andorian-colonized world and are refused? Why, that could take months!"

"Very possibly." The administrator's pinched blue features grew even more pinched as he pursed his thin lips. His antennae twitched with impatience. "But rules are rules. We must not overlook the slightest possibility that some of her kin may agree to take her. Possibly she may find a place in one of the less advanced agricultural colonies, where any pair of hands, no matter how handicapped, might be valued. Tell me, can the child sew? Knit? They say that"—his mouth tightened even more—"blind individuals are often clever with their fingers. Perhaps this child could be trained for some type of manual-sorting job that would not require vision . . ." He sighed, his distaste plain.

Beverly Crusher took a deep breath and counted to ten, first in English, then German, then Vulcan. "Administrator Thuvat. You seem to think that Thala is mentally retarded as well as blind. Such is definitely *not* the case. She is an extremely bright child, and, with proper education, she could be successful at many careers—work with computers, for example, or law, or physics, teaching, writing, hundreds of jobs! And if she were properly outfitted with a prosthetic visual aid, she could perform any function any nonhandicapped person could do! Why, our chief engineer aboard the *Enterprise*, Mister La Forge, has been blind from birth, and he has had an exemplary career as a Starfleet officer!"

"Mmm . . ." was Thuvat's only reply to the doctor's impassioned peroration. The Andorian hesitated, then, evidently realizing that Crusher was not happy about the way the conversation was going, temporized. "You understand, Doctor, this is not my decision. I assure you that my agency will do everything expected of us in this case. I am merely informing you of the regulations concerning orphaned children."

"Suppose that nobody in Thala's family, on any Andorian world, will agree to take her. What then?" Crusher asked tightly.

"Then we will follow regulations, of course, and give her a place here on Thonolan Four."

"A place," Beverly repeated slowly. "What does that mean? What kind of place are we talking about?"

"There are several institutions in our largest cities for the care of those who cannot function in society. These unfortunate individuals are given food, shelter, and humane care."

Humane care! Crusher nearly choked with indignation, picturing it. *He sounds as though he's talking about unwanted pets!* "What about adoption?" she asked, controlling her voice with an effort.

Thuvat blinked in surprise at the suggestion. "I suppose it is possible," he ventured finally. "Perhaps we could find something . . ."

Sure you will, Beverly thought grimly. *Some nice family that needs someone to knit sweaters, or the Andorian equivalent, and sit in the chimney corner and*

45

be grateful for handouts. Damn you! Her heart ached at the thought of Thala—or any child—living in a place where she wasn't wanted.

"Administrator Thuvat," she said finally, "I can put through a request for such a search to be conducted via Federation agencies. But, frankly, that will take a long time. Perhaps if *you* conducted inquiries, you could get faster results."

Thuvat sighed. "Possible. I will do what I can, if you request it." He was plainly hoping that she would *not* request it. A sudden thought seemed to occur to him. "Tell me, Doctor, did this child's unfortunate parent have any property of value? That might make a difference in locating a family to adopt her."

That was the last straw. Beverly Crusher fought a swift and silent battle between her automatic urge to tell the truth and the dictates of her conscience, then shook her head sadly. "I am afraid not, Administrator," she lied smoothly. "There's only a very small trust fund, which will go to Thala herself when she reaches adulthood."

"Oh, that *is* unfortunate." The administrator's momentary interest faded away. "Well, I am afraid that I have other duties, so if there is nothing else? Do you wish me to request that records search?"

"No, thank you, Administrator," the doctor said. "I hate to trouble you further. I'll just let the Federation records people handle it."

"Fine. I wish you good fortune in solving your problem."

"Thank you very much, Administrator Thuvat. May all your problems be as small as this one," Beverly said with poisonous sweetness.

Her sarcasm was lost on the Andorian. "Thank you," he said. "Farewell, Doctor."

With a savage poke, the doctor terminated the connection to Thonolan Four. "Damned little bureaucratic worm," she muttered after the screen was safely dark. Sighing, Beverly ran her hands through her hair, then leaned her forehead against the heels of her palms. She quickly began a meditation-relaxation exercise.

I'll have to tell Selar. Vulcan or not, this is going to upset her. What a mess. Poor little Thala . . .

On the bridge of the *Enterprise,* Wesley Crusher suddenly sat bolt upright in his contoured seat. "Captain, I am picking up an ion trail," he said, unable to keep the excitement from his voice.

"Very good, Mister Crusher." Picard addressed the air, and the computer automatically relayed his voice. "Number One, Mister Crusher seems to have found something promising."

"I'm on my way," replied Will Riker's voice.

The captain waited until his second-in-command was present, while Wesley worked feverishly with the computer. Riker glanced at the board over the young officer's shoulder, then gave him a silent nod of approval. Wesley flushed with pleasure.

"This looks like it, Captain," Riker said. "Exactly what we would expect to find from the *Marco Polo.*"

"She was pulled off her course, Captain," Wesley said. "By some kind of, uh . . . energy . . . field."

"Tractor beam?" Riker asked sharply, with a glance at Lieutenant Worf, who stood manning the security and communications console behind the command center on the bridge. The Klingon head of security's mouth tightened, but his swarthy features beneath his forehead ridges remained otherwise impassive.

"No, sir," Wesley said, then shook his head in puzzlement. "It had the same effect as a tractor beam, apparently, but this type of energy . . . well, it's not anything I've encountered before."

"Confirmed," Data said in response to Riker's

questioning glance. "It is like nothing ever encountered before in Federation, Romulan, or Klingon space."

"A new kind of energy field . . ." Picard got up and paced over to the viewscreen. "Destructive? Any signs of debris that would indicate an explosion or battle?"

"No, sir," Crusher replied. "It works like a tractor beam, but it's based on an entirely different kind of energy. It just pulled them along."

"What about the *PaKathen?*" Worf rumbled. "Any signs of that vessel?"

"No, Lieutenant." The young officer frowned. "But Klingon vessels are designed not to leave ion trails that give away their location, so it could have been pulled off-course in the same way."

"It is also entirely possible that the two disappearances are unrelated," Picard said, gazing out into the depths of space, the starlight reflecting off his austere features.

"Possible, but statistically unlikely," Data added helpfully.

"How strong is this field, Mister Crusher? Could the *Marco Polo* have broken free?"

"I doubt it, Captain." The teenager's thin face was very sober. "A freighter wouldn't have that kind of power, sir."

"What about the *Enter*—"

The captain broke off abruptly as his ship actually *lurched.* Despite artificial gravity fields, stabilizers, meteor shields—all the protective devices the huge ship boasted—for a moment the *Enterprise* shied beneath them like a skittish mare. The red alert automatically activated.

Picard almost lost his footing, but as the ship steadied once again, he was able to regain it without falling. The captain turned to regard his bridge crew and, with an admirable display of *sangfroid,* finished his sentence. "The *Enterprise,*" he resumed quietly. "Could we break free of this unknown energy field?"

"Unknown, Captain," Data said. "However, I suspect we will find that out imminently, sir. The field, whatever it may be, has just snared *us.*"

Chapter Four

"CAN WE BREAK FREE?" Picard demanded.

"Unknown, captain," Data said. "Certainly not without tying in the warp engines. This field is much stronger than any tractor beam I have ever encountered."

A moment of silence followed the android's announcement, then Picard looked up at his Klingon officer. "Lieutenant, request that Mister La Forge join us on the bridge. I want him at the engineering station."

"Yes, Captain."

It didn't take the young officer long to appear. When the ship first encountered the unknown energy field, Geordi had remained in engineering just long enough to verify that the *Enterprise* had suffered no damage. Then, anticipating Picard's order, he'd started immediately for the command center. La Forge was already in the turbolift when the captain's command was relayed.

As soon as the engineer reached the bridge, he glanced around him to identify the inhabitants (their color spectra were as distinctive to the blind officer as their faces were to a sighted crew member).

"I would like your opinion on what we have just encountered, Mister La Forge," the captain said.

"Aye, sir." Geordi headed directly for the engineering console at the back of the bridge. As he studied the readouts there, he sucked in a surprised breath. "Thought I'd seen everything," he muttered to himself, shaking his head ruefully. "Guess that'll teach me."

"Conclusions, Mister La Forge?" the captain asked.

Geordi straightened and resisted the urge to scratch his head. "It's a previously unknown form of energy, artificial in origin, and it's surrounded us, sir. It's beginning to pull the ship along the same path as the *Marco Polo* followed. It's very strong."

"Artificial . . . ," Picard repeated musingly. "That leaves us with two possibilities. One, that this field represents some type of new scientific discovery by beings that we already know, or . . ."

He gave his second-in-command a meaningful glance, and Riker concluded, "Or, that it's generated by something we've never before encountered. Something alien."

"What is our current position, Mister Crusher?" Picard asked, turning to his most junior officer.

"We're being pulled along, sir, just as Mister La Forge said. Our speed is gradually increasing as the field overcomes our inertia."

"If we continue at this rate, what speed are we likely to attain?" Riker asked.

Wesley frowned. Geordi could see the colors on his face ripple as his facial muscles moved. "Well, that depends on what it's pulling us *toward*—I mean, how far away our destination is. I would estimate that we will reach minimum impulse speed in about two hours at this rate."

"Is the force this energy field is exerting constant?" Picard asked.

"Yes, sir."

The captain turned to the operations station. "Can you identify the parameters of this field, Mister Data? Are they also constant?"

"The parameters are indeed detectable, Captain, but they, unlike our speed, are neither constant nor predictable. The *Enterprise* did not simply drift into the influence of this field, sir. I was tracking the phenomenon before we were captured, and it seemed stable—until it actually flowed toward us to envelop the ship. At a remarkable rate of speed, I might add—nearly full impulse power."

"How long did it take to envelop us?"

"Three point one seconds, sir."

"Captain," La Forge said, "I now have warp power at your disposal, so we can try to break free."

"Do you think we can do it, Mister La Forge?"

The chief engineer hesitated. "I'm not sure, Captain. It'll take a fair amount of power. If the force drawing us along remains constant . . ." He shook his head. "Well, maybe."

"Very well," Picard said, and he stood a moment in silent thought. "Lieutenant Worf, can we contact Starfleet Command?"

"Negative, Captain." The Klingon's bass voice sounded not at all regretful. *There's nothing Worf likes better than a chance to take on all comers single-handed,* Geordi thought wryly. *It's been a while since we've faced a real challenge, and he's hot to trot.* "This field is inhibiting transmission and reception on all subspace frequencies, sir. Until we break free of it, any communication—except over very short distances—will be impossible."

The captain turned to his first officer. "Recommendations, Number One?" he asked.

"Recommend we try to pull free now, Captain, and then attempt to follow the energy field to its source, using our sensors to trace it."

Picard considered silently for a second, then shook his head. "No. Now is not the time to try and break free. We have been ordered to find and rescue the *Marco Polo* and the *PaKathen,* and our best chance of locating them lies in letting ourselves be taken where they were taken."

"You mean . . . deliberately let ourselves be drawn into the trap?" Riker asked slowly.

The silence and tension on the bridge were almost tangible.

Picard nodded. "If we attempt to pull free now and fail, we will have strained our warp engines past capacity and still not have reached our goal. Instead, I believe that I will conserve our strength by allowing this 'unknown force' to furnish us with a free ride to its point of emanation, and when we discover that point on our sensors, *then* will be the time to pull free so that we may investigate—and, if at all possible, rescue the two ships."

Riker shook his head admiringly. Picard turned to his Klingon officer. "Lieutenant Worf, is it possible to launch a warning buoy at sufficient velocity so that it could break free of this field?"

The security head made some calculations. "Yes, Captain, I believe that we can."

"Prepare a summary of our mission status, then, and launch that buoy, Lieutenant."

"Yes, sir."

"I want all sensors set for maximum-range scan on all wavelengths, Mister Data," Picard ordered. "I wish to know immediately if any sign of our destination is detected. Please alert your replacement to scan all bands of the spectra."

"That will not be necessary, Captain," Data said.

53

"What do you mean?" The captain glanced at Riker. "Your shift ends soon, does it not?"

"Yes, sir, it does," the android agreed as the first officer nodded confirmation. "But I am prepared to remain on duty for the duration of this alert."

The captain gazed into the viewscreen, his eyes thoughtful. "That is not necessary," he said, then he turned back to the android, and his stern expression softened just a bit. "Though your willingness to take on extra duty is commendable, Data. You may remain on duty if you wish, Commander. I do not believe, however, that we will face any type of confrontation today . . . or, at least, for the next several hours."

"That concurs with my instrument readings, Captain. There is no sign of our . . ."—the android hesitated—"antagonist at the farthest range my sensors extend, which means that contact with our unknown destination cannot occur within the next six hours at the minimum."

"Six hours," Picard repeated dryly. "Breathing space, Mister Data. We must all endeavor to enjoy it while it lasts."

Despite the possible danger of his ship's current assignment, Acting Ensign Wesley Crusher felt rather pleased with life in general as he entered the ship's main lounge, called Ten-Forward. Captain Picard had approved his search pattern, and he had even commented favorably in front of Commander Riker about the innovative way the young man had overlapped the search grids to provide extra conservation of both fuel and time. While the captain was always one to give credit where credit was due, public compliments from Jean-Luc Picard were rare enough that they became things to be treasured, memorized, savored . . .

Smiling faintly at the memory, the youth wandered around the lounge. Ten-Forward was a large, dimly lit compartment, with lighted tables, benches and chairs scattered about, many of them facing toward the many windows, where the moving stars provided a breathtaking background. Soft conversations created a low murmur that overshadowed the music playing softly in the background; absently Wesley identified the piece as a tone poem by the Vulcan composer T'Nira.

"Can I get you anything, Wes?"

The teenager started out of his reverie, only to realize that he'd somehow made his way across the lounge and sat down at the bar, all without being aware of it. Guinan was before him, leaning across the glowing surface of the bar, a faint, knowing smile on her lips. Her brown skin was perhaps a shade lighter than Geordi's, and her features were very human—except that they appeared curiously bare to human eyes. Above Guinan's wide-lipped mouth, her brown eyes sparkled beneath brows so sparse as to be almost nonexistent. Wesley had sometimes wondered whether Guinan had hair on the top of her head, or if it was just long at the back, but he had no way of knowing. The hostess always wore elaborate headdresses that complemented her flowing robes.

"Oh, hi, Guinan. Can I have one of those fruit things you make?"

"You mean a Fomalhaut Frenzy? The pink and green one?"

"That's the one. And a sandwich, please. Grilled Swiss with bacon and tomato."

"Coming right up," she promised, and she turned away to program the food service selector.

Ten-Four's hostess was an enigma to most of the starship's crew. No one even knew precisely which planet she came from. Jean-Luc Picard had personally selected Guinan to run the relaxation center for his ship. Obviously the captain had encountered her before, but if he knew any more about her, it was obviously not information he had any intention of sharing.

Guinan placed the food and drink before the young officer and smiled, one of those gentle, enigmatic smiles that made Wesley wonder, not for the first time, just how old the hostess was. Physically, she appeared to be about Geordi's age, in her early to mid-thirties, but Wes knew she had to be older than that. Exactly how much older was a definite puzzle. At times, she seemed nearly as young as he was, but at other times—especially when he gazed into her brown eyes—the young man felt as though she had lived for centuries and seen nearly everything there was to see.

"You looked pretty pleased with yourself when you came in here," she remarked as he dove into his food with the typical enthusiasm of a teenager.

The young officer nodded around a mouthful, chewed appreciatively, then swallowed. "I was. I mean, I am. The captain gave me an assignment, and when I finished, he said I'd done an excellent job. *And*"—Wes paused for effect—"he said it right in front of Commander Riker!"

Guinan looked suitably impressed. "High praise indeed," she murmured. "So, what's our mission status?"

Wesley shrugged. "The captain called it a breathing space. There's an alien tractor field of some kind that's towing us toward an unknown destination. But at the moment, the captain wants to let it pull us, see where it's taking us. He figures we've got plenty of time to break free later."

Guinan refilled the teenager's glass without being asked. "The captain usually has a good reason for his decisions."

"Of course," Wesley said, then popped the last bite into his mouth. "Terrific sandwich," he said, rather indistinctly. "Thanks, Guinan."

"Want another?"

Wes considered for a moment, then a wide grin flashed on his normally serious features. "Why not?"

When the second sandwich had been dispatched as quickly as the first, Wesley sat back in his seat, watching the hostess as she served Lieutenant Worf to a generous helping of Klingon *gagh*. Wesley glanced at the plate, then hastily averted his eyes. He still couldn't get used to the idea of eating things that moved.

Commander Riker must have nerves of steel, he thought, repressing a shudder, *to be able to go and serve on a Klingon ship and eat in their mess hall. He must also have a cast-iron—*

His thoughts were interrupted by a voice. "Hello, Wesley."

Wes turned on his stool to see Data standing at his elbow. The android was holding several sheets of paper that appeared to be covered with, of all things, handwriting. "Oh, hi, Data. Have a seat."

"Thank you, Wesley, I believe that I will." He sat down on the next stool. Guinan glanced over at them inquiringly to see whether they wanted anything (Data did not need to eat or drink as humans did, but he was able to, and sometimes joined his friends in a toast), but both officers shook their heads.

Wes eyed the pages his friend was holding curiously. "What've you got there, Data?"

"I have a section from the novel I am currently writing, Wesley," the android replied. "I came to ask you if you would consider reading it and giving me your opinion. I have done some extensive revision since seeking Commander Riker's thoughts on the quality of my story."

Wesley hesitated, taken aback by the request. "Uh . . . I don't know, Data. Engineering and science are my strong points, not literature, I'm afraid. I took a test on twentieth-century poets last week, and I completely messed up the section where I had to identify the mythical and biblical references in T. S. Eliot's work. I don't think I'm qualified to act as a literary critic."

"But, Wesley, this book is a novel, written to appeal to a popular audience," Data argued. "You should be able to tell me whether it excites you, makes you want to read more—whether it contains the proper elements for a work of popular appeal. In such a judgment, your opinion is as valid as anyone's."

"Oh," said Wes, unable to think up any argument to refute this. "Yeah, I guess so. Okay, I'll read it. What's the plot?"

"It is an adventure and romance set in the early days of interstellar travel. This scene takes place between a couple on the night before he must leave to captain a ship as it pioneers the paths between the stars."

"Okay."

Data handed the teenager the pages. Wesley began to read:

The mountains of the moon were bright now with the sunrise that lasts for many days, bright except where they were dark with all the blackness of shadow that had never been touched by the light, for on the moon some nights never end. Juan watched the sun and then he watched the face of the *ingles* woman, Maggie, and he thought of many things. *Bueno,* he thought, *good. It is good that she is here with me, for this may be the last time we are together for a very long time. Perhaps forever.*

"We have not much time," he said, seeing that

she knew he spoke the truth. The pressure of her hand in his tightened until it was as searing as the sun on the jagged peaks, making him desire her urgently, intensifying his need of her, filling his entire being with an aching agony of wanting. "Maggie, oh, Maggie," he said urgently.

"Yes. Yes. Yes." She spoke almost fiercely.

Then there was the yielding surface of the space-station flooring beneath them and the faint hiss of the environmental system air filters and the smell of the cleaning agents and the touch of her fingers against his skin that he would remember forever, for as long as he lived, however long that would be, and for her there was the brightness of the unfiltered sun against the dome splashing the mountaintops with light so intense it was painful and she had to close her eyes and even then it seemed that she could still feel it boring into her until she was blind with it, with the feel of the sun and of him. For him it was darkness and a blaze of warmth together, leading to the beginning of the galaxy, before there was anything at all. Time halted in its passage and he felt the galaxy move, shudder beneath them, revolve and spin out away from him.

Then he was himself again, separate, and he smiled at her wearily. "I love you. I cannot bear to part from you, but I know that I must. Did you feel the galaxy move?"

"Yes," she said. "For me it was the same. It is always so."

Wesley reached the end of the handwritten passage and stopped. His face felt hot, whether because of the subject matter or because he was embarrassed for Data, he wasn't sure; the teenager was glad that the Ten-Forward was dimly lit. *This is awful, but what the hell am I supposed to say?* he wondered blankly.

Data's my friend, and this is obviously something he really cares about. I can't hurt his feelings!

"Well?" asked the android, who was watching him intently, a hint of almost human eagerness beneath his habitual calm. "What do you think, Wesley?"

"Well, it's certainly very . . . classical . . . in tone," the youth said, choosing his words carefully. "Matter of fact, if you hadn't told me you wrote this, I'd have thought it was a passage from a Hemingway novel." *A bad one,* he added silently.

Data seemed pleased. "That ambience was what I was striving for, Wesley," he admitted. "Ernest Hemingway is Commander Riker's favorite writer."

"Maybe you ought to show this to him, then."

"Perhaps after our current mission is completed. But tell me, Wesley, did it all seem realistic to you? Did you find it stirring?"

Wes's face flamed again, and he searched awkwardly for words. "Uh . . . well, Data, I can't claim to have had a lot of . . . uh . . . practical experience yet to compare, frankly." He cleared his throat. "As to whether I found it . . . stirring, uh, well . . . I suppose I did. I mean"—he floundered—"that all these parts about what Maggie is thinking and feeling . . . well, I'm not a girl—a woman." He brightened. "Maybe you need a woman's opinion. After all, they read more romances and love stories than men, right?"

"I believe so," Data said, and he took the pages back. "That is a good suggestion, Wesley. I will follow it as soon as possible."

Wesley was vastly relieved to have gotten off the hook. He slid out of his seat and stood up. "I think I'll wander down to engineering," he said. "It's been nearly eight hours since we encountered that field. Maybe something is finally happening. Geordi's monitoring the situation, he'll know what's going on."

"I will accompany you as far as the turbolift, then," Data said.

The two left Ten-Forward, and Wesley spotted a familiar figure just leaving the turbolift. "Hello, Thala!" he called.

The Andorian child stopped and waited for them to reach her. She was wearing, as always, one of the glittery sensory nets over her beige jumpsuit. Seeing her pointed, fine-boned face with its delicate azure skin beneath her antennae, Wesley was reminded, once again, of ancient myths about Earth's fairies.

As the acting ensign approached, the child raised her head, almost as though she could truly see him. But Wes knew that what she was "seeing" was the shape of his body delineated by his own thermal energy, all of him tinted in alien hues that were provided by her color-sensing antennae. "Hello, Wesley!" she said when he halted before her. "Who is that with you? My sensors tell me there's someone, but the thermal readings are all funny."

"That's Lieutenant Commander Data," Wesley said. "He's an android."

"Hello, Thala," Data said formally. "How are you today?"

The child cocked her head at the sound of his voice. "I'm fine. It's nice to meet you. I never met an android before. I've seen robots, but never anyone like you."

"That is not surprising," Data said. "I am, so far as I know, unique."

Wesley had known Thala for several years, for she had already been traveling aboard the *Enterprise* with her father when he and his mother joined the crew. When the child's father, Thev, died, the young officer had talked to the little Andorian girl, trying to offer her as much comfort as he could, from someone who had undergone the same loss. Her people's grief rituals were far different from human ones, but Wesley, his mother, and Lieutenant Selar had joined in Thev's "death chant" and the attendant obsequies.

"I know," Thala replied to Data's statement. "Doctor Soong made you. I heard a tape about it. Are you really as strong as they say?"

"I am quite strong," Data admitted.

"Could you pick me up with one hand?" she asked curiously.

"Certainly," the android said, and demonstrated. Thala gasped as she was swooped high into the air, held suspended for several seconds, then deposited back on the deck so gently that she didn't even bounce as her feet touched the surface.

"Wesley!" she exclaimed breathlessly. "Did you see that?"

"Yeah, I did," the acting ensign said with a wry smile. "Data, what a show-off!"

"Do it again?" she pleaded wistfully, her head turning toward the android.

"Not at the moment," Data said. "But another time, perhaps."

"That would be great!" Her small features sobered suddenly, as if a thought had just struck her. "Wesley, are we due to dock at any starbases soon?"

"I don't know, Thala," the young man replied. "At the moment we're in the middle of a mission, so not for at least a week or so, probably."

Her thin blue features did not alter, but her small shoulders sagged a little. "Oh. Listen, Wesley, will you do something for me?"

"Sure. What?"

"Let me know the next time we're going to dock. You're the helmsman most of the time, so you'll know right away, won't you?"

"If I'm on duty at that time," he said. "I promise I'll signal your cabin, okay?"

"Thanks, Wesley," she said, then addressed herself to Data. "And thank *you* for the boost!"

"You are very welcome," Data said, then both officers started back up the corridor.

"She's a nice little kid," Wesley commented as they reached the turbolift and signaled it. "My mom is worried about what's going to happen to her." He sighed. "Life gets complicated at times, doesn't it?"

Data regarded him with the android's customary unblinking candor. "For humans, it certainly does," he agreed. "I can only envy you that richness of existence. Most of the time, my life seems all too simple by comparison, Wesley."

The lift arrived, and they stepped into it and were whisked away.

Thala watched the flickering outline of the android and the more solid, flesh-and-blood silhouette of Wesley Crusher walk away and, after a moment, step into the turbolift and vanish. Then she turned and headed back to her quarters, a suite of cabins that she had once shared with her father but that now were hers alone. At least for the moment. Thala was under no illusion that they would remain hers for much longer. Soon she would be sent away from the starship, away from all that she knew, and the prospect filled her with fear and the determination to take matters into her own hands.

Even though the child had never set foot on Andorian soil, she knew far better than the humans or Selar that a person such as herself would find no welcome among Andorians. Thala had studied her world's history and customs for years. She'd also learned a great deal about her people from listening to her father while she was growing up, times when Thev had talked frankly to his crewmates, never realizing that his daughter could hear them. Thala's hearing was exceptional, even for an Andorian—one compensation for her lack of sight.

It was a funny thing, the child reflected, that many people seemed to assume that just because you were blind, you couldn't hear, either. She wondered idly whether deaf people got treated as though *they* were also blind.

Resolutely she turned her thoughts back to the matter at hand. Wesley had said that they were on a mission, a mission that would occupy the *Enterprise* for at least another week. Doctor Crusher had told her today that she would not be going to Thonolan Four, so Thala intended to be ready the next time the starship docked—wherever that might be.

Crossing her quarters, she avoided the furniture as much from habit as from the measurements and data that her sensory net supplied her, until she stood before the small statue that was a representation of an ancient Andorian hive-goddess. The sculpture was made of a smooth, cool stone that felt to the child's fingers much like the jade inlays in the hilt of a ceremonial Vulcan dagger that Selar displayed in her quarters. Except that Thala had been told that this stone was yellow, and Selar said the dagger hilt was red.

Red . . . yellow . . . The Andorian girl remembered that Selar had been trying to perfect eyes for her that would allow her to know what those words truly meant, and she had to clench her fingers on the statue's smoothness for a heartbeat before she could gain control.

Why was I born this way? she wondered for the thousandth time. Being born blind was bad enough, but to be Andorian and born blind . . .

Thala experienced a sudden wave of longing for Thev. To his credit, he had managed to overcome the ways instilled into him from childhood; he had had great affection for his daughter and had encouraged her to develop skills that would prepare her for a life away from their people. Thev had planned for both of them to settle on Delma, a planet in the Vega sector, as soon as his diplomatic tour was over. On that world there were many opportunities for bright individuals, and everyone was judged for what he or she *could* do, not what they could *not* do.

Thev and Selar had taught Thala that her handicap was only a handicap if *she* perceived it as such. It had been a terrible blow to the child when they'd told her he was gone.

The Borg ship had blown a good-sized hole in the *Enterprise,* and Thev had been the only non-crew individual in the area when the hull was breached and the section decompressed. They'd never even found his body. Thala *knew* that her father was dead, she *knew* it—but at times she was tormented by imaginings in which Thev had taken the Borg attack as a way to escape from the burden of having a blind child and had run away.

It was hard to mourn properly when one had no body to grieve over. Selar had comforted her by telling her that Thev, in all probability, had had no time to realize what was happening; his ending must have been virtually instantaneous. It had been Selar who had come to her quarters to tell Thala that her father had died. She had been direct and honest, but beneath the matter-of-fact Vulcan delivery had been concern and kindness.

And since Thev's death, Selar had been there every day, sometimes for only a few minutes if she had many patients, but never missing a single time. But soon, even if Thala were to be allowed to stay aboard the *Enterprise,* Selar might not be here. The thought was enough to make the Andorian girl want to keen aloud again.

But after a moment, the child swallowed, then squared her small shoulders resolutely. If she allowed herself to think about never seeing Selar again, she wouldn't have the resolve to do what was necessary.

Grasping the smoothly carved statue with one hand and its base with the other, Thala twisted. The sculpture came apart. It was hollow inside, and she turned the top piece so that its contents cascaded down into her hand.

The cool feel of metal, the faceted hardness of jewels, her mother's antennae webs filled her hand. Slowly, carefully, Thala counted the jewels one more time.

Sixteen natural Rigellian sun crystals, ranging in size from a quarter-carat to nearly two carats. The stones were not particularly rare, but she had been assured that they were flawless and of excellent color—a brilliant reddish orange, the color of one of the Rigel system's stars. They were set in old-fashioned settings of *oriri,* an alloy of gold, copper, and iridium that her people prized greatly.

The Andorian girl had only a vague idea what the stones and the metal were worth on today's market, but she was certain that they would bring enough to buy her passage to Vulcan and keep her there for long enough to get a job.

Thala planned to work as a translator-scribe. She spoke three languages fluently—Andorian, Vulcan, and English—and people were always needed who could transcribe and translate. Despite the invention of the Universal Translator a century ago, many Vulcan or Terran merchants still preferred to have a living being act as interpreter during trade negotiations. They claimed that translations rendered by living interpreters more accurately reproduced the other speaker's subcontext and inflection—elements that could prove crucial during delicate bargaining sessions.

And once she was on Vulcan and had earned enough to support herself without working for two years—Thala had only a hazy idea of how many years the attainment of this goal would take—then she would begin classes at the Vulcan Science Academy. And she would see Selar again. They could be . . . friends.

Thala thought of how long that might take, and her throat tightened, but her mind was made up; nothing was going to shake her resolution. She would *not* go to an Andorian world.

On her homeworld she could hope for nothing but a bare, friendless existence in an institution, surrounded by those who, unlike her, had not been trained to surpass their limitations. Andorians who bore disabling illnesses, wounds, or other imperfections were thought honorable only if they did not burden the living with their presence or their care.

An institution was certainly her most likely fate, but if she were very, very lucky—although to Thala it seemed luck only in the blackest, most ironic sense of the word—she might be spared the institution and be adopted by one of the clans that had lost population to one of the planet's endless blood feuds. Her blindness was not the result of any genetic cause, and so she might be deemed fit for such an adoption, because in a year or so she would be old enough to bear and nurture young. She would be placed in one of the clan's hive harems, impregnated with boy babies by selected males at medically safe intervals, and then her children would be taken away from her at a young age to be trained as warriors.

Thala thought that her people were right in at least one thing. Death would be preferable to either of those options.

She stood thinking and planning, making a mental list of what she should take and what she would abandon, all the while allowing the fine-spun *oriri* chains holding the jewels strung together to slip through her fingers, over and over . . .

"Doctor Crusher?" A hesitant voice came from the doorway of Beverly's office, which she'd left open.

The chief medical officer looked up. "Data? Can I help you?"

"Am I disturbing you?" he asked, his unnaturally pale features showing a trace of almost-human anxiety.

If I didn't know that's impossible, I'd think he was nervous, Crusher thought. Aloud she said, "No, not at all. Come in, won't you?"

He stepped inside, then paused on the threshold. "I would not want to interfere with your work, Doctor."

"I'm not particularly busy at the moment, Data," she said. "So please, sit down. What's on your mind?" She leaned back in the chair, thinking that she'd never seen Data so unsure of himself.

The android seated himself, his features serene, but something about him still seemed unsettled. "Doctor Crusher . . . ," he began, then stopped.

"Data, when we're just talking like this, why don't you call me Beverly?" She gave him a quick, speculative glance and said, "Because, correct me if I'm wrong, I don't think you're here on ship's business."

"You are indeed correct," Data said. "Very well, Beverly . . ." He paused, then continued quickly, almost in a rush, "I need a woman's honest opinion on something I have written, and I wondered whether you would give me yours."

"Something you've written?" She was taken aback and struggled not to show it. "You mean . . . creative writing?"

"Yes, Doctor," he said, and, reaching beneath his uniform jacket, the android withdrew a sheaf of folded pages covered with handwriting. "I have done several drafts of a novel about the early days of space exploration and a romance between the captain of a ship and the woman he loves. This scene is set on Earth's moon, the night before he is to depart." He glanced up at her hopefully. "I rewrote the book to be more overtly masculine in tone, which Commander Riker recommended. Then, when I asked Wesley to read it, he commented that, since this scene is a love scene and includes a woman's point of view, I would be well advised to seek a woman's opinion."

"Did he specifically suggest me?" Crusher asked, thinking that the next time she saw her son she'd have a word with him about passing the buck, but Data shook his head.

"No, he did not. However, you and Counselor Troi are the two women with whom I work most closely, and she is not available, so that left you."

"I see . . ." Beverly mustered a smile. "Well, Data, I'm honored that you think my opinion might be worth something, but I have to say that I'm not very experienced at literary criticism."

"That is fine, Doctor . . . Beverly. My novel is written for a popular, not a literary, audience." He held up the sheaf of manuscript. "Shall I read it to you?"

"No, I think I'd do better to read it myself," she said, reaching across her desk. Taking the handful of manuscript, she began reading, acutely conscious of Data's hopeful gaze fixed on her. It made concentrating difficult, to put it mildly.

She read the scene over twice, once to catch its flow

and pacing, the next to study the style and content. Then she looked up. "I don't really know what to say, Data," she said honestly. *Because I can't tell you the truth, which is that this is awful!*

"Just tell me whether it moved you," Data urged. "Is that the way a woman really feels during a sexual encounter?"

Not any woman I ever met, Crusher thought grimly. *This reads like some adolescent juvenile male's fantasy of how women feel—sunlight and Juan boring into her . . . I'm afraid that "boring" is only too apropos . . .*

"Well," she began cautiously, "every woman does long to meet a soul mate, someone who really needs her and will express his love for her, and uh . . ."—she glanced at the flimsy—"uh, Juan . . . certainly seems to do that," she said, sounding unconvincing to her own ears. "As for making love in an airlock, or wherever they are, it doesn't seem to me to be a very romantic spot. I mean, with the smells of cleaning agents and the hiss of the environmental systems . . . things like that are too commonplace and graphic to be very romantic. Maybe you ought to rethink your setting."

Data's expression brightened. "Finally, some concrete criticism! Your suggestion is most welcome, Doctor. I can indeed alter the setting to a more romantic location, by having the hero and heroine meet in the Luna Botanical Gardens."

"Umm . . ." Crusher shrugged. "That might do it. Also, Data, uh, well, while I enjoy a good potboiler as much as anyone else . . ."—she smiled ruefully— "don't tell anyone, but I have an entire collection of Jacqueline Susann's works—but, anyway, for me to become truly emotionally involved with the characters, I prefer love stories where people don't just fall down on the ground together and, uh . . . have intercourse, but where they *talk* to each other. Where they develop a relationship over a period of time, and that relationship grows into love."

"Can you give me any examples?" he asked.

"Well, my favorite author is Jane Austen, whose characters always expressed their sentiments so clearly, and so wittily, that the emotion comes through, not to mention that it's a pleasure just to read her elegant prose."

"Jane Austen," Data repeated thoughtfully. "I will consider what you have said, Beverly. And I do appreciate your taking the time to read my work."

"Oh, you're very welcome," she said, uncomfortably aware that she certainly had not delivered the "honest opinion" that he'd requested. "You might consider asking for another woman's opinion . . . maybe more than one," she suggested, thinking that perhaps if Data asked enough people, he'd be able to put two and two together for himself.

"I shall do so," Data said solemnly, and he gathered up his manuscript. "And I shall do some rethinking about what constitutes romance in a work of fiction."

"Maybe you ought to read *Gone with the Wind,*" Beverly suggested. "And *Jane Eyre.* Or Hightower's *Flame of Darkness.*"

"I have read them," Data replied, "but I will review them, I assure you."

"Good," she said, and she racked her brain for more examples of successful romances. Just then, Lieutenant Selar paused in the doorway, hesitated, then started away.

"Selar!" Crusher called with relief. "It's okay. Lieutenant Commander Data and I were just finishing our discussion. You can come in."

The android rose to his feet and greeted the Vulcan

doctor as she stepped into the office. "Thank you again, Doctor. I will keep your comments in mind," he promised, and left, manuscript in hand.

"I did not mean to interrupt," Selar said. "These inventory reports could have waited until you were free, Beverly."

Crusher leaned back in her seat and sighed. "I *wanted* you to interrupt," she said. "I needed rescuing. I wasn't enjoying the role of literary critic."

Selar's only comment was a raised eyebrow.

"Commander Riker," said Lieutenant Worf suddenly, "I am picking up a transmission, sir."

"A transmission?" Riker sat bolt upright in the command seat. "From how far away? Can you identify the source, Lieutenant?"

"It is coming from approximately point five light-years away, Commander," the Klingon said in his deep rumble. "As for the source . . . I cannot be positive, sir. The signal is weak, but I believe that it may be from the *Marco Polo.*"

"Can you boost the signal enough to bring it in clearly? Is it repeating?"

"No, Commander, it was only the single transmission. And I will attempt to amplify the recording so that we can make it out, sir, but . . ." The Klingon trailed off as he worked, frowning. Riker spoke up. "Riker to Captain Picard."

"Picard here."

"Sir, we may have something. Lieutenant Worf believes that he is picking up a transmission from the *Marco Polo.* He's trying to boost the signal now."

"On my way, Number One."

By the time the captain reached the bridge, the Klingon officer had managed to amplify the weak signal. "Onscreen, Lieutenant," the commanding officer ordered.

"Sir, there is no visual. Just audio, Captain."

Picard raised his eyebrows in surprise but nodded. "Very well, Mister Worf. Play the audio portion."

"Yes, Captain." The head of security touched a control, and a whine overlaid with the crackle of static filled the air. Worf winced and made an adjustment in the volume control.

A voice, so hoarse and gasping that for a moment Riker had trouble identifying it as human, emerged: ". . . invaded . . . can't identify . . ." A rattle of static, then: ". . . symptoms vary . . . eight suicides, three murders . . . helpless against it . . ." The voice was gabbling now, nearly sobbing: "oh, God, the dreams are killing us! Please, *help*—but . . . oh, God, you can't! Don't! Stay away! No more deaths, please . . ."

The message trailed off into inarticulate sobs, then static reigned once more.

"Is that all, Lieutenant?" Picard asked. Riker, who was gripping the back of his seat as he stood beside it, experienced a moment of shock that the captain could sound so calm, then he noticed the tension in the way the captain held his shoulders, the tightness of the older man's jaw muscles. *It got to him, too,* the commander realized. *He's just got too much control to show it.*

On the other hand, Wesley Crusher, who was on duty at the conn station, looked pale and shaken. Riker didn't blame the young man. There had been such terrible despair, such *agony* in that hoarse, pleading voice.

The captain raised his voice slightly. "Doctor Crusher, please report to the conference room." He stood up. "Commander Riker, Lieutenant Worf, Counselor, Mister Crusher . . . please assemble." He turned to the android. "Mister Data, you have the conn."

When they were all seated around the long, polished

table, Picard ordered the message to be played twice-more, then he gazed at them, his eyes grave. "Opinions, please?"

"They spoke of invasion," Worf said. "We must be ready to do battle against an alien force."

Doctor Crusher shook her head. "I don't agree. It sounded more to me as though they had contracted some kind of unknown plague. You could call that an invasion. Remember, the man spoke of symptoms."

"I agree that we are dealing with some type of medical problem as opposed to a military force," Counselor Troi said. "Could it be some kind of plague that infects people's minds? He spoke of dreams killing them . . ."

Wesley Crusher looked skeptical but interested. It was obvious that the youth's agile brain had seized the idea and was running with it. "Some kind of illness that induces lethal dreaming?" he asked slowly. "Is that possible?"

"Nightmares can be extremely stressful to the body," Crusher said. "They cause the heartbeat to accelerate, adrenaline to be secreted, and blood pressure to rise."

"I can certainly attest to that," Riker said. "When I was bitten by that alien bug and the medical staff had to use nightmares to kill it in my cells, I felt as though I'd gone twenty rounds in an anbo jyutsu match with the galactic champion! Every muscle in my body was sore, and I was exhausted."

"But can dreams kill?" Picard asked slowly.

"Under the right circumstances, possibly," Crusher replied slowly. "An individual with a weak heart or one who is suffering from some debilitating illness might be so shocked by a terrible nightmare that he or she could expire from the strain . . ."

"But from that transmission, it seems clear that all

the crew was affected," Riker said. "It's hard to believe that they all had bad hearts. Besides, that wouldn't account for the suicides or murders he spoke of."

"Dreams are tied in with the unconscious mind," Counselor Troi put in. "Perhaps they are experiencing soom kind of alien mental invasion that is compelling them to kill themselves or each other. This mental invasion could be expressing itself also in bad dreams."

"That is possible," the captain said slowly. "It has happened before."

Riker glanced around the table and saw that everyone remembered, as he did, the time when a revenge-crazed Ferengi captain had used an alien machine to produce just such an effect on Jean-Luc Picard's mind. Memories of his lost ship, *Stargazer*, had tormented the captain in vivid dreams.

"If it is some kind of mental invasion, does that mean that we're facing Ferengi?" Riker thought a moment, then shook his head. "This just doesn't have their stamp, sir."

"I concur, Number One. The nature of this energy field suggests to me that we are dealing with a force or being that is unknown and alien to us."

Slowly Picard rose and leaned over the table, resting his weight on his outspread hands. "I believe that the time has come for us to break free of this field. We should be close enough to the *Marco Polo* now to pick it up on our sensors." He straightened and glanced over at Riker. "Number One, I'll want Mister La Forge on the bridge to monitor the engineering station."

"Understood, Captain."

Picard turned his gaze to the rest of his bridge crew. "All hands to their stations."

The conference room emptied rapidly.

Scant minutes later, Geordi La Forge looked up from his controls on the bridge and nodded. "Warp power at your disposal, sir. Ready when you are."

Picard in turn nodded at his young conn officer. "Proceed on our new heading, Mister Crusher. Engage."

All his attention on his controls, Wes activated the ship's powerful engines. The *Enterprise* began to vibrate almost imperceptibly, while the navigational schematics showed that they were turning in relation to their previous course. "That's it, Captain," the young helmsman said, never taking his eyes off his instruments. "We're breaking free—"

He broke off as the *Enterprise* abruptly shuddered beneath them, nearly as violently as it had when they had first encountered the alien energy field. "Captain!" Geordi said tensely. "The field is strengthening. The more power we put into breaking free, the stronger the force is holding us! If we keep this up much longer, we'll overtax the warp engines, and then we'll be in *big* trouble!"

Picard glanced over at Riker. "Cut power." His voice was tight with anger, though Riker thought you'd have to know the captain as well as he did to realize just how angry Jean-Luc was.

Riker glanced at the instrument readings over Data's shoulder. "That field didn't just strengthen enough to hold us, sir," he reported. "It moved with us, to keep us in its center."

"Like a spider that doesn't want to give up its prey," Picard said grimly. "I don't like this, Number One."

"I don't like it either, Captain."

Data suddenly straightened in his seat. "Captain, I am picking up something dead ahead. I believe we have finally reached our destination, sir."

Jean-Luc Picard's eyes narrowed, and he whispered something very softly.

"I beg your pardon, Captain?" Data said. "I did not hear your order."

"I said, 'increase power to the shields, Mister Worf.'" The captain's voice was tight with tension.

Will Riker was careful to keep his face under control, so as not to reveal that he knew the captain was lying. He'd heard his commanding officer the first time, and Picard had *not* said, "increase power to the shields."

What he'd murmured was an expletive in his native tongue. Jean-Luc Picard had said, *"Merde."*

Staring at the viewscreen, wondering what was going to happen now, Riker couldn't have agreed more with the captain's sentiment.

Chapter Five

"SHIELD POWER INCREASED, CAPTAIN," the Klingon officer announced.

"At our present rate of speed, what is our ETA, Mister Data?"

"Our speed has increased until we are moving at nearly maximum impulse power, sir. We will encounter the source of this field in . . . twenty-two minutes, Captain."

"Why didn't you pick up our destination earlier on the sensors, Mister Data?" Picard was simply asking, not accusing.

"I do not know, sir," the android replied, sounding puzzled. "It is possible that the alien energy field distorts the sensor readings."

"What do your sensors tell us about our . . ."—the captain hesitated, then continued with grim irony—"our host, Mister Data?"

"The central object within the energy field appears to be approximately five kilometers at its greatest length."

Picard pursed his lips slightly. That made the thing the size of some starbases. "Its shape, Mister Data?"

"I would judge roughly rectangular, sir, but the energy field is continuing to distort my readings, which makes its precise parameters difficult to determine. I also cannot identify the substance from which it is constructed. The only known alloys or materials registering on my sensors come from the vessels surrounding the alien artifact."

"Vessels?" the captain queried sharply. "Plural? How many vessels?"

"I cannot be sure, Captain. Some of them are so close together that their readings overlap. However, I would estimate that there are at least one hundred."

"One *hundred?*" *Could it be an alien armada?* "Are they similar in design and construction, Commander?"

"No, sir, they vary widely."

"Are they docked?"

"No, sir, they appear to be stationary, just . . . drifting."

Could that thing have captured so many ships? Picard glanced quickly over at Riker, who raised his eyebrows. "How does that number compare with the number of vessels that have gone missing in this sector?"

"Between fourteen and twenty vessels of known registry have gone through this sector and apparently vanished, Captain. I could not be more precise than that, because several of the small, privately owned freighters were not meticulous about recording all ports of call. Presumably because they were—or are—engaged in shipping activities that fall outside the bounds of Federation law."

"You mean smugglers, Data," Geordi said dryly from the other side of the bridge.

"Precisely."

"I see," Picard said. "Can we get a visual yet?"

"Not at this moment, sir. But we should be able to in about ten minutes."

Time limped by, while the bridge crew sat silent and tense in their seats. Picard glanced around him, noting the rigidity in La Forge's, Worf's, and Riker's shoulders, though the officers betrayed no other sign of nerves, well trained as they were. Deanna Troi sat composedly, her hands folded in her lap against her turquoise skirt, but Picard saw the troubled expression in her black eyes. Wesley Crusher was rather pale, but the young officer's hands were steady as they moved across his instrument panel.

He'll make a starship captain one day, Picard thought, not for the first time. *That is, if he doesn't decide to become an engineer or a scientist.* For a fleeting second, Jean-Luc remembered the being they had called the Traveler, and his prediction that Wesley Crusher was destined for greatness. *Only if he lives to fulfill that destiny,* the captain thought sourly. *And at this point, I'm beginning to wonder whether any of us will be alive tomorrow . . .*

"Mister Worf," he said, "can you pick up any transmissions from either the *PaKathen* or the *Marco Polo?*"

"Negative, sir," the Klingon's bass rumble responded a minute or so later. Picard sighed softly. "Keep trying to hail them at regular intervals, Lieutenant." *Just in case someone remains alive to answer . . .*

"Understood, Captain."

"Sir." Data suddenly turned in his seat to regard the captain, his strange yellow eyes holding Picard's unblinkingly. "I believe I can give you a visual now."

"Onscreen," the captain ordered. "Mister La Forge,

if we get a good look at this thing, I would like you to examine its visible light spectrum."

The chief engineer nodded. "Aye-aye, Captain."

Data busied himself at his controls, and the starfield steadied. "That object in the immediate center of the viewscreen is our destination, sir," Data reported. "It is mainly discernible because it is blocking out a portion of the Eta Carinae nebula. The object itself *is* illuminated . . . however, at this distance, and seen against the brightness of the stars, it appears dark."

Picard fixed his eyes on the viewer, then, after a moment's study, he could make out a small, dim blotch against the bright haze of the nebula. "Magnification factor ten, Mister Data."

The viewscreen wavered, then the object was suddenly much larger, but still too small to allow any detail to be seen. It was simply a dark blob against space.

The *Enterprise*'s captain waited another five minutes, until Data reported their distance from the artifact as one hundred thousand kilometers, then he spoke again. "Magnification factor one hundred, Mister Data."

The viewscreen wavered again, then the alien artifact was visible as a dimly lit shape, though it was blurred because of the extreme enlargement. As Data had predicted, it seemed to be roughly rectangular, though most of its surface was obscured by the floating hulks that must be derelict spacecraft of all shapes and sizes.

Picard eyed them, trying to identify any of them by shape, but they were still too far away, and there were too many. *They must all be derelicts,* he thought. *Brought here throughout the years. There could be ships hundreds of years old out there,* he realized suddenly. *Mon dieu, there could be ships thousands of years old . . . or millions.*

"They're trapped," he heard Geordi whisper. "And *we're* going to be, too . . . just like the Sargasso Sea . . ."

Automatically Jean-Luc's mind supplied the reference, and he had to agree that it was an apt one. "Mister Crusher, can you get fixes on the orbits of those ships, enough to plot us a course close to the location of the *PaKathen* and the *Marco Polo?*"

"I've been working on that, Captain," the young acting ensign replied. "We can maneuver in a limited fashion, as long as we don't try and break free. I believe I can plot a course."

"Good. Make it so. Keep shields on full, Mister Worf. We'll need them to avoid hitting one of those derelicts."

As the starship moved within fifty thousand kilometers of the artifact, Wesley Crusher spoke again. "Course plotted, Captain."

"Can you slow us down?"

"I'll try, sir." The young officer's hands moved capably, and their headlong rush toward their alien destination visibly slowed. "The tractor effect has lessened, Captain," Wesley said, sounding surprised.

"It doesn't want us to crash into it," Picard guessed. "None of these other ships show signs of impact, do they?"

"No, sir."

"Sir," Riker said urgently, "perhaps we could break free now."

"I doubt it, Number One," Picard said quietly. "And if we engage in a tug-of-war with that thing, we're likely to find ourselves ramming into some of those derelicts. Let's wait until it has us where it wants us. The tractor beam may let up entirely then. And don't forget, our orders are to rescue any survivors from those ships." He straightened in his seat. "Mister Crusher, you may engage your course when ready."

"Aye, sir!"

The *Enterprise* began weaving a complex pattern through the field of ships. They were still moving quickly enough to make some of their encounters seem entirely too close, but Wesley's course was a good one.

As they passed through the floating vessels, Picard's trained eyes quickly identified a Ferengi trade vessel, a Romulan warbird, a Gorn cruiser, an Akamerian Gatherer's battered corsair, a Klingon cruiser (*the* PaKathen *or another,* he wondered), a Delosian courier, a Promellian battle cruiser, a Benzite trader, an Orion slave ship, a Deltan passenger vessel—it was like a catalogue of ships, past and present, and there were many, many vessels that were totally unfamiliar to him.

The *Enterprise* slowed and came to a full stop within twenty kilometers of the *Marco Polo* and some fifty kilometers from the Klingon vessel.

"Forward viewscreen on the artifact, Mister Data. Let's get a good look at the thing," Riker ordered.

The screen wavered for a moment, then filled with their alien captor. It lay 250 kilometers in front of them, full in view. Picard focused his gaze on the artifact—

Then, almost immediately, he was forced to look away. Beside him, Deanna Troi gasped. He heard Riker grunt softly, as though he were in pain, then Wesley made a choking, gagging noise.

With a giant effort of will, Picard *made* himself stare full at the thing. As soon as his eyes focused on it, he was immediately aware of a disorientation so great that his eyes, used to sane angles, predictable parabolas, straight lines that stayed straight, were unable to follow the shapes of the thing without causing his brain and body acute distress. Insane, alien colors seared his vision. Dizziness assailed him; controlling his vertigo with an effort, the captain snapped, "Data! Filters on! That's a shipwide order!"

The android did not acknowledge the command until after he had implemented it, but under the circumstances Picard was not inclined to be fussy about protocol. The filters softened the outlines of the artifact, muted the colors that made a human brain reel, and in general made the thing somewhat more bearable to look at. The captain found that he could now stare at it for nearly a full two seconds before he had to look away.

Picard finally stood up, breathing deeply. His knees were weak, and he paced a few steps until he felt in better control. Then he turned and gazed around him at his bridge crew. None of them was looking at the artifact, either, except for Geordi. *And who knows what he sees when he looks at it?*

Deanna Troi was chalky pale as she balled her fists with white-knuckled intensity. Will Riker's face was white beneath the darkness of his beard. Wesley was definitely green around the gills. Even Worf looked as though he'd gotten hold of some bad *gagh* and was having trouble keeping it down.

Only Data and Geordi seemed unaffected by the sight of the thing. Picard had to force himself to regain his customary calm; the faint current of air from the life-support system turned the sweat beading on his forehead clammy.

"Mister Data, are there any life-form readings from that thing?" he demanded.

"It is impossible to be sure, Captain, because the alien field creates considerable distortion in our instrumentation," the android said. "However, I am detecting nothing that my sensors recognize as organic life."

The android adjusted a control. "And none from the *PaKathen,* sir." Picard glanced at Worf, saw the Klingon's mouth tighten, but he did not otherwise react to the news. A moment later, Data continued, "However, I am detecting seventeen life-forms aboard the *Marco Polo.*"

"And their condition?"

"The distortion makes that difficult to say for certain, sir. Most of them are not moving about, as though they are asleep, or unconscious."

The captain turned to the counselor. "Can you sense anything from the *Marco Polo?*"

Troi concentrated, eyes closed. "I can feel them," she said in a low voice. Suddenly she put a hand to her head, moaned, then swayed in her seat.

"Counselor!" Picard said sharply, but she did not answer.

With a sudden leap, Riker was by Troi's side, bending over her. "Deanna!" he cried, touching her shoulder gently. "Are you all right?"

Blindly she put out a shaking hand, and the first officer caught it, gripped it tightly. His grasp seemed to steady her, but still the half-Betazoid woman shuddered all over, as though some fever were gnawing at her bones. "Captain . . . ," she began in a hoarse whisper. "They're dying over there . . . oh, God . . . we must save them . . ."

She swayed again, then crumpled out of her seat in a dead faint.

Will Riker caught her before she could hit the floor of the bridge. The tall officer scooped up her slight form as easily as he would a child. Her long black hair streamed down over his arm like a river of ebony as he straightened up.

Picard raised his voice to address the intercom. "Bridge to sickbay. We need medics up here on the double!"

A voice he did not recognize replied, "Yes, sir!"

Riker walked up the curving ramp and waited near the turbolift doors. Seconds later, they opened, and two people, one of whom carried an antigravity stretcher, bolted out. "She passed out," Riker said as they carefully eased the counselor's limp form onto the stretcher.

One of the medical personnel passed a scanner over the unconscious Troi, then nodded briskly. "She just fainted, sir. She should be fine."

Riker made a quick involuntary movement as if to follow them as they carried the counselor into the turbolift, but he stood his ground. His blue-gray eyes were shadowed with anxiety as he came back down the ramp, but his step was determined.

Doctor Crusher's voice was heard on the bridge. "Captain? I was in my quarters and am on my way to sickbay. What happened?"

"Counselor Troi just collapsed on the bridge. The medical team is taking her to sickbay."

"Any idea what's wrong with her?"

"From what your medical team said, I gather that she simply fainted. We just got our first look at the alien artifact that is apparently causing all our troubles. The sight was . . . unsettling, to say the least." He paused as a thought struck him. "Hold a moment, Doctor." Then he turned to Data and ordered, "Order all viewing ports darkened, Mister Data. I don't want anyone else passing out from the sight of that thing."

"Yes, Captain."

"Doctor," Picard continued, "this . . . *thing*—whatever it may be—is so alien, so outside our frame of reference, that gazing upon it is physically distressing. The counselor, I believe, was reacting to that. She was also able to pick up very disturbing emotions from the *Marco Polo* crew. Our sensors indicate that there are seventeen of them still alive, but the counselor told us that they are dying."

Picard knew exactly what Beverly Crusher would say next, and she did not disappoint him. "Request permission to assemble a medical team to beam over there and rescue them, Captain."

"I am not sure yet whether it will be possible to use the transporter," he replied.

"Then we'll take the shuttlecraft," she responded promptly.

"Doctor, I will consider your request and get back to you shortly," the captain said in his most formal voice.

"But—"

"Picard out. Mister Data, will it be possible to drop the shields to use the transporter?"

"Our position is stationary, sir. The tractor field appears quiescent, now that we are here. Dropping the shields to allow the transporter to function should pose no danger . . . at least to the structure of the ship, Captain."

Picard understood completely what the android was hinting at. "Yes, but dropping them may leave us open to whatever mental assault the *Marco Polo*'s message mentioned. I get your drift, Mister Data."

Riker turned to Worf. "Can you pick up any log entries or tactical data on the condition of the *PaKathen,* Lieutenant?"

"The last log entry was made by Captain Khlar when his ship had come to rest, Commander. He reported dissension and assassinations among his crew, and logged his decision to blast their way out of this trap. That is the last entry."

Riker gave Picard a speculative glance. "Can you scan their weapons' status, Lieutenant?"

"Readings from their gunnery station indicate that all forward disrupter banks have been discharged, sir."

"Confirming Lieutenant Worf's information," Data said. "I am detecting ionized particles in this area that would indicate a volley of disrupter fire."

"And yet the artifact remains untouched," Picard mused softly. He considered options for a moment, then sighed. He didn't like the idea of dropping the shields for any reason, but theirs was a rescue mission, and risks were often necessary to fulfill orders. "Lieutenant Worf, I have decided to send a medical team over to the *Marco Polo* to bring the survivors back," he said to the Klingon security chief. "You are ordered to assemble an adequate security force to deal with whatever you may find over there, and to head that force personally."

"Yes, Captain!" Worf, as always, preferred action to waiting.

"Captain," Riker said urgently, "request permission to accompany the security team."

"Denied, Number One," Picard said evenly. "I want you here. If this . . . mental invasion should begin aboard the *Enterprise,* then you and I must be prepared to watch each other for signs of instability. *And* be prepared to act on the results of our observations. Do you understand?"

"Yes, sir, I do," replied Riker with equal gravity.

"Lieutenant Worf, assemble your security team. Use Transporter Room 3. Have Chief O'Brien signal the bridge when you are ready to beam over, so that we can drop the shields."

"Yes, sir!" The Klingon officer beckoned to an ensign to replace him at his station, then he strode into the turbolift.

The captain spoke to the air. "Doctor Crusher, this is the captain. What is Counselor Troi's condition?"

"Physically she's unharmed, but I've had to sedate her to blunt the effects of having the *Marco Polo*'s crew at such close proximity," the chief medical officer replied. "Apparently many of them are insane. Sir, how soon can we beam a rescue team over?"

"Doctor, I am approving your request for a medical team to help the survivors aboard the *Marco Polo*," Picard replied formally. "However, as chief medical officer, I want you to remain here. If this . . . dream illness, mental plague, whatever it is, should invade the *Enterprise*, I will need you above all others, thus I can't afford to risk you. Can you recommend someone to head the emergency medical team? Preferably someone who is extremely . . . stable."

"Lieutenant Selar, Captain. She's a Vulcan. Need I say more?"

"No indeed. An excellent choice. Have the lieutenant and your emergency team join Lieutenant Worf and his security people in Transporter Room 3 as soon as possible."

"Yes, Captain," she replied briskly.

Having half expected her to argue with him about wanting to lead the medical team personally, Jean-Luc Picard breathed a silent sigh of relief.

Selar was on her way to Thala's cabin to talk to the Andorian child when the summons from the chief medical officer reached her. "Lieutenant Selar here," she said, touching her communicator.

"Selar, I've recommended you to lead the medical team for the rescue party that will board the *Marco Polo*," Beverly Crusher said. "Counselor Troi reported that the crew was experiencing some kind of mass mental disorder. We're having trouble getting accurate readings because of the energy field the alien structure is emitting, but, as far as we can determine, there are seventeen humans alive over there, most apparently unconscious, but a few who are still ambulatory and may be violent. If you beam over with a security party, how many of our people will you require to stabilize those patients, then transport them back to the *Enterprise?*"

Selar made a quick mental calculation, then spoke with barely a pause. "Myself and six others."

"Whom would you recommend for your team?"

"Doctors Logan and Chandra," Selar said immediately. "Also Nurse Johnson, Nurse Selinski, Doctor Gavar, if she will volunteer to serve on this mission, and Nurse Itoh."

"I don't know about Chandra," Crusher objected. "She's pretty far along with her pregnancy. If there *is* some kind of malign mental force over there, what could it do to a fetus?"

Selar nodded. "A good point. Very well, I request Doctor Grunewalt instead."

"Approved. I'll have them assemble in sickbay immediately."

"I am on my way," Selar said, and she tapped her communicator to close the channel. Quickly, she turned back toward the turbolift, wondering if there would be time to ask Beverly to check on Thala while she was gone with the rescue party. She hadn't seen the child since her emotional outburst yesterday, and she was concerned.

"Selar! *Wait!*" A familiar voice broke into her thoughts.

"Lift hold," the Vulcan commanded, and a second later Thala flung herself through the doors, panting hard, obviously having run to catch her. "I was just on my way to see you," Selar told the little Andorian girl. "However, our visit will have to wait until later. I have just been ordered to take a medical team over to the *Marco Polo.*"

Thala's small blue features were pinched with anxiety. "Selar, what's going on, anyway? Everyone says all the ports are dark! Is the ship in some kind of danger?" She swallowed hard. "Have the Borgs come back?"

"We are trillions of kilometers away from Borg space," Selar said reassuringly. "No, our current situation does not involve them."

The child relaxed slightly. "Then what's going on?"

"I have not yet been fully briefed," replied Selar truthfully. "And I probably could not discuss what I knew if I had. But I do not believe we are in any immediate peril. After all," she pointed out reasonably, "Captain Picard has not continued the red alert, has he?"

"No," Thala admitted. "That's true."

"Then I suggest you try not to concern yourself. I promise that I will come and see you as soon as I am able."

"Okay," Thala whispered. Then she blurted, "Selar, it won't be *dangerous* where you're going, will it?"

"I do not know," the Vulcan said, forced by the direct question to respond with the truth. "However, I will have a security team with me, and I am sure that Lieutenant Worf will be able to protect us from any menace."

Thala nodded, seemingly mollified. "Yeah, I guess he can. He's awfully big, and Wesley says he's very strong and the best shot on the ship . . ." She trailed off, then continued excitedly as a sudden thought struck her, "But not as strong as Data! Selar, you'll never guess what happened when I met Lieutenant Commander Data!"

"I cannot guess," Selar began, but just then the lift whined to a halt. "At least, I cannot guess *now,*" she amended, "but later on, when I see you, I will try. At the moment, I must go."

"Okay," Thala said softly. Then, as the Vulcan

stepped out of the lift, she suddenly grabbed the woman's hand in both of hers. "Be *careful!*" she whispered fiercely.

Selar nodded. "I will, Thala."

The lift doors closed on the child's farewell wave.

The doctor walked briskly down the corridor and into sickbay. There she found a buzz of activity as her emergency crew gathered supplies. She had chosen these six because all of them, like herself, had had some experience in psychiatric wards, and all were of a calm, unflappable nature—even Doctor Gavar, the Tellarite physician from the Starfleet exchange program. Most Tellarites were pugnacious and easily excitable, but Gavar was atypical. Selar was pleased that she had chosen to volunteer for this mission. She was as strong as a *sehlat,* in case any of the patients were indeed violent. From the briefing Beverly Crusher had given her earlier, Selar gathered that there had been both murder and suicide aboard the *Marco Polo.*

Doctor Logan was a short, plump, gray-haired woman who had been with Starfleet since graduating from medical school. Selar had chosen her for this mission because she had interned in a human psychiatric ward.

Selinski was a tall, strapping man in his mid-forties. He was an excellent nurse, efficient, conscientious, and protective of his patients.

Nurse Itoh was a tiny woman with slanted, almost Vulcan-appearing eyes; Nurse Johnson was a huge, muscular woman with very dark skin and hair. Their natures, however, were utterly opposite to what most humans seemed to expect upon seeing them—though large in size, Johnson was soft-spoken and timid, while the smaller Itoh was assertive, extremely talkative, and noisy, given to loud laughter and fond of raucous, vulgar jokes.

Johannes Grunewalt was a small, wizened man,

without much physical strength (which was why Selar had not made him one of her first choices). But he was a competent physician, if a little unimaginative in his diagnostic skills.

Gathering up their assorted medical supplies and the portable antigravity stretchers, the medical team followed Selar up to Transporter Room 3. There the Vulcan found Lieutenant Worf with three armed security guards that he introduced as Clara Bernstein, Ricardo Montez, and Caledon. O'Brien informed the captain that the away team was ready.

Moments later, the security party stepped onto the platform and dissolved in a wash of light. Selar nodded to her team, and they stepped onto the transporter. The Vulcan officer nodded to Transporter Chief O'Brien. He manipulated his controls, and she felt the familiar sense of dislocation seize her.

The *Enterprise's* medical team materialized on the cargo deck, which was the one space large enough on the freighter to allow them all to beam over together. It was cold because of the refrigeration, and deadly silent. Selar shivered slightly, feeling the cold more than a human would, and experienced a strange mental disquiet. The *Marco Polo* was silent—too silent. She saw Johnson tremble and Grunewalt glance uneasily over his shoulder.

The security team waved at them to stay where they were, then, phasers ready, moved around the main stack of cargo toward the entrance of the deck. Each member of the landing party had been provided with a schematic of the freighter.

A moment later Selar heard Worf's gruff tones. "Doctor, we have found someone, but I fear we are too late to help her."

Selar moved quickly to join the security team, her people following her. Worf and his team were squatting beside a limp figure that was sprawled in the open doorway. A thin spatter of red blood marred the light gray of the deck, its source hidden beneath the facedown form.

"The body is cold," Worf rumbled as Selar reached him with a few running steps. "And I cannot locate a pulse."

Dropping down beside him, Selar ran her medical scanner over the woman, then she nodded brusquely. "She's been dead for at least two hours." Already knowing what she would see, because of the tricorder's readings, she turned the human over.

The corpse rolled onto her back, a once-attractive woman in her late forties with soft golden curls. An ornamental dagger was embedded in her chest. The blade had pierced the left ventricle, and death had been virtually immediate—which accounted for the relatively small amount of blood.

The body was icy cold from lying in the refrigerated compartment. Selar looked up at her team, noting that Johnson looked wide-eyed with fear and making a mental note to keep the woman with her.

"We will search in teams of three," the Vulcan ordered crisply. "One doctor, one nurse, and one security officer to each team, is that understood?" They nodded. "Doctor Grunewalt, you and Nurse Selinski will make one team." Worf gestured to Bernstein to join the designated medical personnel.

"Nurse Johnson and I will make another team." Again Worf gestured, and Caledon, a small, dark-haired man from Proxima II, stepped up to join the Vulcan and Johnson. "Doctor Logan, you and Nurse Itoh will make up the last team." Worf himself prepared to accompany Logan's team.

"What about me?" Doctor Gavar asked.

"You and Yeoman Montez will be remaining here on the cargo deck," Selar said. "Chief O'Brien reports that the energy field surrounding both ships is causing some distortion in his instrumentation. So, on his request that we allow a margin for error in the transporter coordinates, we will be beaming all patients back from the cargo deck. Gavar and Montez will assume the care of the patients waiting for transport."

She glanced around at all of them. "The process of transporting will provide full decontamination procedures, as usual, but from what Doctor Crusher and I have observed so far, we are not dealing with a pathogen. Instead, we believe that we are dealing with some kind of malign alien mental invasion, possibly generated from the artifact." She paused. "I have been conscious of *something* ever since I beamed over. Have any of the rest of you?"

All of the medical and security people nodded—even, after a second, Lieutenant Worf.

"But I thought we had scanned no life-forms over there," Doctor Grunewalt said.

"We have not. However, there have been many new discoveries in connection with this mission, so we cannot be certain that our instrumentation will correctly evaluate everything connected with the artifact," Selar pointed out. "But, for the moment, we are concerned only with this vessel. My point is that whatever affected the crew of this ship may affect us, too. If you should observe signs of mental deterioration in a team member, you are hereby charged to report your observation to me and to the other unaffected team member immediately. Is that understood?"

Everyone nodded, casting uneasy sideways glances at one another. "Good. Team One"—she indicated Grunewalt and Selinski—"you will take the forward lounge, the officers' quarters, and the galley . . ."

A minute later, she had finished assigning the teams, and they were all on their way.

Selar followed her tricorder to the location of the first survivor. On the way they passed six bodies, two fully clothed, one in a sleep shirt, and three nude. The two clothed people had killed themselves, one with an overdose of tranquilizers (the woman was either the ship's medic or had forced the lock on the pharmaceutical stores), the other with a phaser blast to the head. But the ones who were sprawled in the doorways of their cabins appeared to have been roused from sleep, staggered into the corridor, then died. Selar quickly checked the cause of death as they passed and caught Caledon's eye. "Heart failure," she said.

"Looks to me as though something scared 'em to death," he said.

"Dreams?" asked Nurse Johnson faintly. Despite her dark coloring, she appeared pale.

The survivor, when they found him, was a man in his late fifties, curled up into a fetal ball so tight that it seemed impossible for bone and muscle to compress that much. Selar and Johnson bundled him onto the stretcher, then took him back to the transport point.

Within the next forty-five minutes, they located and rescued another five survivors. The other teams reported similar successes, save for one crewman who turned violent as they were putting him on the anti-gravity stretcher, gibbering and shrieking so loudly that Selar's sensitive ears picked up the sound a deck away. The man then expired on the spot, despite all of Doctor Grunewalt's resuscitation efforts.

As they loaded up the last survivor in their assigned area, Selar's communicator beeped. She tapped it. "Selar here."

"Logan here!" came a breathless voice. "It's Nurse Itoh! She attacked Lieutenant Worf, screaming that he was a dirty Klingon spy, and then, when I tried to help him, she attacked *me!* Together we managed to wrestle her down, but when I turned to get a tranquilizer from my bag, she literally *threw* the lieutenant off her and escaped! I never saw such strength!"

"Where is she now?"

"I don't know! She disappeared in the direction of the galley, but that leads into a main corridor, so she could be anywhere by now!"

"Please calm yourself, Doctor. Where is Lieutenant Worf?"

Logan drew a deep breath, and when she spoke again, her voice was steadier. "He is with me."

"Lieutenant?" Selar said.

"Here, Doctor," came the bass rumble.

"Have Doctor Logan transport back, then rendezvous with my party immediately. We are in the crew quarters on Deck A. We will head directly for the transport coordinates from here."

"Understood. Worf out."

Selar gestured to Nurse Johnson and Caledon to guide the antigravity stretcher and headed back up the corridor. Even though she was alert, every sense attuned to pick up another presence, she had no warning. One moment she was walking cautiously around a bend in the hall, the next a piercing scream blasted her ears, and a kicking, clawing, berserk fury was atop her, teeth snapping at her nose.

Selar stiff-armed Itoh, managing to hold the woman away from her face, but just barely. The madwoman's insane strength was, as Doctor Logan had reported, unbelievable. A hand raked the Vulcan's face, fingernails scoring grooves in her cheek. The flare of pain gave Selar the impetus to throw the woman off, away from her. The nurse scrambled to get up, and Selar plunged forward, still on all fours, crashing headlong against the nurse's knees and sending her flying again.

The blow stunned the human woman for a precious

second as Selar clawed her way up Itoh's body; a heartbeat later, the Vulcan's fingers found the nerve between her neck and her shoulder. The nurse sagged, unconscious.

Breathing hard, Selar rolled off the limp body and sat up, her face smarting. Tentatively she put fingers to her cheek, and they came away smeared green. Selar summoned her inward vision to assess her injuries and was relieved to find nothing more than the scratches and bruises.

Nurse Johnson and Caledon were staring at her, frozen with shock, still holding the straps of the antigravity stretcher. "We'd better put her on it, too," Selar said, climbing to her feet wearily, bracing her knees so they would hold her. "We must hurry. Lieutenant Worf will be wondering where we are."

As she stared down at the slack face of her unconscious friend, Nurse Johnson abruptly turned a sickly greenish-gray color and began shaking all over. For a moment Selar wondered whether she were about to have another one run mad, but from some inner wellspring of strength the big woman rallied. Straightening her shoulders, she matter-of-factly picked up Itoh's feet while the security guard picked up her shoulders, then they deposited her on the stretcher beside the *Marco Polo* crewman.

When the team reached the transporter coordinates on the cargo deck, they found Worf, phaser drawn, staring suspiciously at Doctor Gavar, who was sitting atop the unconscious body of Yeoman Montez.

"What happened?" Selar demanded, wondering whether Gavar, too, had been affected by whatever it was that had affected Itoh and the *Marco Polo*'s crew. But the Tellarite physician's small, weak eyes beneath her bushy brows were sane.

"He began saying that the shadows of the dead were

coming to life and gathering around us," the doctor replied, her voice filled with unconscious drama. "Then he drew his phaser and fired at one of them." She waved at a stack of seed-grain sacks with a blackened area. "By that time I knew he was, as my people would put it, paddling a boat with a sieve instead of an oar. I agreed to help him kill the shadows and managed to get close enough to him to shoot him full of chlorpromazine. Then, to make sure he didn't go anywhere, I sat on him." A thought occurred to her, and she added, "The other teams have already gone back."

"On my order," Worf added.

Selar nodded wearily and beckoned to the Tellarite to get up. She did so, and the Klingon officer stepped forward and hoisted up the drugged human, slinging him easily over his shoulder.

"Good work, Doctor Gavar," the Vulcan said, and the Tellarite flushed with pride. Selar tapped her communicator. "Chief O'Brien?"

"O'Brien here," came the immediate response.

"Beam the remainder of the landing party—plus the last survivor of the *Marco Polo*—back, please."

She felt the familiar sensation seize her, saw the walls of the dead freighter fade, only to be replaced by the clean, bright bulkheads of the *Enterprise*.

"Selar?" The voice of Beverly Crusher reached her from the communicator. "Are you all right? Doctor Logan reported trouble with Nurse Itoh."

"We have returned to the *Enterprise*," Selar reported. "I am undamaged, and Nurse Itoh is unharmed physically, though I had to render her unconscious. Apparently whatever affected the crew of the *Marco Polo* also affected Nurse Itoh and Yeoman Montez."

"They aren't the only ones." The chief medical

officer's voice sounded as though she were holding herself together with a bare effort. "It started as soon as we dropped the shields to allow your party to beam over. We've had two attempted suicides and an attempted murder over here. Whatever got to the *Marco Polo*'s crew is now spreading to the *Enterprise.*"

Chapter Six

THALA STUMBLED THROUGH *the rubble of the deck,
hands out before her, blind and despairing. Her sensory
net was useless, its functions shorted out by the explosion on Deck 18, when the Borg weapon had penetrated
the starship's shields. She smelled fire, heard the air
hissing away into space.*

*Catching her toe in something wet and slimy, she fell
headlong, landing on something yielding. Stunned by
the impact, she felt around blindly, trying to determine
where she was, what had tripped her. A body, broken,
eviscerated, lay beneath her. Her hands sank into cold
wetness, and she felt the bulgy shapes of organs. A loop
of entrails was wound around her foot, serpentlike.*

*Gagging with disgust, she pushed herself up and felt
the body, irrationally trying to find a pulse, even though
she knew the person was dead. As she tried vainly to
locate the throat or the side of the face, Thala felt her
questing fingers sink into something quiveringly soft,
then jar against hardness. Sickness clutched her stomach as she realized that she had just sunk her fingers
knuckle-deep in the corpse's eye sockets . . .*

Retching, whimpering, Thala snatched her fingers away from the sticky, punctured jelly that had been eyes. "I'm sorry," she whispered, and she felt the body shudder with pain as it came back to life.

As if under compulsion, Thala's fingers quested again, found a sharp-boned face, fluffy hair—and then, with a horror that gripped her like giant jaws, antennae.

Thev. It was her father's body, and it moved beneath her, making a rusty, mewling sound. His hands touched her face, pawing at her, probing for her eyes.

"They won't do you any good, Father!" she screamed. "I'm blind!"

But the living corpse was holding her in a terrifying grip, and the hands were digging into her eye sockets. Thala felt pain such as she had never experienced before, and a full-blown shriek burst from her throat—

—and she sat up in her bed, safe in her cabin aboard the *Enterprise.* Her heart was pounding so hard that it hurt, and for a moment she could only press her clenched fists against her chest and rock back and forth in agony, a whimper issuing from the back of her throat.

Then she began to keen aloud, terrified and alone. Only one thought kept her, she thought, from dying from the fear and loneliness.

Pulling on her sensory net over her nightgown, she swung out of the bed and ran for the door, burst out into the corridor.

"Selar," she moaned as she pelted headlong for the lift, and then louder and louder until she was screaming so hard her throat was on fire—

"Selar. *Selar. Selar!* SELAR! SELARSELAR!!!"

* * *

Jean-Luc Picard faced his crew across the conference table again, hands folded before him on the polished surface, his expression grim. Just before calling the briefing, he'd had a hot cup of his favorite Earl Grey tea, but the brew had done little to alleviate the crushing weight of weariness that seemed to enfold him like a garment. "How are the survivors from the *Marco Polo?*" he asked Beverly Crusher.

She shrugged tiredly, her usually silky red hair hanging limp and dull. Dark shadows marred the fair skin beneath her eyes, and she looked haggard, older than her actual age. Picard wondered for a moment how long it had been since *she'd* slept.

"We may lose one of them today," she said quietly, "if we can't bring him out of whatever dream or fugue state he's in. His metabolic functions are going to short out. Nobody can exist for long in that much fear." She sighed. "But the others are stable. Most of them are catatonic. Selar says the Vulcan Science Academy has telepathic healers who may be able to go into their minds and bring them safely out of their withdrawal. Even so, they'll probably need months of therapy to cope with the experience. Many of them may have committed murders, don't forget, under the influence of whatever that alien thing is."

"Are any of them able to talk rationally? So we could find out what happened?" Riker asked.

"Perhaps the first officer, after he comes out of nerve regeneration treatments. When we were preparing him, he managed a few sentences and seemed fairly lucid. But he'd lost so much blood that he was in critical condition, and soon after he slipped into deep shock. We almost lost him."

"He was physically injured, then?" Picard asked.

"He'd been stabbed twelve times—by his own captain, or so he told me," Crusher answered bluntly.

"He also said that he was the one who sent the distress call."

Visualizing the scene, Picard shook his head, repressing a shudder. "How is Counselor Troi? She might well be the one who could offer us the best guidance in dealing with this situation."

Beverly looked grim. "Captain, I'm having to keep her sedated. I'm afraid for her sanity if she regains consciousness. The mental agony of the *Marco Polo* crew is apparently causing her distress even when she is not awake."

"Do you think the alien artifact is affecting her, too?" Riker asked.

"I don't believe so. She was awake and conscious up to the point where the *Marco Polo* survivors were beamed aboard, but she blacked out from the shock the moment the first group was transported over." Her mouth tightened, and she looked down at her hands. "Before I sedated her, she nearly went into fibrillation. If I allow her to regain consciousness, it may be not only her sanity that's in jeopardy."

"I see . . . ," Picard said slowly.

A moment of leaden silence passed, then the captain straightened his shoulders with an effort and sat up in his seat. "Let us, for a moment, review our situation. We are being held by some kind of tractor field that is unlike any we have encountered before, one that apparently is capable of proportionately increasing its strength to keep captive whatever it has managed to trap." He took a deep breath. "The source of this field is an artifact that was obviously constructed by some beings extremely alien to us—so alien that even to look upon an object they constructed is extremely disorienting to human vision.

"Our instruments detect no life-forms aboard the artifact, but the energy field surrounding it interferes considerably with our sensors. Still, since our hails have produced no response, and there is absolutely no indication that anything organic exists aboard the structure, for the moment I am going on the assumption that the artifact is either functioning by remote control or obeying programming given it by beings who are either dead or gone.

"From using the library computer to identify as many ships as possible in this . . ."—Picard glanced over at La Forge—"this space Sargasso, we have been able to determine that the artifact has apparently been ensnaring vessels not only since before the Federation was formed but before either the Romulan or the Klingon empires arose."

Wesley Crusher's eyes widened at the idea of such age.

"Each of the vessels is, as far as we can determine, in perfect operating order. Not marred from cosmic dust accretion, no signs of meteor impacts, nothing. Something about this field apparently preserves them as well as imprisons them."

Picard looked around at each of his officers. "When I first saw the alien artifact, it was difficult to see, because my eyes did not want to follow its contours. My emotional reaction was that I should look away, because the thing was not put together in any sane fashion that my brain could readily comprehend. Then, when I forced myself to concentrate on its shape and colors, I experienced such vertigo that I felt vaguely nauseated. What about the rest of you?"

Riker, Wesley, and Worf all agreed that they had experienced similar reactions. Beverly Crusher, who had watched the record of the event after the fact, announced that she, too, had been sickened by the sight of the artifact. The captain turned to his third-in-command. "Mister Data, how did the sight of the artifact affect you?"

The android officer considered for a moment. "I did

not experience the emotional distress, repugnance, vertigo, or nausea that the artifact apparently generates in humanoids," he said finally. "However, my circuitry is not calibrated to allow me to *see* the thing in any meaningful way. To me it is a blur, though I can make out a few details. Its colors are such that they overload the color-sensing circuits in my positronic brain, and I perceive it mostly in shades of gray, values of light and shadow."

Picard nodded, then turned to the chief engineer. "Mister La Forge, how did the artifact appear to *you?*"

Geordi shrugged. "Captain, I examined it thoroughly, and it didn't look like anything I ever saw before . . . but it didn't bother me to look at it." He smiled ruefully. "And I may sound crazy saying this, but it had a . . . symmetry about it that I found, well . . . beautiful. The colors harmonize with the shapes of the various pods that stick out of it."

Taken aback, Picard glanced at his second-in-command. Riker raised his eyebrows, then shook his head in silence. "Mister La Forge," the captain said, "can you sketch the artifact as it appeared to you? At least a rough approximation of its actual shape?"

"I'm no artist, but I can try, sir," Geordi said, and he activated the controls in the table, so that what he produced would be shown up on the viewer for all to see.

Moving his fingers hesitantly, Geordi "sketched," using the computer, manipulating the colors, lines, and depths of the three-dimensional image until he produced a shape that appeared vaguely rectangular but with many small protrusions branching off it. Every shape on the thing was an "almost." Some protrusions were almost spheres, some were almost rectangles—except for one strangely parabolic side— some were almost squares or triangles or rhombohedrons. There were also shapes that Picard could find no approximation for at all. The entire thing was fired with wild shades of color that looked like the palette of some mad, brilliant artist.

The *Enterprise*'s officers sat gazing at Geordi's creation for several minutes in silence. Riker was the first to break the spell cast by the strangely compelling object. "What can it be?" he wondered aloud.

"A weapon of some kind," Worf said immediately. "One designed to blast and warp minds instead of bodies. Truly a diabolical creation."

"You mean some kind of ultimate weapon designed to kill in such a way that only the living beings aboard a vessel would be affected, thus leaving the ship unharmed?" Picard found the notion repugnant. "Hardly a pleasant idea."

"But not a new one, Captain," Data put in. "Back in Earth's late twentieth century, there existed a weapon called the neutron bomb that was designed to destroy life, while leaving structures intact."

Worf gave the humans a surprised glance. "I had no idea that humans were capable of coming up with something as hideous and efficient as that," he rumbled.

"It is not something we're proud of, Lieutenant," Picard said sharply. "And that was hundreds of years ago."

"Now that we've rescued the survivors from the *Marco Polo,* Captain," Wesley Crusher said, "perhaps we ought to try and break free again."

"I have been considering that," Picard admitted. "It is only the proximity of the other ships that has me worried. Crashing against them as we fought the tractor field would eventually short out our shields."

"We could disintegrate the ones closest to us," Worf said. "I was going to suggest that for the warriors aboard the *PaKathen,* so they could receive, in death, an honorable end."

"But if the artifact is a weapon," Geordi said, "it's possible that it has defense systems that would be triggered by firing on the ships, or firing on the artifact itself."

"We don't know yet that it *is* a weapon," the captain reminded them.

"What else could it be?" Worf asked, but nobody had any suggestions to offer.

The captain sighed. "Our examination of the *PaKathen*'s last log entry and sensor analysis of its weapon banks indicate that the Klingons *did* fire at the artifact, remember . . . with no apparent effect."

"The *Enterprise* is a far larger, more powerful ship," Riker pointed out. "Perhaps our phasers could damage it, where the *PaKathen*'s weaponry could not."

Picard thought for a moment. "Nothing ventured, nothing gained, Number One," he said. "I believe an experiment is in order." He addressed the tabletop. "Computer, restore normal viewing mode to the conference room viewscreens."

The bridge crew turned their heads away as the darkened ports suddenly filled with the stomach-wrenching sight of the artifact. Only La Forge remained facing the alien structure. Picard then tapped his communicator. "Ensign Whitedeer, this is the captain."

"Yes, sir?" came the voice of the young security officer who was on current duty at Worf's station.

"Prepare to fire a five-second contained burst from the forward phaser banks directly at the artifact, on my order, Ensign."

"Yes, sir." There was a few seconds' pause, then, "Ready on your signal, Captain."

"Fire, Ensign."

"Firing, sir!"

Quickly the bridge crew swung around, squinting, as the deadly beams shot out, filling the viewport with a wash of golden, coruscating light. Mentally, the captain counted the seconds off, then the five-second burst was over. The glow faded away.

Leaving the artifact completely unchanged. The captain glanced away from the unnerving sight. A murmur of wonder and distress filled the conference room as the bridge crew reacted. Whitedeer's voice reached them. "My instruments show no damage whatsoever, Captain." He hesitated. "As a matter of fact . . . the thing appears to have *absorbed* ninety-two percent of the phaser energy, sir."

"I see. That will be all, Ensign," Picard said. He sighed. "Computer, darken the viewports again."

The artifact vanished from sight.

Will Riker shook his head, his bearded face grim. "Nothing ventured, nothing gained is right."

"What about photon torpedoes, sir?" La Forge said.

"The backlash from such a close-range detonation would be quite likely to damage the *Enterprise*," Data warned. "Unless, of course, the energy field absorbed it all, as it did the phaser blast."

"But we could try it," Riker said. "With all power transferred to our forward shields, we might not sustain too much damage."

"That would be an extremely high-stakes gamble, Number One," the captain said. "One that I would like more information about before attempting." He turned to the chief medical officer. "Doctor Crusher, what is the mental condition of the crew? Exactly how many incidents have there been?"

"Five, Captain," she said softly. "Two attempted suicides, one attempted murder—the man is now in the quarantine cell in sickbay—one case of hysteria, an Andorian child, a couple of hours ago. And one case of fugue withdrawal, like the ones we beamed back from the *Marco Polo.*"

Picard pursed his lips thoughtfully. "Five. We have been within the sphere of influence of the artifact for nearly ten hours now. Doctor, how long had the twenty-six casualties aboard the *Marco Polo* been dead when the away team examined their bodies?"

"Two had been dead for about eighteen hours, but most had been dead for fifteen hours or less," she reported. "Remember, one died while they were examining him."

"To me, that suggests that whatever killed them is not infiltrating the *Enterprise* with nearly the success that it had with the *Marco Polo,*" the captain said slowly. "And I would speculate that it is our shielding that is providing the protection."

"It's certainly true that the onset of many of the cases occurred when our shields were down to allow the away team members and their patients to beam back," Crusher said.

"No wonder it affected the *Marco Polo* so much faster!" Riker said. "A freighter is not equipped with shielding beyond standard navigational shields."

"But *PaKathen* had shields," Worf reminded him. "It was a military vessel."

"The Klingon vessel was also captured several days before the *Marco Polo,*" Riker said. "Besides, the effects may have been more immediate and severe with Klingons."

"Have you felt any distress, Lieutenant?" Crusher asked anxiously.

The security chief drew himself up. "Certainly *not,*" he began, then hesitated, his face taking on the expression Worf wore whenever he faced a conflict between duty as a Starfleet officer and his dignity and honor as a Klingon. He finally nodded reluctantly.

"While I was aboard the *Marco Polo,*" he confessed, "I did feel a certain amount of mental . . . stress." He glared at the assembled company. "Everyone in the landing party did. *Including* Lieutenant Selar."

"I see . . . ," Picard said, careful not to smile. He got up to pace slowly back and forth, hands behind his back, as he considered all options. "I have decided that we have a small margin of relative safety here," he said at last. "And we will use that time to discover more about our antagonist. Mister Crusher, you and Lieutenant Commander La Forge, with Lieutenant Commander Data's help, will attempt to recalibrate our sensing devices so that we can get an idea of what is inside the artifact. Search especially for any sign of control devices or machinery that may be generating that field. Try and find out how it absorbs our phaser bursts. You have eight hours."

The captain turned to the chief medical officer. "You, Doctor, will please have sickbay provide me with hourly updates on the mental and emotional status of the crew and passengers."

"I understand, sir," Crusher said, pushing herself up by bracing her hands on the table. "I'll see to it personally."

"No, you won't," the captain said evenly. "At least not until you have gotten some sleep yourself. I need you clear-headed, Doctor, not sodden with exhaustion. Is that understood?"

Beverly Crusher drew herself up regally, then, as the captain's eyes held hers, her tight mouth relaxed into a weary but still impish smile. "All right, I'll agree to rest, Captain," she said, "as long as *you* agree to do the same. Commander Riker can receive those hourly reports while you sleep. I wouldn't want to have to declare *you* unfit for duty, either."

Nobody still seated at the table looked at Jean-Luc Picard—everyone was suddenly fascinated by their fingernails, or the tabletop, or imaginary threads on the sleeves of their uniforms. Even Data's customary candid gaze was averted.

The captain took a deep breath, then nodded. "Consider it a bargain, Doctor."

Jean-Luc Picard sat woodenly in the copilot's seat aboard the shuttlecraft that slowly maneuvered through the Maxia-Zeta star system. Every nerve and muscle in his body was screaming with agony from the physical stress he had just undergone . . . but his body was in topnotch condition, compared with his mental state.

The captain could not move, could barely blink, and every lurch and movement of the small craft seemed to explode inside his head with pain. The smell of smoke and the stench of burning instrumentation pervaded his nostrils; the reek seemed to have permanently bonded with the charred fabric of his uniform.

And all that was as nothing to the pain in his mind and heart.

I have lost my ship. I have lost my ship. I have lost my ship. *The words repeated themselves in his mind like some kind of insane mantra, until Jean-Luc Picard thought that it would be infinitely easier to curse all the gods there ever were, then die—or go silently mad. Gazing at the smoldering, abandoned hulk with the identification code NCC 2893 that had, an hour ago, been a gleaming Constellation-class starship, Picard felt the fabric of his existence crumble and fall apart.*

I have lost my ship. *They had entrusted the deep-space exploratory vessel* Stargazer *to his care, and he had lost her to an unprovoked attack by an unidentified vessel. The ship floated in the viewport of the slowly withdrawing shuttlecraft like a scarred and burned toy, hardly seeming real anymore.*

Let it be a dream, a nightmare, *the captain thought, childishly squeezing his eyes shut and willing time to turn back*. Let it be *then*, not *now*. Let it not have happened.

But when he opened his eyes many heartbeats later, Stargazer's *black-marked hulk was still there, slowly dwindling in size. Soon she would vanish altogether, lost to him forever.* What could I have done to prevent this? *Picard wondered, absently rubbing left-handed at the filth smeared across his face, smelling again the burning and the fumes from his uniform's sleeve.* There must have been something. And even if there hadn't been, what am I doing here? A good captain is supposed to go down with his vessel . . .

Someone touched his shoulder gently, but Picard did not start, nor look around. "Captain." *The first officer's voice reached him, soft in the stillness.* "The medical officer can see you now."

Stargazer *was growing ever smaller as the little fleet of shuttlecraft grouped into formation for the long voyage to the nearest Federation outpost. Picard silently shook his head at the young officer. No doctor could heal the wound in his soul, and he did not deserve the oblivion of sleep, because he had lost his ship.*

"Sir," *the man tried again, a note of unwonted gentleness in his voice,* "the medic would like to see you now."

"I'm all right, Commander," *Picard managed to say, his voice hoarse from shouting orders above the noise, and from inhaling the fumes.*

"Respectfully, sir, you are not. *You're injured, Captain. Your right arm . . .*"

Dully Picard looked down at his arm and noticed, for the first time, that a deep, ragged gash extended from below the elbow up through the deltoid muscles. Blood was oozing out of it sluggishly, dripping off his fingers. There was a puddle of it soaking into the shuttlecraft's deck covering. His uniform hung from his shoulder like a rag, and seared shreds of fabric clung to the wound.

Reddish second-degree burns were beginning to swell the skin of his shoulder, forearm, hand, and wrist.

In the rush of directing the battle, of saving his crew, (and losing his ship, a mocking voice reminded him yet again), and of overseeing the abandon-ship procedure, he had felt no pain, nothing . . . and he still felt nothing.

"This can wait, Number One," he said, "until all the other injuries are attended to." He swallowed, the inside of his throat feeling as though fire had seared it. "Updates on casualties?"

"No deaths since the first two, Captain." The commander paused, then said slowly, "Sir . . . it's a long way back to civilization, a large part of it through uncharted space."

Mentally, Picard pictured their most direct route, then he nodded silently.

"Sir?" The first officer's tentative voice spoke again after a long moment.

Jean-Luc sighed; he'd rather hoped that the younger man had gone away. "Yes, Number One?"

"Respectfully, sir, may I remind the captain that we're going to need him, or we haven't a chance in hell of making it back?"

Slowly, Picard turned away from the receding Stargazer and looked up at his second-in-command. "We'll make it back," he said finally.

"I know, sir," the man said. "But only if you're in command. To be honest, sir, I can't do it alone." He nodded at the captain's wound. "So will you please come see the medic, sir?"

It was the hardest thing Jean-Luc Picard had ever done, but slowly, slowly, he straightened his shoulders. He nodded, then, unsteadily, he climbed to his feet and stood unassisted. Feeling light-headed from reaction and loss of blood, he managed to speak in a level tone.

"You're right, Number One," he said. *"This wound needs attention. Where is the medic?"*

As he turned to follow the commander into the cargo section of the shuttlecraft, which had been turned into an impromptu sickbay, the smoldering wreck that was the Stargazer *caught Picard's eye for the last time.* I have lost my ship . . .

Deliberately, Jean-Luc turned his back on it and walked out of the pilot's section on his own two feet. There will be a court-martial, *he thought.* I may well be stripped of my commission. I could even face criminal charges . . .

He knew also that they had barely embarked upon a journey that was every bit as perilous as the one the ejected captain and loyal crew of the Royal Navy ship Bounty *had faced, hundreds of years ago. Braving the void in the tiny shuttlecraft was, most people would have said, hopeless insanity. But somehow Picard knew that he'd told his first officer the truth. They would make it back. It wasn't over yet.*

Next to the loss of his ship, the charges, the court-martial, the void to be crossed—all of it seemed as nothing. I am a captain who has lost his ship, *he thought.* Nothing worse can happen to me . . .

In the darkness of his cabin aboard the *Enterprise,* Jean-Luc Picard opened his eyes, then sat up unsteadily. "Lights," he said quietly, and the room was obediently illuminated. He swung his legs out of the bed, his left hand going up to touch his shoulder, rub at it, trying to erase the ache that throbbed there. *A phantom pain,* he thought. *A memory of pain, awakened by the most realistic dream I have ever experienced . . .*

He padded into the bathroom to pull on a robe, then he walked over to the wall slot. "Tea, Earl Grey, hot," he ordered from force of habit, but when it arrived he had no urge to drink it; instead he took the mug out and set it down on the dresser, scarcely feeling its heat against his fingers. "Water, cold," he commanded.

When the water glass sparkled before him, he raised it and gulped the cold liquid gratefully, feeling it wash over the rawness of his throat. *Memory of what it was like to inhale those fumes?* he wondered. *A psychosomatic reaction?*

He rubbed his aching arm again. The doctors had managed to heal it so well that there was virtually no scar. But Picard could still trace the path of the old injury.

If other people are experiencing dreams that real, no wonder they're going mad, he thought, picking up his tea and walking back to sit on the edge of his bed, feeling the softness of the carpet pleasantly tickle his bare soles. He sipped the tea, closing his eyes and savoring the taste, glad to be back in the here-and-now, rather than then, no matter how dangerous their current situation aboard the *Enterprise.*

I relived an actual event, he thought, *and I came out of it feeling every bit as terrible as I did the day it happened, when I think I must have been the closest to committing suicide that I have ever come in my life. Reliving a real event that traumatic with such a degree of verisimilitude was terrible enough . . . but what if that damned artifact over there could invest a nightmare with that same sense of reality? Mon Dieu, no wonder their hearts are stopping!*

Briefly, he wondered whether Beverly Crusher had experienced one of the dreams, too. *If so, I hope it was a pleasanter experience than mine,* he thought. Shedding the robe, he walked into the head, then turned on the sonic shower to "massage."

Feeling it pummel his body, slowly manipulating

the tension out of his muscles, he was able, finally, to relax. The captain smiled grimly as he adjusted the shower to "hot water" and began lathering himself. *Not what Beverly had in mind for a restful experience. I feel as dragged through a knothole as I did on that very day . . .*

After he was clean, and clad again in a fresh uniform, Picard looked over at his bed and smiled grimly. *So much for "sleep that knits up the raveled sleave of care,"* he thought. *It will be a long time before I lie down to sleep again with any kind of anticipation.*

He stood thinking, remembering, all the while absently rubbing the path of the ancient, almost invisible scar that traced the skin of his arm. *A long, long time . . .*

Chapter Seven

"HEY, GEORDI!"

Lieutenant Commander La Forge glanced up when Wesley Crusher called his name. "Yeah?" he said, raising his voice to be heard over the muted throb of the matter-antimatter engines and the dilithium crystal generators that regulated the power to the life-support systems and the *Enterprise*'s shields.

"Will you and Data come up here for a moment?"

"Okay," Geordi called, and he beckoned to the android, who was assisting him in his systems checks.

The two officers climbed to the upper deck in engineering, where the teenager stood before the sensing devices, duplicates of those located on the bridge.

"What've you got, Wes?" La Forge asked.

"I've been analyzing that energy field the artifact is generating," Crusher said, a puzzled look in his eyes. "And something is very weird about it."

Data glanced at the readouts, then back up at the youth, with an inquiring expression. "Could you be more specific, Wesley? Since all of our information about the artifact indicates that it is a construct completely outside our frame of reference, I would say that there are many 'weird' things about it, not 'something,' which usage implies a single thing."

Geordi grimaced. "Data, sometimes you sound like you swallowed a dictionary."

"I never swallowed one," the android said seriously. "However, my memory core does contain—"

"Never mind," Geordi interrupted resignedly. "Wes, what did you mean, there's something weird about the artifact? Data's right, there are a helluva lot of things that are weird about that critter."

"I know," Crusher agreed, "but my readings on this energy field that's surrounding us indicate that the tractor field effect is only one small part of the total output of that field. Actually, it would be more accurate to say that the artifact is emitting many different kinds of wavelengths that blend together to form this field that's encasing us."

Geordi examined the readouts for himself. Wesley pointed to one green line in the visual representation of the spectral analysis of the artifact's field.

"See this one portion of the wavelength? That's what's keeping us here. All the rest of this"—his fingers swept over the remainder of the spectrum band—"is something else. Or maybe a lot of different things. We're being bombarded with these kinds of energy, all of them of a type I never encountered before, but I can't figure out what any of them do—except for the tractor field, and even *that's* weird."

"How is it weird?"

"It's as though the tractor effect is a by-product of the field, not the main purpose. I don't think it was designed to do what it's doing. Instead, I think it was designed to have a completely different effect on vessels that were totally unlike any that humans or humanoids use for space travel. Whatever creatures constructed the artifact, their whole approach to science was different—physics, mathematics, everything!"

"How so?"

"From what I can tell, the beings that created the artifact moved through space not by warping it, so they could travel at FTL speeds, but by going *around* it."

"How does one go *around* space?" Data asked, obviously intrigued.

"I can't be sure, but I think they popped into another dimension where everything is very *compressed.*" He made a squeezing motion with his hands. "A universe that's much smaller than ours, so they had only a very short distance to go, and when they snapped back into the point of correspondence in this universe, they would have traversed incredible distances in our space in just hours. Only they didn't travel within this space-time continuum, they bypassed it completely."

Multiuniverse geometry and theoretical physics had never been Geordi's favorite subjects. He preferred the here-and-now, the good ol' universe where E was equal to mc^2—except, of course, that humans had long ago found ways to warp space so that Doctor Einstein's edict didn't apply.

La Forge scratched his head. "But you've never seen one of their vessels, unless the artifact is one."

Wesley shook his head. "I'm positive it's just a structure, like a space station. It can't travel under its own power."

"Then if it isn't a vessel, what makes you think you know what kind of ships they had?"

Frustrated, the boy bit his lip. "I don't *know,* Geordi! It seems as though they had a different way of looking at physics, at the way the universe works, and

I really don't understand it yet. So I guess you'd have to call this a theory that isn't backed up by much data, very little observation and no certain facts. It's just a feeling I have, when I look at the way they made this energy field function."

"You mean a hunch."

"I guess so," Wesley admitted, his shoulders sagging dejectedly.

Geordi smiled. If that statement had been made by anyone else, the chief engineer would have rolled his eyes. Engineering was *facts:* mathematical formulas, the laws of physics, scientific theory, and data plus observation—*not* hunches. But he'd known Wesley Crusher for years now, and he knew damned well that the kid had something the rest of them didn't. A sixth sense, a spark of genius that at times allowed him to leap *past* facts, to arrive at intuitive solutions that were correct—not to mention brilliant.

So Geordi considered Wesley's words seriously.

"Even though the interweaving energy fields are alien, they appear harmless," Data interjected. While the two humans had been discussing space-time theory, his strange eyes had been moving over the readouts.

"I know, but some of them must be the cause of the insanity, the depression, and all the other mental and emotional distress that's been affecting the crew," Wesley said.

"Could some of these broadcasts be picked up . . . absorbed . . . by portions of the human—or humanoid—brain?" Geordi asked, trying the idea on for size.

Wesley got a faraway look, then quickly entered several commands. Another wavelength band appeared above the first, and the youth let out a cry of triumph and pointed triumphantly. "Geordi, you're a genius!"

La Forge grinned. *No I'm not, I just work hard. You're the genius, kid.* But aloud he said, straight-faced, "I am?"

"You sure are! Look there, that one peak of alien energy is very close to the EEG pattern of human alpha waves! Waves the human brain gives off all the time, but *especially* when people are *asleep!*" The youth's voice broke in his excitement, but Geordi did not tease him about it. He could still remember vividly what it was like when his own voice had changed.

"Hey, I think you're really on to something here, Wes," La Forge said, studying the patterns, taking in the similarities. His VISOR could correlate and compare the two wavelengths even better than normal human vision. "It's not an exact match, but it's close. That portion of the energy must be what's affecting people as they sleep."

"Is there any way to insulate against it?" Data asked practically.

"Our shields are absorbing some of it, but not all," Geordi said. "And we've got the shields on full power. It's a damned good thing we're not moving, or we wouldn't have enough power to keep them up for this length of time."

Wesley gave him a sour look. "It's a *bad* thing we're not moving," he corrected, "as in 'moving away from here.' The artifact is really messing up people, don't forget."

"I know," Geordi said with a sigh. "I went down to sickbay this morning to see Thala, and the poor little kid looked like she'd been through one of Worf's Klingon Rites of Ascension."

"My mom told me she came screaming into sickbay like she'd seen a ghost," Wesley said absently, studying the readouts with narrowed eyes.

"She did," Geordi said heavily. "I was there when

she described the dream the damned artifact so kindly sent her, and before she was done I lost my appetite for lunch. Eviscerated corpses and punctured eyesockets . . ." He shuddered. "I've been scared to close my eyes ever since."

"You've got to sleep sometime," Wesley said.

"I know," Geordi agreed grimly. "Which is why I'd rather put about a hundred light-years between me and that thing"—he jerked his head in the approximate direction of the artifact as it lay off their starboard bow—"before I hit the sack again."

"Wesley," Data said, "perhaps you should tie in to the medical computer and ask it to search for more correlations among brain waves."

"Good idea," the teenager said, and did so.

Moments later, they had their response, which was that several of the waves the energy field was generating *did* correlate marginally with wave patterns in the brains of humans, Betazoids, Andorians, Klingons, and Vulcans. Oddly enough, there were no waves that correlated with the brain patterns of Tellarites, which possibly explained Nurse Gavar's immunity to the psychosis that had struck Montez, the security guard.

Wesley then instructed the library computer to search for correlations within the brain patterns of all known sentient races. "Working," replied the computer, and the officers turned their attention back to the structure of the artifact itself, knowing that the search would, in all probability, take several minutes. The *Enterprise*'s computer was a marvel of state-of-the-art cybernetic engineering, but there were a plethora of known sentient races . . .

"Hey," said Wesley a minute later, "this is interesting. I've been scanning the actual structure of the artifact on all wavelengths, all spectra, sonic probes, everything—even X-ray scans, since we don't think there's anything alive over there that could be hurt by them . . ." He paused and made an adjustment. "And guess what?"

"The suspense is killing me," said Geordi dryly.

"It has chambers inside it, as strangely shaped as the pods we can see on its outside. There are hundreds . . ." He touched a control. "Correction, one thousand and ninety-two chambers and pods over there."

"That's weird," Geordi said, unintentionally borrowing Wesley's favorite expression; the youth gave him a feeble grin, making him realize what he'd just said. "What do you suppose the chambers are for?"

The young officer shrugged. "Your guess is as good as mine."

"They vary in shape and size," Data said, scanning the X-ray image. "And presumably in function, or why would they be constructed so differently?"

"There could be a number of reasons, Data," Geordi said. "Religious edicts, tradition, personal preference of the architect who designed the thing . . . or some reason so alien that we'll never guess it." He hesitated, thinking, then asked, "Any sign of living quarters? I've wondered whether this thing wasn't some kind of barracks in space, or possibly even a space station."

"I've wondered the same thing," Wes said. "But we don't know anything about what these people looked like, so how could I identify living quarters?"

"Is there anything you can identify as furniture? Any repetition of shapes that would indicate the equivalent of beds, or storage compartments, or chairs . . . tables . . . anything like that?"

"Not a thing. There are some objects in some of the rooms, but each object is totally different from all the others. And I would estimate that seventy percent of the chambers are empty."

"Any signs of weapons?"

"Nothing that I can identify as being a weapon or a guidance system," Wesley said. "No radiation that's detectable by our sensors."

"Well, that's comforting," Geordi said. "Maybe we will be able to blast the thing to smithereens and get the hell out of here."

"It would be a shame to destroy the artifact," Data said.

"Why?" Wesley asked. "It's dangerous."

"Yes, but it, and the ships it has trapped, constitute an invaluable historical and archeological treasure," Data replied. "Scientists could learn much about the history of our galaxy from studying—"

The android broke off as the computer suddenly beeped. "Requested analysis of data complete," the neutral female-sounding voice announced.

"Go ahead," Geordi commanded.

"Comparison of energy field wavelengths with brain patterns generated by known intelligent species are as follows," began the computer. "Andorian: point four-two correlation. Betazoid: . . ."

The results of the computer's search were intriguing, Geordi thought several minutes later. Only one kind of known being had a high correlation rate: Medusans.

"Medusans!" La Forge muttered. "I guess I shouldn't be surprised that they might be related to the builders of the artifact. God knows they're so alien that we can't even stand to look at them—just like normal humans can't stomach looking at the artifact."

"Did the Medusans ever have colonies or anything?" Wesley wanted to know.

"None recorded," Data said. "Frankly, I find it doubtful that the Medusans themselves actually built the artifact. I believe rather that the unknown creators of the artifact had mental processes that were similar to the way Medusan brains function."

"That makes sense," Geordi said thoughtfully. Then the engineer sighed. "Listen, finding a race that *might* be distant kin to the Medusans is all very interesting, but it doesn't help us break free from this space Sargasso."

"Right," Wesley agreed. "But *this* might!" He pointed to a readout. "They've got an oxy-nitro atmosphere over there!"

"You're kidding!" Geordi said, then he whistled softly. "Weirder and weirder, huh, Data?"

"I do not believe this finding is as extraordinary as you seem to believe, Geordi," the android said. "After all, the Medusans are oxygen-nitrogen breathers, are they not? Then why should you be surprised to discover that the artifact's creators were also?"

Wesley shrugged, smiling wryly at the engineer. "He's got a point."

"But discovering that there are chambers over there and that we could breathe the air without suits gives me an idea," La Forge said. "Maybe we could beam over a landing party and find the controls for the tractor field and shut them down! Then we could get out of here, and that thing wouldn't be able to capture any more ships."

"I don't know," Wes said. "If just looking at the artifact is disorienting, what would exploring its interior be like?"

"If it's anything like the outside, pretty damn strange," Geordi conceded. "But it would be worth the risk, if we could break free. Is there room in any of those chambers to beam over a landing party?"

"Most of them are fairly small, but there are several that are almost the size of a small shuttlecraft deck," the teenager replied.

"Good. Materializing inside a bulkhead is not my idea of a good time."

"Is there any indication of machinery or power generators that would allow us to pinpoint a target location for a landing party?" Data asked.

"Not anything I can be sure of," Wesley reported. "Like I told you before, it's really"—he grinned at Geordi apologetically—"*weird* over there."

Fifteen-year-old Will Riker was on his first one-day pass away from Starfleet Academy, and, after a day spent sightseeing in San Francisco, he stood marveling, as so many had marveled before him, at the beauty of the Golden Gate Bridge. It hung there against the sky, reflected in the water of the bay, looking like the bridge into Valhalla or Vorta Vor, the Romulans' warrior paradise. The bridge to forever . . .

The boy's eyes traced every line, enjoying this triumph of human engineering that had stood for so long. Shafts of light from the glorious purple-clouded sunset touched the amber towers, turning the suspension cables to threads spun from red gold.

He drank in the beauty of it, feeling the wind blow through his hair as he stood on Land's End, with Golden Gate Park behind him and to his left, only a couple of kilometers' pleasant walk from here.

Will had enjoyed the park very much. It had been great to walk on grass and see trees and birds—natural things instead of classrooms and corridors and starship mockups. Adjusting to the Academy hadn't been easy. Will came from Alaska and was far more accustomed to a rugged outdoor life—camping, hiking, and fishing —than he was to city living.

Not to mention that he'd written to his father twice, only to get a message today from one of his father's friends that Carl Riker had been called away to advise

127

Starfleet Command on a tricky situation somewhere in the Procyon system.

Of course, telling his only son where he was going would be too damned much trouble for him, *Will thought bitterly. I'm getting tired of always being at the tail end of his lists of priorities. He probably wouldn't even care that I got the highest grade in the—*

"Didn't anyone ever warn you that if you scowl like that your face might just freeze that way, Cadet?" inquired a light, amused soprano voice.

Will started violently and swung around to see a woman standing beside him. She regarded him with wide, laughing eyes that were the color of the water in the bay below, a luminous greenish gray. Her face was exotic, arresting, with high cheekbones, a generous mouth with strong white teeth, and a pointed chin. Fashionably styled dark hair blew around her face like a fluffy cloud, and even though her features were not classically regular, she was the most beautiful woman he had ever seen.

She wore a red dress of some silky material, and the wind blew it around her, molding it against her, outlining the shapes of her small, high breasts, the slight curve of her hips, the narrowness of her waist. Her legs were long and beautifully shaped. "I'm sorry if I startled you," she said, smiling, though he knew she'd done it deliberately. "But you looked just like a thundercloud. You're too young to be that mad."

She was making fun of him, he knew it . . . but somehow he didn't mind. Will looked down at her, realizing that, even though she was tall for a woman, he towered over her. He'd reached his adult height the year before; his weight was only now beginning to catch up to his length. He was still thin, but, because of faithful workouts in the Academy gym, he was beginning to fill out in his shoulders and chest. But most of the time he still felt skinny and gawky and homely. It was always a shock to realize that he was taller now than almost everyone he met.

He smiled back at the woman tentatively and managed to say, "My mom used to kid me about scowling and my face freezing, but that was a long time ago. I guess I forgot." His grin broadened. "Sorry if I scared you."

"Oh, you did," she said, straight-faced. "But I forgive you." She extended her hand, the mocking smile softening, growing more genuine. "Hi, I'm Paula Andropova."

"Will Riker," he said, taking her hand in his, feeling the warmth of her long, strong fingers. With a dim memory of an old book he'd read called The Scarlet Pimpernel, *he bent and kissed her fingers, expecting to mess it up somehow, expecting to be embarrassed at his ineptness, his lack of finesse. But for the first time that he'd attempted any sort of grand gesture, he did not mess it up. His bow was graceful, and he came over looking like an aristocrat of a previous century, rather than a clumsy adolescent.*

And, for a wonder, at just the right moment, she caught up the skirt of the red dress and executed a perfect curtsy!

He held her fingers, supporting her as she rose, then let them go at exactly the right second. "I can't believe it," he said, sounding, even to his own ears, quite witty and urbane. "Someone else who loves old romances? I thought I was the only one who still read novels like The Scarlet Pimpernel!"

She laughed, her teeth flashing. "Guilty as charged, kind sir. As a matter of fact, I not only read The Scarlet Pimpernel, *I danced it once upon a time."*

"A dancer!" He took in her long, graceful neck, her muscled legs, and nodded. "I should have known."

The wind struck her again, and this time she shiv-

ered. "Oh my," she said, looking around them. "I'm afraid we've missed the last of sunset."

"Are you cold?" he asked, wishing he had a jacket that he could offer her. Then perhaps she'd stay a little longer.

"To be honest, I am," she admitted. "But I'd love to talk to you more. It's not every day that I meet a member of the aristocracy. Could I buy you a drink?"

His pass was good until midnight. "I'd like that," he managed, and he gallantly took Paula's arm, realizing for the first time that she was actually picking him up—that this beautiful woman was interested in spending time with him, with all-elbows-and-knees, lumpy-Adam's-apple Will Riker. For a brief, devout second, he thanked all the gods in the universe that his complexion was, for once, fairly clear.

They drank synthehol together, first giving the traditional toast "To the Ferengi!" because the Ferengi had invented the drink, which relaxed and mellowed a person like ethanol, but the effects of which could be voluntarily dismissed by the imbiber.

Then they talked for hours, of books they'd read and music they'd enjoyed and plays she'd seen. He discovered that she'd been a ballerina but that a persistent knee injury had ended her career. She told him about the ballets she'd danced, and he told her about what it was like to see the sun on the snows of Mount McKinley from a nearby peak.

Finally, he realized that it was nearly time for his pass to end, and he had just time enough to report back to the Academy. "I have to go," he said regretfully. "I wish I didn't, though." He hesitated, then took the plunge. "Uh . . . look, do you think we might be able to see each other again? I don't know anyone in San Francisco except other cadets, and this has been . . ." He smiled and shrugged. "Wonderful," he finished.

The Eyes of the Beholders

"I'd love to see you again, Will," Paula said seriously, *and she gave him her address. "Come over the next time you get a pass. Just give me twenty-four hours notice, okay?"*

"Is that so you can chase out all your lovers?" he asked, greatly daring.

Paula smiled. "Oh, no, I never chase them. When they become tiresome, I feed them to my Aldeberan shellmouth, Archibald." She glanced again at the chrono. "Now run—you don't want to be late!"

Riker did run, nearly all the way back to the towers of Starfleet Headquarters, and past them to his dormitory. Only part of the reason he was running was to be sure to make his deadline. The main reason was that he was so excited, so full of energy that he couldn't just walk! He felt like shouting aloud in his exultation but managed to restrain himself.

She likes me! She wants to see me again! A woman like that, who could have anyone—!! *His head spun with the wonder of it . . . the wonder of Paula herself.*

And when I get that pass, I'll be going over to her place. What will happen there? Will she want to go out? What if she wants to stay in? If she does want to stay in, will we just . . . talk? *he wondered as he undressed.* That would be wonderful, but something about the way she smiled tells me that she had more than conversation on her mind . . . I think . . . I hope . . .

Unsophisticated as he was, Will still recognized a come-on when he saw one. What if she wants to go to bed? *The thought filled him with a mixture of fevered anticipation and near panic.* She'll know it's my first time, there's no way I can hide it. What should I do?

Finally, he managed to calm down, even study a little for his next-day advanced calculus class. Maybe she won't want to see me. I might as well not worry

131

about it until I get my next pass. Hell, maybe I won't even earn a pass for the rest of the year . . .

But he had earned one, the next month. Will called her, and she invited him up to her apartment, obviously delighted to see him, and she wanted to talk, and no, they didn't go out. And what with one thing and another, their conversation eventually languished, then ceased altogether . . .

If she guessed that it was Will's first time, Paula was wise enough not to say so. And, as in all his other subjects, the cadet proved an amazingly quick study.

Their affair continued for the next three and a half years. Paula remained a woman of mystery, sharing little of her former life with him. He knew that she worked as a liaison between a large theater and the performers who came to entertain there, but that was all he knew. He never met her business associates.

She did, however, introduce him to many city entertainments—concerts, the theater, ballet, opera. On his rare weekend passes, he took her hiking and backpacking in the Sierra. Paula seemed equally at home wearing jeans and a lumberjack shirt while pitching a tent in a meadow, or wearing a stunning long gown and waltzing in a crystal-chandeliered ballroom.

Riker knew that she had been married and was now divorced, but he was not sure of her age. Older than he, of course, but she was so beautiful, with her dancer's passion for fitness—the difference in their ages just didn't matter.

When Will was a couple of months from his nineteenth birthday, he was assigned to duty on his first posting as an ensign aboard the cruiser Nogura. *He was wildly excited about actually getting out into deep space, and his only regret, he told Paula, was in leaving her.*

"I'll miss you so much," he whispered to her as they lay in bed after making love; he was shipping out the next day at noon.

"I'll miss you, too, Will," she said softly, sadly, her eyes glistening a little in the moonlight flooding through her bedroom window.

"But it won't be forever, Paula," he reminded her earnestly. *"Just a year, probably, until I come back for leave and refresher classes here in San Francisco for another year. I've decided to go for line officer training."*

"Good," she said. *"You belong in command, Will, you really do. You inspire confidence, and when you give orders, people want to obey them. Not everyone has that ability."*

He smoothed her hair back from her face, then kissed the side of her throat, barely listening. There was something else on his mind. "Just a year," he muttered. *"That's not very long. You'll wait for me, won't you?"*

Will felt the muscles of her shoulder go taut against his cheek as she tensed. He pulled back, trying to see her face, but she rolled away from him, onto her back, pulling the sheet up over her breasts.

"What is it?" he demanded anxiously, confused. *"I thought that you . . . well, that you felt the same as I do. You do, don't you?"*

"Will . . ." Her voice was very gentle.

"Paula . . . ," he said, his own voice roughening as fear touched him. Dammit, I love her! She must know how I feel! *"I love you,"* he said urgently. *"You must know that. And you love me."*

He heard her draw in a deep breath. "No, Will, I don't," she said evenly.

With a muttered curse, Riker turned on the bedside lamp. Paula's face in the dimness was strained and a bit pale, but her eyes were steady as they met his.

"I'm sorry, Will," she said.

"Sorry about what? Sorry that you don't love me? What kind of thing is that to say? It's not true, I know it!" But a terrible fear was gnawing at the edges of his mind, because she sounded so certain.

"It is true. I'm very fond of you, Will, and in a way I do love you. But not in the way you're talking about. Not in the way you think you love me."

"Think!" He was struggling for control. "I don't think, I know! Paula . . . why . . ." His voice was having trouble staying steady, and it sounded plaintive even in his own ears. "Why don't you love me?"

She sighed and turned back on her side to face him, her expression gentle. "Will, darling, I don't love you because we're not equals."

He could only look at her, completely taken aback. Paula smiled faintly. "Oh, I'm not turning into some kind of social snob or something, never fear. I just mean that insofar as age and experience go, we're not equals, and we never will be. The gap is too wide. By the time you could possibly catch up, it would be impossible. I'd be too old."

He started to protest, and she put a hand over his mouth gently. "Will, do you know how old I am?"

"Older than I am," he admitted grudgingly. "But, hell, that doesn't mean anything! What's five or six years? Or ten?"

She smiled faintly. "Bless you, Will. I chose well that day down by Land's End. You have the instincts of a diplomat and a silver tongue to express them with. You're going to cut quite a swath with the ladies of the galaxy." Paula hesitated, then said flatly, "Will, I have a son who is five years older than you are."

He stared at her, momentarily stunned, but rallied after a second. "I don't care! What difference does that make?"

"I told you what difference it makes," she said. "Will, you'd be crazy to tie yourself down at your age to anyone, let alone someone who doesn't have time to wait for you to come back from a long mission."

"Doesn't have time?" he repeated numbly. "You're not trying to tell me you're sick or something?"

"Of course not. But at my age, I don't have time to waste on waiting. And, to be honest, I don't want to wait for you. I've been in this situation before, and it's better just to break off now, believe me."

He felt numb. "You don't want to see me when I come back?"

"No, Will, it wouldn't be wise. I'd be lying if I said I would, and I've never lied to you, darling."

He knew that was true.

Paula leaned over and kissed him tenderly. "Now get some sleep," she said, mock-sternly, "so we can have some time together in the morning. I want to send you off to those distant stars with beautiful memories."

But after she was breathing regularly, Will slipped quietly out of bed, located his clothes by touch, and carried them out into the hall to dress. He let himself out of the apartment, inwardly debating over whether he should leave a note, but it seemed as though everything had already been said. He didn't want to hurt Paula by not staying the night, but he didn't think he could face her again, knowing that she didn't love him.

San Francisco was silent and moonlit as he walked along, head down, thinking. Tomorrow he would head out into deep space for the first time. Tomorrow everything about his life would change . . . had already changed. Already he felt different—harder, stronger, older.

At the end of the block, he stopped and turned back, his eyes unerringly picking out the window of her *apartment.* I wonder whether she was really asleep, or only pretending, *he thought, and rather suspected it was the latter.* She knew it would be easier on both of us this way, *he realized.*

Smiling faintly, he blew a silent kiss back in the direction of the apartment building, then turned and walked away, into the night . . . and the future.

Commander Will Riker opened his eyes on darkness, then sat up. The blond woman who had been snuggled beside him made an inquiring noise and opened one blue eye.

"Time to get up?" she mumbled from the depths of the pillow.

"No . . . go back to sleep," he whispered.

"Okay . . ." She closed her eyes.

Riker got up and stood looking down at her for a moment, wondering whether she was dreaming, too. He supposed that he'd been lucky. His dream, while as real as the others he'd heard described, had at least been benign.

But he felt oddly desolate as he realized that he hadn't thought of Paula in years. He wondered where she was now, what she was doing. That had been . . . God, it had been damn near twenty years since he'd first met her. They'd had some good times . . .

You know something, Paula? he thought. *You were right about so many things, but you were wrong about one important one. I did love you. I only just realized it, but I truly did love you. There've been a lot of women since you*—an image of Deanna Troi's face flashed into his mind involuntarily—*and I've loved a number of them, and now I know what it feels like, and that was certainly what I felt for you.*

Softly, he tiptoed out of his sleeping room into the study and activated the intercom on the desk—audio only, as he was not dressed. After a moment, he heard Lieutenant Selar's precise tones. "Sickbay. Selar here."

"Doctor, this is Commander Riker. I'm calling to find out how Counselor Troi is doing."

"Her condition is stable, Commander. We are keeping her under sedation, to prevent further emotional and mental trauma."

"Any further problems with the crew, Lieutenant?"

Her unemotional Vulcan accents changed, became tinged with regret. "We lost one of the *Marco Polo* crewmen, sir. A fugue case. His heart couldn't take the stress. And we had a suicide this morning . . ."

Riker drew in a deep breath and forced himself to ask evenly, "Who was it, Lieutenant?"

"One of our nurses, sir. Penelope Johnson."

"I see . . . ," Will said. "I understand, Lieutenant. I'm sorry to hear that. Riker out."

He then signaled the bridge. "Captain?"

"Number One?"

"Yes, sir. I just spoke to sickbay. We've lost a crew member."

"I know," the captain said heavily. "I only hope that Geordi, Data, and Wesley will be able to come up with something. Their deadline is up in two hours."

"Sir, about the dreams . . . ," Riker began, then he hesitated.

"Yes, Number One?" Picard encouraged after a moment, when his second-in-command did not continue.

"I understand now, sir. What you were saying earlier, about how real it was . . . it was just as though I were living it all over again, every moment . . ."

Picard's tone grew gentler. "A bad one?"

"Not really, Captain. Nothing like what you described. But it was very, very real."

137

"I know, Will." Picard sounded grim. "And apparently for Johnson, her dream was *too* real."

"I'm going to go check on Geordi and Data," Riker said. "The idea of catching another hour or two of shut-eye has lost its appeal." His voice was grim.

"Good idea. I quite understand," Picard said dryly.

"Riker out."

Chapter Eight

"DOCTOR?"

Beverly Crusher looked up to see Lieutenant Selar standing in the doorway to her office. "Come in," she said.

Selar entered. "You sent for me, Doctor?"

"Yes," Crusher said, indicating a seat. "I wanted to find out how the staff is doing. In regard to Johnson's death, I mean." She smiled wanly. "People always tend to put on their best face when the boss is inquiring."

The Vulcan nodded, understanding. "The staff is reacting as well as could be expected, I would judge. Nurse Johnson was well liked, but her death is regarded as an unfortunate by-product of our current mission, not as any reproach for words or actions left unsaid or undone by her friends. I have not observed any of the typical human 'if only I had' behavior that is characteristic of a guilt reaction in any of her coworkers."

"Well, that's something." Crusher slowly shook her head, biting her lip. "I wonder what made her do it?"

Selar raised an eyebrow. "There is little point in indulging in speculation. No matter what dream or hallucination initiated Johnson's unfortunate reaction, the artifact is ultimately responsible."

"Have you had one of the dreams, Selar?" The chief medical officer's gaze slid away, not meeting the Vulcan's eyes.

"My people rarely dream," the lieutenant replied evenly. "So far, I have been spared."

"I had one," Crusher announced, raising her greenish-blue eyes to meet the dark ones opposite hers, straightening her shoulders with a sudden air of decision. "It made me understand why Penny might have been moved to do what she did."

"Logically, you would not have mentioned that you had been the recipient of one of the artifact's dreams if you did not wish to discuss it," Selar observed, relaxing her official stance somewhat in the light of Crusher's personal revelation. "What did you dream, Beverly?"

There was a long pause. "I dreamed about the happiest day of my life," Crusher said finally. "Only at the moment I didn't know that it was, of course. It was only later, after Jack died, that I realized that that day had been the closest I'll ever come to achieving perfection"—she smiled faintly, sadly—"at least in this life, I suppose."

"You dreamed of your deceased husband?"

"Yes . . ." Crusher clenched her fists on the desktop. "Selar, it was so *real.* I thought I was there. There was no sense that this was a dream—and no worry, as is so often the case with pleasant dreams, that I would awaken and it would be gone. While I was there, I was *there.*"

She took a deep, steadying breath. "It was when Wesley was just a little fellow," she said, an unconscious note of maternal wistfulness tinging her calm delivery. "Jack was home on leave—a long leave, the longest he'd ever gotten since Wesley was born. One day we took a flyer out to the Black Hills. It was summer, the most beautiful part of summer, and there were blossoming plants everywhere. The sky was the bluest I'd ever seen, and the mountain slopes were green with pines and hemlocks and spruce. The meadows were lush with grass, and there were animals grazing on them in the far distance—deer or elk, I suppose.

"We went for a walk, with Wesley riding on his father's shoulders, and I can remember him demanding that we name everything we passed, everything around us. We began laughing after a while, and threatening to make up names, because neither of us could identify *all* those plants. We teased Wesley, calling him our Elephant's Child."

Selar raised an inquiring eyebrow, and Beverly paused and smiled. "That's a reference to a story by Rudyard Kipling, about a young elephant who was possessed of insatiable curiosity. It's like a fairy tale designed to explain, for a child, why elephants have those long trunks."

The Vulcan nodded. "I understand. Humans have a propensity for romanticizing everything."

Beverly chuckled. "So we do. Anyway, after Jack and I had walked a couple of kilometers, we sat down by a brook and dangled our feet in the water. It was soooo cold! Felt as though it had come down from a glacier . . . which I suppose it had." She shuddered theatrically, smiling. "We got silly and kicked water at each other, until we were really wet, and we laughed like fools."

The lieutenant's eyes were a bit skeptical, as if she could not comprehend the notion of pleasure connected with being sluiced with icy water, but she did not remark on it, merely waited for Crusher to continue.

"Then we lay down in the grass, and Wesley took a nap. Jack and I . . . we wanted to make love, but we didn't quite dare, with Wes there, so we just cuddled together . . ." Beverly's voice failed, and she stared down at her clenched hands, struggling for control.

"If it distresses you to speak of this . . . ," Selar began, but the other's red hair swung as she shook her head no.

"It's important that the medical staff try to understand what's happening here," she said softly. "Since you haven't had one of the dreams—and, from what you say, aren't likely to—you need to understand what they're like. Also, when humans have an upsetting dream, it helps them to relate it to someone. I don't really know why . . . perhaps it helps us distance ourselves." She rose from her chair and paced back and forth in the small area of the office. "I just . . . need a moment, that's all."

Finally, she resumed her seat and her narrative. "So after the water battle we fell asleep, too, and when we woke up we were dry again, and hungry. We walked back to where the flyer was parked, to have lunch. I had made that lunch myself, and it tasted so good!" She looked up at Selar. "I can remember every mouthful—and do you know, for about the first half-hour after I woke up, I wasn't even hungry? Usually I'm a breakfast person, but I felt physically full—satiated, as though I'd really eaten all that food."

She smiled. "I had made a cheese soufflé and put it in the stasis unit, and it was perfect." She sighed. "The cheddar was just right, it was puffed up like one of the white clouds overhead. And to go with it I had bread that I'd made myself, with real butter and honey. Fruit, too, pears and apples, and Wesley had a banana . . . he loved bananas . . ."

"You are making me hungry," Selar said dryly, and the doctor smiled wanly.

"Then, for dessert, we had chocolate mousse. Homemade. Oh, it was indescribable! Jack said it was the best he'd ever had."

She paused, and after a moment the Vulcan said hesitantly, "Then what happened?"

The chief medical officer shrugged. "Nothing spectacular, to an outside observer. We packed up the flyer and went home—and after Wesley went to bed, we made love and fell asleep. That's all . . ." Her voice broke, and tears welled up in her eyes.

Finally, she whispered, "And the whole time it was happening, I never realized that it was the happiest day of my life! If I had, I would have savored it more—every minute, every second. I wouldn't have left Jack's side for a moment. After we made love, I wouldn't have turned over and gone to sleep. I would have stayed awake and loved him all night long . . ."

"And you awoke from the dream fully conscious of what you had not done," Selar said.

"Yes," Crusher replied softly. "When I woke up, I experienced the sorrow, the desolation of Jack's death all over again—just as though it were the first time. While I was dreaming, he was truly alive again, and when I awoke, it was as if he'd just died. I had to go through all of it over again."

"I grieve with thee," Selar said, her voice taking on a formal note that told the chief medical officer that she was translating literally from her mother tongue. "Have you spoken to anyone else about this?"

Beverly shook her head. "When I made the hourly sickbay update last time, the captain told me that he'd dreamed about losing the *Stargazer*. It was apparently one of the worst moments of his life. He didn't go into any details, but I know him pretty well by now . . . Anyway, it must have been extremely difficult for him."

She sighed deeply. "Then he asked me whether I'd dreamed, and I lied and said I hadn't. It would have been too painful to tell him. Jean-Luc is the one person I could never share my grief over Jack's death with. Doing so would bring up feelings that I'm trying to overcome, not to mention that it would be cruel to Jean-Luc. I know now that Jack's death was in some ways as traumatic for him as it was for me."

"So I have gathered," the Vulcan said. "I believe that you should tell the captain that you have experienced a dream but, if asked about the subject matter, decline to discuss it. I am certain that the captain, being a man of diplomacy and sensitivity, will not press you for details."

"You're right, Selar," Beverly agreed. "I will. But now I know why the 'fortunate' victims are slipping into catatonia, and the unfortunate ones wake up so desperate and depressed that they are driven to seek oblivion in death. Many people have dark ghosts in their pasts, and if they felt they would be forced to relive those moments over and over again *as if they were really happening,* while we're under the influence of that *thing"*—she gestured bitterly in the approximate location of the artifact—"well, I can understand why they're killing themselves."

"Yes," Selar said. "There are moments in my past that I would not wish to experience again."

Crusher straightened her shoulders. "I suppose it's an indication of the greater mental stability of those who successfully complete Starfleet training that only two *Enterprise* crew members have turned their anger or fear against their comrades, the way the people on the *Marco Polo* did. And, thank God, Itoh and Montez were stopped before they could seriously harm their intended victims."

"It is possible that you are correct," Selar said. "However, it is also apparently true, according to your son's findings, that the *Enterprise*'s shielding is insulating us from the artifact's full effect, which was not the situation for the crew of the *Marco Polo*."

"Wesley . . ." Beverly ran a hand through her hair distractedly. "My God, I wonder whether he's had one of the dreams."

"Not when I last spoke to him, an hour ago. He requested data from our medical banks on brainwaves of intelligent beings."

"For his research, I suppose." Her smile was a bit strained. "The captain has a lot of confidence in Wesley, to give him assignments that involve the safety and sanity of the crew. I just hope it's not too much responsibility too young."

"From what I have observed, Wesley thrives on challenge," Selar said. "He is nearly a grown man, Beverly, don't forget."

"You're right." She shook her head. "It seems like yesterday that he was Thala's age. By the way"—she glanced up—"how is Thala doing?"

"Better." Selar's mouth tightened a bit. "Although she received a considerable shock. She is technically well enough to leave sickbay . . ."

She trailed off, and Beverly finished the phrase. "But . . ."

"But she pleaded so fervently not to be sent back to her cabin that I have kept her here." Selar looked as though she were wondering whether she'd have to defend her action and, if so, how she would successfully do so.

Beverly waved at her subordinate reassuringly. "Don't worry about it. We're not that crowded . . . yet. The poor thing deserves any feeling of security we can give her, after all she's been through."

"Did you discover whether Thala could legally be sent elsewhere than an Andorian colony, if the cost of her passage were paid?" Selar asked.

"Yes, I talked to Lieutenant Greenstein a couple of days ago, right after I spoke to the administrator on Thonolan Four." She slanted a sideways glance at the Vulcan. "By the way, when you speak of finding someone to pay her passage—which from this sector would be a considerable expense—do you by any chance have someone in mind?" Crusher asked the question as if she already knew the answer.

"I would pay it," the Vulcan said unhesitatingly. "To see Thala have a chance of continued proper medical care and schooling, I would be pleased to do so."

Crusher nodded. "Well, from what Howard said, sending Thala to Vulcan would constitute a rather shady deal." At Selar's raised eyebrow, the doctor translated: "It would be against the letter of the law."

The lieutenant's dark eyes betrayed disappointment. "That is most unfortunate."

"However, just between you and me"—Beverly leaned forward, holding the Vulcan's gaze with her own—"I doubt that the law would ever enter into it."

"Why not?"

"Because the Andorians don't want her, and if she were to conveniently disappear, they wouldn't ask a single question about her whereabouts."

Selar raised an eyebrow. "Indeed?"

Crusher's usually generous mouth thinned angrily. "The only reason any of the officials I talked with could think of to offer Thala a place would be to collect any inheritance she has." She gave a bitter laugh. "Frankly, for all they care, we could sell the child to a brothel as long as we split the money with them! Their callous attitude makes me sick."

Beverly took a deep breath to regain control, then managed to smile faintly. "Selar, if you want to pay Thala's passage to Vulcan, to see her placed in an institution there, where she'll receive good medical care and a real education, I'll take my hat off to you."

Selar's eyes were puzzled. "Your hat?" she said blankly. "I have only seen you wear a hat once, when you were on your way to the holodeck, wearing those impractical shoes with stilts for heels."

The doctor rolled her eyes. "No, no, what I meant is that I'll help you any way that I can."

"Oh." Selar's expression lightened fractionally. "Thank you, Beverly. I am grateful for your support."

"I'm the one who's grateful," Crusher said. "I want you to know that during the past few days it's been so reassuring knowing that I can rely on you to keep things on an even keel around here. Don't think I don't appreciate it."

"I know," Selar said, then she, in turn, took a deep breath. "Beverly . . . I must tell you something."

"What?"

"I have been offered another position, a very good one, with the Vulcan Science Academy, as head of bioelectronic research. If I accept it, I will have the opportunity to accomplish much more than I can in Starfleet, working on improving prosthetics for people like Geordi La Forge and Thala. I am seriously considering accepting the offer." She paused, then a hint of wry humor touched her mouth as she continued. "Assuming, of course, that we all survive our current mission."

"Congratulations, Selar, that's a great honor! You'd

be terrific at it, with the way you can handle both electronics and medicine. Of course, we'd miss you terribly here, but I think you should take it, if it's what you want."

"I am not sure it *is* what I want," the Vulcan said seriously. "I know that it is what I *should* want, what I have worked for the past fifteen years to achieve, but . . ." She trailed off, not meeting Crusher's eyes.

"But what?" Beverly asked gently. "Don't you want to go back to Vulcan?"

Selar's head came up with surprise; her eyes widened slightly. "How . . . ," she began. Then she finished heavily, "How did you know?"

"We've worked together for a long time," the doctor said. "I've seen your reaction"—she smiled—"however slight, whenever your homeworld is mentioned. And Deanna commented once on your aversion to talking about your family. Vulcans are hardly blabbermouths, in comparison to humans, but the other Vulcans on board talk far more about home than you ever have."

"That is because my family regards me as . . ." She thought a moment. "I believe your idiom is 'a black cow.'"

"Sheep," Beverly corrected, managing not to smile.

"Thank you. I did not marry the man they selected for me, and they were not sanguine about it. They have never let me forget my transgression, my flouting of tradition. Every few weeks I receive communications from them, and nearly every one manages to remind me of my disgrace and of how successful my former betrothed has become."

She sighed. "It was an immense relief to me when Sukat finally married, so that at least I did not have to hear them tell me that it might not be too late, and that if I would only return to Vulcan and abase myself

148

in his presence, he might do me the immense honor of taking me back."

Beverly shook her head sympathetically. "I can just imagine it. Families . . ." She made a face. "I have—had—an uncle who was a fast-talking shyster, and the biggest pain in the . . ." She trailed off, then shook her head. "Well, it's a long story, but I know what you mean. Our friends we can choose, but our relatives . . . we're stuck with them."

"Indeed," said Selar, with equal irony. "It is bad enough to receive such remonstrations while parsecs away, but what would it be like to have to live on the same planet with my kinspeople?"

"Sounds to me like you ought to just tell them to get off your back about it," Beverly said. "If you made it clear that you weren't willing to put up with . . . remonstrations, then they would let you alone eventually. After all, it's not as though you're still a kid, fresh out of school. You'd be going back as an honored professional."

Selar nodded, as though the idea was something she hadn't thought of before. "And I could make it clear that if I marry, it will be by my own choice," she said.

"Sure! If they fuss about it, tell them to write down their complaints, fold them up, then stick them where the sun never shines," the chief medical officer suggested, a twinkle in her eyes.

"Where the sun—" Selar broke off as she figured out the colorful metaphor. "Excellent advice, Doctor," she said, straight-faced.

"No charge, Doctor," Crusher said with equal gravity.

By the time Selar finished her patient checks, it was nearly lunchtime. She went looking for Thala, to suggest that they go up to Ten-Forward again. Finding the child bent intently over a computer link, she greeted her. "Hello, Thala. Would you like to join me for lunch?"

The girl's white head jerked up, startled, then she hastily turned off the computer before the Vulcan could catch more than a glimpse of what was on the screen. It appeared to be some kind of grid the child had been tracing with her fingers, as the computer's voice identified each area. "Oh, Selar!" she said a little breathlessly. "I didn't know you were there!"

"I regret having startled you," the Vulcan said. Then, curious about what the child had been doing, she remarked, "Apparently you were studying."

"Yes . . . yes, I was." Her blue features twisted uncertainly, as though she were wondering what the other had observed of her "studies." "I was studying the layout of the starbases near here," she conceded finally. "Memorizing where everything is, in case I ever get to visit one again . . . then I can find my way around."

"You have visited starbases before," Selar said, still puzzled, but certain that there was some hidden purpose here. "And you should not plan on wandering around a starbase alone. That would be most unwise."

"Yes, I've been to starbases, with my father," Thala admitted. "But this was different. I wanted to . . ." She hesitated, then continued in a rush, "Wesley promised to take me the next time we docked at one, and I want to impress him by knowing where everything is!"

"I understand," Selar said, admitting to herself that the explanation was perfectly logical . . . but that still didn't make her believe it.

For a moment, the doctor considered telling the child about her own decision to pay Thala's passage to Vulcan and see that she was properly placed in one of the excellent learning and medical institutions on her world, but she decided against it. She would speak of it later, after their current mission was completed (assuming they *did* successfully make it back) and all the arrangements were firmly in place. Better not to raise the child's expectations until she was sure everything would work out; after all, there was still plenty of time.

Besides, Thala was still overcoming the effects of the terrible shock she'd received from her artifact-induced nightmare. Emotional upsets—even happy ones—should be avoided until she was completely over the effects of the trauma she'd undergone.

So, instead of asking the questions in her mind, Selar only nodded. "What about lunch? Or should I go by myself?"

"I'm coming!" Thala leaped up happily, her small features brightening. "I'm starved!"

The small boy walked barefoot on the side of the road, feeling the warm dust rise up grittily between his toes. It was hot in the light of the double suns, hot and bright. The rainy season on Khitomer was still many days away, and the brown and grayish-green countryside shimmered with the afternoon heat. Small puffs of whitish dust rose up around Worf's bare legs as he trailed along behind LengwI', his pet Targ.

The Targ *was a large gray animal, heavily muscled, with a snouted face and small beady eyes. The beast stood taller than the boy's waist, even though the child was big for his years. Worf was still a long time from his first Rite of Ascension, but already he dreamed of it—dreamed of the day that he would be a warrior, traveling the star paths in a battle cruiser. The boy dreamed also of the day that he would command such a ship, imagining himself in the central seat, feeling in his mind the weight of leather and metal on his shoulders.*

The Targ *suddenly snorted and dashed ahead into the shadow of some trees. Whuffling and grunting savagely, it rooted beneath them, its tusks tearing into the earth, uprooting the pale green ground covering. There was a sudden terrified scuffling, then a triumphant squeal from the* Targ *as it pounced, striking something with its sharp-hooved forefeet, then seizing the small, furry creature in its jaws. Blood gushed from the unfortunate burrower's throat as the* Targ's *sharp teeth ripped it nearly in half, then the Klingon animal dispatched its prey in two messy swallows.*

"Good boy, LengwI'!" Worf praised. The Targ *grunted and wriggled with pleasure, shoving its sticky snout into the boy's hand for a pat. "You got that burrower! You're the best hunting* Targ *on the whole planet!" He stroked the beast's thick gray ruff, careful to avoid its sharp spines.*

LengwI' snuffled, not knowing, of course, that he was the only Targ *on this backwater of the empire, the planet named Khitomer. Worf's small face drew into a scowl even more pronounced than usual. At least his family had let him bring his pet along to the small Klingon settlement—he couldn't imagine what it would be like to be here without LengwI' to take hunting and provide company.*

Worf sighed. He didn't like being stuck here on this remote, underpopulated colony world while Mogh, his father, worked on setting up the planetary communications system. They'd already been here half a season longer than Mogh had thought they would be when they'd first come.

Absently, Worf scuffed his big toe into the hole LengwI' had dug, pushing the clods back around the roots of the tree. If only Mogh would take Worf, LengwI', Mother, and Worf's nurse, Kahlest, back home, then everything would be fine again. Back home there would be other children to practice battle strategies and unarmed combat with. There were few children anywhere near Worf's age on this colony world, and most of them were females.

Not that there was anything wrong with females, basically, Worf thought. Some of them were very good fighters indeed, making up for their smaller size and lesser strength with quicker reflexes, greater cunning, and, when in battle frenzy, ferocious savagery. But females weren't the same as having boys his own age as friends.

The boy sighed, and LengwI', catching his mood, grunted inquiringly and thrust a bristly muzzle into Worf's hand. When the boy looked down at his pet, he saw the Targ eyeing him with a certain glint in its small eyes that the boy recognized. "You just ate," he pointed out. "Are you hungry already?" LengwI' snuffled agreement. "Well, it's not time for you to be fed yet, so if you're hungry, you'll just have to catch something else. So hunt, boy. Kill!"

The Targ's bristly, moist snout quivered as it scented the air, then it began jogging purposefully toward another tree. Worf watched proudly as the Targ promptly dug up, dispatched, disemboweled, then devoured another burrower, even larger than the first. "Good boy!" he praised.

Worf glanced at the sky, seeing that the small, reddish sun was nearly down to the horizon. His own stomach churned with hunger. Soon it would be time for dinner, and Mama was making Rokeg blood pie tonight!

The boy's stomach grumbled eagerly at the thought. Waving to the Targ to abandon the last few juicy scraps of burrower, Worf turned around and headed back. Behind him he heard the Targ's hooves crunching the dry ground cover, and, with a shouted challenge—

"This time you won't catch me!"—*he broke into a run for home.*

Worf's eyes opened, and he sat up, glancing around him at the solid familiarity of his own quarters. The dream had been so *real!* The smell of Khitomer's dust and vegetation seemed to linger in his nostrils. His stomach was rumbling hungrily, and his mouth watered at the thought of eating real *Rokeg* blood pie, hot and slippery and salty in his mouth. The *Enterprise's* food synthesizers, accurate as they were, just couldn't manage to reproduce that raw, fresh-killed flavor.

He rose from his narrow, austere bunk. Worf's quarters were stark, almost monastic in their simplicity and sparseness.

Quickly Worf dressed in his uniform. He draped his sash over his powerful shoulders, checked its placement in his mirror, and checked the charge in his phaser. He smoothed back his hair—not as long as most Klingons wore theirs, but Worf strove to balance his appearance between that expected of a Starfleet officer and that of a Klingon warrior.

Then the security chief walked toward the door, but suddenly he stopped halfway there, his body stiffening. That dream . . . it hadn't been just a dream. It had been a memory. That day had actually happened. He remembered now—

—remembered being roused in the middle of that same night by his father, who had hauled him and Worf's mother and Kahlest, the boy's nurse, down into the gunnery bunker.

Soon the air had been filled with the smell of destruction and death, the stifled groans of the wounded and dying. His mother had clutched him tightly in her arms, ignoring her small son's protests that he wanted to fight—to kill—the opponents who had attacked them in such a cowardly fashion.

154

The Romulans' attack on the Khitomer colony had been both unprovoked and unexpected. Before the next day's light dawned, four thousand Klingons, including all of Worf's family as well as his pet *Targ,* lay dead. Federation officers had found the small Klingon child clawing feebly at the rubble he was buried in, and had pulled him back out into the light of day. The first sight to greet his eyes had been a Starfleet uniform, like the one he now wore.

Worf had lived the rest of his life among humans . . .

That meal of Rokeg *blood pie was the last time we were together,* Worf realized. He remembered feeding bits of it under the table to LengwI', remembered his mother's resultant scolding, and heard in his mind the echo of his father's gruff, booming laughter . . .

The Klingon resumed his walk. Enough of such memories. Sorrow and loneliness had no place in a Klingon warrior's heart. He had work to do, duties to perform.

With quick, decisive steps, Worf left his quarters. His stomach rumbled hungrily again, but, strangely, he discovered that he had no further desire for *Rokeg* blood pie.

As soon as the research team's findings were assembled, Picard called a meeting in the conference lounge, so that the team could relate its findings to the senior officers. Data, La Forge, and Acting Ensign Crusher took turns relating all that they had discovered, with Wesley providing the summary of results and conclusions about the artifact. The junior officer was a bit nervous at first, and it showed, but as he warmed to his subject, his hesitancy vanished, and he spoke concisely and clearly about the results of their sensor readings and the correlations with the medical scans.

Picard nodded when the young man had finished. "Thank you, Mister Crusher, that was most informative. Discussion, anyone?"

Actually, the captain had already made up his mind about his course of action, but he preferred to hear all relevant viewpoints before announcing his plans. Of course, given strong enough new information, he was prepared to change his mind.

That was not to happen this time. The captain listened to several minutes of discussion, some of it repeating previous speculations and theories. Worf and Riker believed that the artifact was a weapon and that the *Enterprise* should take the risk of attempting to destroy it. La Forge was in favor of beaming over a landing party to attempt to shut down its systems. Beverly Crusher, on the other hand, warned against any contact with the alien environment.

Picard heard them all out, then raised a hand for quiet. "I have decided to act on Lieutenant Commander La Forge's suggestion and authorize an away team to beam over and attempt to shut down that energy field that is holding us here." He turned to Will Riker. "Number One, you will lead the away team."

Riker nodded, his bearded countenance sober but serene. Leading such teams was a major part of his job, but he'd obviously been braced for an argument if Picard had expressed the wish (as he occasionally had) to lead an away team himself.

"Lieutenant Worf, you will be the security officer on this detail."

The Klingon officer did not smile, but something like a faint growl of pleasure emerged from his otherwise unmoving countenance. He was plainly eager, as usual, for action.

"Commanders La Forge and Data, I want you to accompany them, and use your unique vision and perceptions—both of you—to discover as much about that place as possible."

"Yes, sir," both officers murmured.

"Captain, I'd like to recommend one more person for the away team," Riker said.

"Yes, Number One?"

"I'd like to request that Doctor Crusher allow Doctor Gavar from her staff to accompany us. If Tellarites are indeed immune to the artifact's brain-altering fields, then Gavar's presence could prove an asset."

Picard nodded. "I agree. Doctor Crusher?"

The chief medical officer hesitated. "I agree that it may be wise, since Gavar demonstrated on the *Marco Polo* that she has some resistance to the artifact's effect. However, I would prefer not to order her. She's here as part of the Starfleet officer exchange program, after all. If she wishes to volunteer . . ." She trailed off.

"Very well," Picard said. "On a volunteer basis, then."

The doctor tapped her communicator. "Doctor Gavar?"

"Yes, Doctor?" came the Tellarite's voice.

"The captain is sending an away team over to the artifact, in an attempt to free us from its tractor field. We have discovered that apparently the reason you withstood the psychosis that struck Montez is that Tellarite minds are not affected by the artifact's energies. Captain Picard is therefore looking for a Tellarite to volunteer for the away team."

There was a moment's hesitation, then the doctor said quietly, "Inform the captain that I am volunteering to go."

"Thank you, Gavar," Crusher said. "I will tell him. Crusher out."

She tapped her communicator again to close the channel, then nodded at Riker. "When do you want to go?"

The commander stood up with an air of decision. "I for one would like to put this place far behind us." He gave Picard a quick, inquiring glance. "So I suggest that the away team beam over as soon as possible."

The captain nodded. "Make it so, Number One. And good luck."

Chapter Nine

As THEY ASSEMBLED outside Transporter Room 4, Commander Riker surveyed his away team critically. Data, Geordi, Worf and Doctor Gavar, like Will himself, were dressed in heavy-duty uniforms with insulated jackets. Data's and Wesley's sensor readings indicated that the temperature aboard the artifact was quite chilly—barely above freezing.

Riker checked the settings and charge on his phaser one final time, and the away team followed his example. Even though they had detected no life-forms aboard the artifact, there was no telling what kind of automatic defense systems it boasted. Also, despite their sensor readings, Will wasn't entirely convinced that there were no living beings over there. So many things about the artifact had proved so alien as to be virtually undetectable by their sensing devices.

He glanced over at the Tellarite, who had a pouch clipped to her belt. Noting his look, she patted the thing with her stubby, hooflike hand.

"Medical kit," she explained in her gruff voice.

"I doubt you'll need it where we're going," Riker

said. "But I suppose it's best to be prepared. Would you like a phaser, Doctor?"

"No, sir," she replied, wrinkling her snout. "I'm not a very good shot. I'd be afraid that I'd trip and shoot something—or somebody—by accident."

Worf did not quite roll his eyes, but the Klingon security chief's expression was eloquent.

"That's all right, Gavar," Riker said hastily. "We're all armed. By the way, I would like to thank you personally for volunteering to be part of the away team."

"It's my medical duty, sir," she replied steadily, her small, weak eyes within their folds of pink flesh very serious. "Anything I can do to help save patients in this crisis, I'll do."

"Commander Data, I want you to record everything we see and experience," Riker instructed. "Understood?"

"Yes, Commander," the android replied, and he gave one final check to his tricorder.

"Everyone ready?"

At their nods of assent, Riker led the way into the transporter room, where Chief O'Brien stood by at the controls.

"O'Brien," Riker said, "I want you to keep a fix on us at all times, so you can transport us out immediately if we run into trouble over there."

"Yes, Commander," said the chief. "But in order for me to do that, you'll have to keep the away team together. The distortion caused by that field makes tracking and locking on to individuals nearly impossible."

Riker nodded. "I understand, Chief O'Brien." He fixed his away team with a stern look. "Everyone will stay together, is that clear?"

"Yes, sir," they all replied.

"Good luck, Commander." O'Brien's broad, usually good-natured features bore a strained expression, and Will thought he saw new lines around his eyes and mouth. Riker wondered for a moment whether the sandy-haired transporter chief had experienced one of the dreams.

If so, he would only be one of many by now. More and more crew members were wearing haunted expressions, their eyes bleak and empty or, worse, filled with fear. Doctor Crusher had reported that nearly forty percent of the crew and fifty percent of their family members had experienced one of the "real" dreams the artifact induced. Not all of the dreams were unhappy ones, but the nightmares tended to outnumber the pleasant experiences.

There were other statistics even grimmer. Seventeen suicide attempts, one successful, and one more not expected to live. Five attempted murders. Forty-three cases of catatonia. Eighty-four nervous breakdowns. One hundred sixty-two under treatment for severe depression and withdrawal. And, of course, one Betazoid who could not be allowed to awaken for fear that the emotional and mental trauma pervading the ship would destroy her life or her reason.

On his way to the transporter room to join his away team, Will had stopped off in sickbay. For a moment he'd stood gazing down at the counselor's lovely, unconscious features, framed by those masses of glossy black curls. *Sleeping Beauty,* he thought, and he had to swallow against a sudden tightness in his throat. The sight of Troi asleep awakened a surge of memories and feelings that he'd thought long buried.

Taking her limp hand in his, Riker directed a thought at her, hoping somehow that it would reach beyond the drug-induced sleep. *Hang on, Deanna. We're going to get out of this, I promise you, darling. Just hang on . . .*

As he'd walked out of sickbay, he'd been disturbed

to note that every bed was full and that nearby lounges and sleeping quarters had been appropriated by the medical staff for care of those incapacitated by the artifact's mental assault.

The shortage of duty-ready personnel was beginning to impinge on the ship's efficiency, and there were additional cases admitted to sickbay every hour. *We've got to succeed in shutting down that field,* Riker thought, *or we'll have to take the risk of blowing up the damned artifact.*

The team mounted the transporter, standing poised and ready. Worf had his hand on his sidearm. Riker thumbed on his flashlight, in case they emerged in darkness, and nodded at the transporter chief.

"Energize," he ordered.

The walls of the chamber shimmered around them, growing indistinct. Riker felt his own body phase out of one space, then emerge into another—a feeling of profound displacement, but now familiar to him after all these years.

Cold air struck his face and throat, light and color surrounded him, sound filled his ears—Riker had barely a second to realize that the beam-over was complete, before he was hit with a sense of vertigo so profound that it made the dizziness he'd experienced when he first gazed at the artifact seem as nothing.

The commander gasped for breath. He was blind, deaf, surrounded as he was by alien colors, alien sounds, none of which was meant to be assimilated or even tolerated by human eyes, human ears. An alien odor assaulted his nostrils—sweeter than claret, more bitter than bile.

Doubling over, retching, Riker staggered a few steps, trying to close his eyes, to clap his hands over his ears, but the hideous shrieking colors and impossible shapes smote him, assaulted his vision, even as the sounds of insanity ripped into his mind via his eardrums, making him wish he were deaf, that he were dead. The very air tortured the skin of his face and hands, making his flesh creep and shrink until it seemed as though his bones would burst through.

Stop! he wanted to scream. *God, please, stop it! Stop!*

But his mouth and tongue did not obey. His body was slipping sideways, out of control, unable to stay upright, because it was not *his* anymore—

Neither was his mind. And that assault was the worst of all.

Birth agony, death agony, orgasm, pain—raw physical and emotional experiences, all jumbled together as his mind was wrenched and wrung, attempting vainly all the while to function, to comprehend images, events, feelings that were totally, irrevocably, alien to it.

Emotions assaulted him, each alien, each intense, each fundamentally *wrong*—skewed, distorted, twisted. The commander felt those emotions ripping at his sanity, shredding it, sending his psyche gibbering away, back into the deepest recesses of his consciousness, as his essence, his anima, his sense of self—his *soul*—tried and failed to take refuge from this ultimate violation.

Will Riker had one fleeting moment of clarity to realize that he was lying on his side, curled up, the stink of his own vomit filling his nostrils, and that he was either dying or going insane. In that last second, he prayed desperately for death, knowing that no archaic conception of an eternal hell could equal what now awaited him within the depths of his own mind, should he by the worst stroke of fortune imaginable remain alive.

Geordi La Forge was screaming, but he could not hear himself. All he was aware of was the turbid cacophony of sound that surrounded him, the pandemonium of noise echoed by the chaos within his own mind. His skin was a prison of icy fire, and a taste filled his mouth that was so sour his tongue seemed to shrivel.

He had lost all sense of direction or location. He no longer knew where his comrades were. The engineer reeled along, crashing against walls and into shapes, screaming as he went, until finally his boots caught on something solid and he fell heavily.

Movement had apparently helped him hold the mental assault at bay, he discovered, for as soon as he was still, it tunneled into his mind with a savage intensity, seeking to reform, rechannel, reshape his very brain configurations. He could feel his body trying to breathe in an alien rhythm, his blood attempting to flow in nonhuman patterns, his flesh straining to reshape itself into a different envelope.

Oh, God, make me deaf! he thought, stuffing his fingers in his ears, trying to focus his mind on the multiplication table, natural logarithms, square roots —anything that was reasoned and ordered, anything that would protect him from the chaos.

And all the while he fought his losing battle, Geordi's head swung back and forth, up and down, as he scanned with his VISOR, fighting the blackness that wanted to carry his mind into blessed oblivion. He concentrated, trying for one more minute, one more second, one more heartbeat of consciousness, because he could not bear to stop *seeing*.

Moments later, the blackness won out, and La Forge sank into nothingness, conscious only of a terrible regret that he could not endure—had not proved worthy—of his own vision.

It was the *may'QeH*, the battle madness, filling him, and it was good. Snarling, Worf raced through the halls, not sure whether they were, in fact, physical places or alien labyrinths imposed upon his mind—or perhaps he was on some other plane of existence, it was impossible to know. Nor did it matter. He was here to fight, and the lust for it filled him past all other knowledge or goals.

Forgotten was his struggle to maintain the demeanor of a Starfleet officer. That was over now. The fire had taken possession of his blood, casting out the weak inhibitions imposed by his upbringing and his Starfleet training. There was only the drunken, soaring knowledge of the enemy and the single-minded pursuit of victory.

He knew there was danger, but that knowledge was like the heat of *HIq* in his blood, as though he had indeed imbibed some heady liquor such as Romulan ale, not the feeble synthehol the humans drank. Blind with rage—or was he blind from the light exploding within his vision? It did not matter! Roaring, he struck out, sending his fist—it should be armored, where was his battle glove?—smashing against an unyielding surface.

Deaf from the glorious war chant singing in his blood—or was he unable to hear because his ears were filled with alien sounds? That did not matter, either. He was here, and he would fight!

But where was here? Confused, Worf spun around, unable to tell whether he was still in his own body, or whether he was now fighting some enemy within the recesses of his mind. He could not be sure what was real and what was illusion, but that did not matter, either! Trying to decide which was which and what was what brought agony, but that did not matter. A warrior used pain only as a lash, a goad that could spur the valiant on to greater glory!

Worf blinked, suddenly realizing something disturbing. His phaser! It was no longer in his hand! When had that happened? He must find it! With the phaser, he could wreak real destruction, more than he could with his hands or his feet, strong and ably trained as they were.

Spinning on his heel (but had he really moved at all? it was impossible to tell . . .), he strode in search of his weapon. It must be here someplace, and with it in hand he would be able to achieve the ultimate in glory. They would feel his fury, and so would this place (but was it a place? or was it the inside of his own mind?).

Shaking his head, Worf bared his teeth and narrowed his eyes, trying to focus them, but as hard as he strained, he could only see the alienness, not his phaser! He began to howl curses, because the *QI'yaH*-bedamned colors and images and shapes were in his *ghuy-cha'* way! And, worst of all, he could not even hear his own obscenities because of the *Qu'vatlh* alien sounds!

"naDev vo'ylghoS!" he roared, ordering the images, the colors, the sounds, to go away!

But they did not. Worf stumbled around a corner, seeing behind the screen of colors a darker, quasi-familiar moving shape. At last, something concrete for him to kill!

He lunged at it with a bellow of berserker rage, and it dodged his outflung hand (but was it really there?). Something caught his leg, sending him sprawling, but with a warrior's trained reactions, he was on his feet again in an eyeblink, poised to spring.

Only the colors and the images and the shadows that had invaded his mind mocked him—there was nothing there, nothing . . .

Worf's rage to battle dimmed suddenly, cooling like coals drizzled with water. Where was his phaser? He should be shooting, assaulting the enemy, making the kill! What was wrong with him now? The Klingon officer struggled to see, to focus—

—and, still struggling to act, to think, to fight, he fell like a severed limb, to hit the unyielding surface beneath his feet with a boneless thud, where he lay facedown, unmoving.

Gavar knew she was in trouble from the first moment she materialized. Colors bludgeoned her small, weak eyes, and she saw disturbing, impossible shapes, even as sounds ripped into her small, folded-over ears. Sickeningly sweet odors assaulted her sensitive nose. *My senses,* she thought frantically, squeezing her eyes shut. *I can't trust them . . .*

Something fell next to her feet, something heavy. A body. Kneeling, Gavar ran her stubby two-fingered and single-thumbed hand over the form below her and touched a face, feeling "flesh" that was smoother than any human or Klingon skin could ever be. Commander Data. The android's circuits must have shorted out from the sensory overload.

Fumbling blindly at her medical kit, the Tellarite got it open and managed to locate by touch the roll of bandage material within, as well **as** her surgical scissors. Fighting the urge to open her eyes, and trying desperately to ignore the alien sounds that seemed determined to bore into her ears like angry insects, she clipped off wads of the bandage and stuffed each deep into her ears, twisting them until they blocked out the worst of the sounds. She drew a long, relieved breath, then wrapped a length around her head so they would be held in place.

Now for her eyes. Carefully, Gavar measured off a length of the stuff and wound it around her head, covering her eyes. She squinted through the translucent cover and gave a grunt of satisfaction. The bandage softened the stomach-churning colors and muted the edges and impossible angles of the shapes and images surrounding her, the images that had made her nauseated and dizzy.

She wondered how long it had been since the beam-over. Not more than a minute or so, she supposed. She tapped her communicator, wondering if her own voice would be heard and understood above the sounds. "Gavar here," she said in her husky, snuffling voice. "Terrible sensory distortion. I've had to cover my eyes and ears or risk madness. Commander Data is unconscious . . . or shorted out . . . whatever. I can't hear you, because I can't risk uncovering my ears. I'm going to try and get the landing party together so we can beam back. Do *not* attempt rescue until you hear from me. This place—it's terrible, like being inside an alien nightmare . . ." She trailed off, then said, "I'll signal again soon. Gavar out."

Faintly, she heard a different sound, the noise of human pain, a noise that she had heard only too many times before. This one reminded her of the sounds she'd heard when she'd been detailed to a human psychiatric ward—a thin, high-pitched screaming that went on and on, keen as a knife edged with madness.

Catching the shape of a dark bulk moving toward her, Gavar scuttled back on her rear, out of the way, and the human, whoever it was, blundered into Data's inert form and fell hard. For long seconds he scrabbled, struggling—Gavar could dimly see his dark form moving before her, screaming all the while in that thin, piercing way. Then, abruptly, he was still.

The Tellarite scrambled back over to check for a pulse. The man was breathing and alive, but his pulse was fast and thready. Her questing fingers found the crescent shape of the VISOR across his face. It was La Forge.

Gavar left him where he was, his legs resting across Data's back, and, lurching to her feet, she fumbled her way along the wall, searching for any familiar shapes among the alien ones she could half glimpse.

Her sensitive nostrils twitched, discerning a familiar odor among the alien stenches. Human vomit—she squinted and made out a dark shape outlined against the colors of madness. *Commander Riker?* she wondered, and moments later, touching the man's forehead, she had her answer.

He was alive, though, if anything, she judged, in even worse condition than La Forge. Grasping the folds of his jacket, she began dragging his heavy body back toward the others. Gasping, she let him go when he lay within a handsbreadth of his fellow officers, then straightened up. The Klingon . . . where had he gone?

She tapped her communicator. "Gavar again. I've found the humans. They're alive. I'm going after Worf now. Gavar out."

Wondering where to try first, she decided to risk loosening the bandage in one ear. She'd listen for only a second . . .

That second nearly proved her undoing. Gavar sagged against the wall, knees weak, feeling the hinges of her mind rattle as insanity pushed against the puny barriers she'd raised against it. But she'd heard a distinct roar that was nothing like the alien, undefinable sounds that surrounded her. It had come from, she thought, her right . . .

The nurse hesitated, thinking, considering. Insane humans were one thing, but a crazed Klingon was something else again. For a moment she was tempted to abandon the security chief and tell the *Enterprise* to beam them back. Then her chubby features tightened, her stocky, porcine body stood taller. She had to at least try. She couldn't leave a fellow creature to die in this hideous place.

As she turned to head right, her fingers touched her medical kit. Gavar paused, then opened it quickly, as a sudden thought struck her. If she could just locate the right ampoule . . .

Removing the injector, she searched her memory for the location of the medicines within, striving to bring to mind a mental image of their arrangement. Crusher conducted frequent drills with her people, drills where they had to function without gravity, with poor or no light, among simulated wreckage.

Got it, she thought as her stubby, hoofed fingers closed over the correct sedative. At least she prayed to all the Tellerite goddesses that it was the right one. If she'd guessed wrong, Worf might very well die.

Lifting the bandage away from her ear again for the barest instant, she discerned again that demented roaring. It had to be the Klingon.

Hugging the wall, loaded injector clutched in her hand, Gavar edged to her right. When she reached a branch that her groping arms revealed as a cross-corridor, she called out, "Lieutenant? Are you there?" She did not expect a rational answer, but she at least hoped that he might hear her and roar with rage again.

It took her nearly a minute, measured by her racing pulses, of calling and listening in the briefest of flashes, before she heard him again. To the right again . . .

Finally, beneath her shoulder as she edged along the new corridor, she felt a vibration, as though a heavy body had struck the unyielding surface. Gavar froze, wondering whether she dared raise her bandage even by the smallest amount, straining her eyes through the sheltering bandage for any sight of a dark bulk before her . . .

The wall vibrated again, harder. Easing the lump of bandage away from her ear for a heartbeat, Gavar heard the Klingon's enraged bellow.

Mother of Many, she thought with a clutch of fear. *I forgot about the phaser!*

She braced herself, half expecting to be roasted or vaporized at any moment.

Before her eyes a darkness loomed. Worf—it had to be!

He lunged for her, and Gavar skipped aside, nimble on her hoofed feet despite her bulk. The Klingon reeled against her, arms out, grasping, his breath hot on her cheek for a second, then the Tellarite jerked her leg hard against his shin, and he went down. Quick as a thought, she was beside him, the injector pumping the sedative into his body, she knew not exactly where. The shoulder, she guessed, leaping away, behind him now, as he lunged to his feet.

Gavar counted seconds by the pounding of her own heartbeats—ten, twelve, fifteen . . . *Oh, Mother, didn't it work?*

Seventeen, twenty . . . twenty-two . . .

And the surface beneath her hooves vibrated as the Klingon went down like a monument falling.

Thank you, Mothers, all of you, Gavar thought fervently as she hastily checked Worf's pulse and respiration by touch. He was thoroughly unconscious —she'd given him the entire dose, because she hadn't been able to set the calibrator on the injector—but he was definitely alive. She'd used the correct medication.

Grabbing the back of his jacket in both hands, she began dragging him along. But she had too far to go, that was no good, her back was in agony from hunching over after just a few steps.

Hastily, Gavar tugged her own jacket off, turned the

Klingon over, and tied her garment around his head by its sleeves. Then she walked around him, turned so her back was toward him, then stooped and picked up his booted feet. Pulling them up into the crooks of her elbows, she grasped his heels in her hands. Much better. She started forward—

—then halted, her heart slamming. Was she headed the right way?

She spent a moment trying to remember whether she'd gotten turned around, so she was now facing in the wrong direction, and decided, finally (all the while knowing that a wrong decision could mean both their deaths), that she had. Slowly, Gavar shuffled around until she was facing the opposite direction, then she began dragging the Klingon along as he lay on his back.

She kept her left elbow brushing against the wall, searching, searching for the way she'd come . . .

Then her arm met only air, and, praying all the while that she'd chosen the correct direction, she turned left down the branch.

Surely she hadn't come this far before! She must have missed her way back there, and now was wandering lost in this labyrinth of madness! Gavar hunched her shoulders determinedly and began counting paces, wishing that she'd thought to do that on the way out. *Twenty-five, twenty-six, twenty-seven* . . .

She would turn around and try to retrace her steps, she decided, at the count of fifty . . .

Forty-three, forty-four, forty-five, forty-six—

Her hoofed foot struck something yielding. She had found them!

With a gasp of relief, Gavar dropped her burden, careless of where the Klingon's heels landed. She tapped her communicator. "This is Gavar," she panted, winded as much from the mixture of terror and relief as from exertion. "I've got them all. We're together. Beam us back, O'Brien!"

Blind, she could not see the transporter beam forming around them, but after a second she could feel its blessed melting feeling seize her.

Even as they materialized, she ripped at the bandages over her eyes and ears, hearing a babble of voices, feeling the touch of hands.

The sane, clean sights of the *Enterprise*'s transporter room and Doctor Chandra's face filled her vision. Gavar's people did not weep, but her knees sagged, and she would have collapsed if not for the human woman's support.

"Are they alive?" she demanded, looking down fearfully at her sprawled companions. Beverly Crusher was running a scanner over Commander Riker. Medical priorities reasserted themselves in her mind, and the doctor struggled to regain her professional demeanor. "Doctor Crusher," she managed in a steadier tone. "I had to sedate the Klingon—twenty cc's of *Qong-Hergh.*"

Beverly Crusher glanced up, her expression terribly worried, but not holding the bleakness Gavar had feared to see. "They're all alive, Gavar," she said reassuringly. "Thanks to you, they're all alive."

Jean-Luc Picard entered sickbay with strides so hurried they were almost a run. Beverly Crusher had rarely seen him so visibly agitated. When he saw her standing over the diagnostic and treatment couch where Will Riker lay unconscious, Picard halted, then approached cautiously, as though he could somehow awaken her comatose patient. "How is he?" he asked in a low voice.

Beverly sighed. *If only he could awaken Will by mere noise! It's not going to be nearly that easy.*

Aloud she said, "Physically, he's fine now. But he's withdrawn deep into his own mind, probably in a last-ditch effort to hang on to his sanity."

Picard glanced around the medical facility. "What about La Forge, Worf, and Data?"

"Recovering, all of them," she reported crisply. "Geordi came out of it within a few minutes of his return to this ship, under the influence of a small dose of tricordrazine. Worf is still asleep—Gavar gave him a hefty dosage of that Klingon sedative—but his brain patterns indicate normal activity. He should awaken naturally in about eight hours. Doctor Selar and Commander La Forge are currently engaged in restoring Data to full function. They say it won't be much longer."

"What happened to Data? Why did the artifact affect him? Surely the mental trauma couldn't disturb him, since he's an android."

"Apparently his positronic brain went into a full-system shutdown when confronted with the unstable and contradictory sensory environment aboard the artifact. He was the first to lose consciousness."

"I'll want to talk to them—except, of course, Lieutenant Worf—as soon as possible." Picard gazed down at Riker's bearded features. "Is he in a coma?"

"No," Crusher replied. "His condition at present resembles the mental withdrawal into catatonia that so many of the other victims of the artifact have evidenced."

"Will he recover naturally, or can you bring him out of this?"

She sighed. "I don't believe he will recover without intervention. At the moment, I'm considering alternatives. I thought of asking one of the Vulcans to attempt a mind-meld, but none of our medical personnel is a psychological healer. That's a specialty on Vulcan, just as psychiatry is on Earth. The doctors at the Vulcan Science Academy might be able to help him . . ." She trailed off with a shake of her head.

"I can't afford to wait for a hypothetical future cure!" snapped the captain. "Dammit, Doctor, I *need* Commander Riker, and I need him *now.*" Picard's hazel eyes were filled with concern and . . . yes, fear —something Beverly Crusher had never seen there before. "This crisis is growing worse by the moment. Within another twelve hours, the *Enterprise* is likely to be in the same shape as the *Marco Polo.*"

Crusher's mouth tightened with frustration, and she gestured angrily around her at the crowded sickbay. "Nobody knows that more than I do, sir. But I can't sanction any treatment that would pose a danger to my patient's health or sanity!"

"What about Counselor Troi? She and Will share a special . . . bond. Is it possible that if she called to him, using her empathic abilities as well as her voice, she could reach him?"

Crusher hesitated. "That might be possible. But if I awaken Troi, she'll be subjected to all the mental trauma that's pervading the ship. It would be risky."

"You could monitor her condition, and if the stress was too great, you could sedate her again." Picard glanced over at the counselor's sleeping form. "If Deanna knew that Will needed her, she would want to help him, no matter what the risk to herself," he said quietly. "I know that, and you do, too, Beverly."

The red-haired chief medical officer stared down at Riker's face for nearly a minute in silence, then she looked back up slowly, her blue eyes brightening. "I may have thought of a way," she whispered. "If only it would work . . ."

"If only *what* would work, Doctor?" Picard demanded.

"When Commander Riker contracted that illness from the alien plant, they monitored nearly every area of his cerebral cortex while they were attempting to discover which kinds of memories would kill the invading virus," Crusher began.

"Go on," the captain said.

"Thus, I have extremely complete data on the commander's brain—more so than I have for nearly anyone else on board. If I could bring Counselor Troi into consciousness but get her to channel her awareness so that she is only linked with Commander Riker, instead of open to receive the mental trauma of the entire ship—" She pounded her fist into her palm, her expression growing increasingly excited. "She could focus on the proper area of Riker's mind and let him know that he's safe. Jean-Luc, it could work!"

The captain nodded, his eyes glinting with satisfaction and respect. "Make it so, Doctor."

Beverly nodded. "I'll let you know when we make the attempt." Picard nodded and turned to go. "And Captain . . ."

He turned back. "Yes, Doctor?"

"I intend to recommend Doctor Gavar for a Medal of Valor."

"I was going to suggest something of the sort myself, Doctor," the captain said. "I will gladly second your recommendation. By the way, I would like the doctor to be present at the away team's debriefing." He glanced down at his unconscious second-in-command. "As soon as Commander Riker can join us."

"I understand, Captain," Crusher said. "I'll begin immediately."

"What is it?" asked a voice. The sound penetrated, awakening, for the first time, conscious thought. *"It's not human, is it?"*

Knowledge entered, an automatic reply to the questions, knowledge that had been stored, waiting, for a moment such as this. The being who responded to the personal designation of "Data" opened his—

(Am I a "he"? he questioned the automatic self-designation that had come to him, and the immediate internal response was: Yes, my programming and body were designed with male attributes.)

—eyes and gazed upon the first sights he had ever consciously beheld.

Faces surrounded him, faces his programming recognized as belonging to the category of "human." Two men and one woman. He was pleasantly surprised to realize that he had no difficulty in distinguishing the gender differences.

(I must have been programmed with extensive information and discrimination capabilities. That is good. Information is valuable, and contributes to knowledge and wisdom.)

"Looks like some kind of robot," replied a different voice.

Again knowledge sparked, and Data found his body's mouth opening. "I am not a robot," he said. "I am an android. I am called Data."

The humans drew back, startled and somewhat distressed. "It talks!" the first human male to speak blurted.

"Indeed I do," Data replied. He sat up and moved his head to regard his surroundings. He was sitting upon a smooth slab of stone within a rock-walled niche. Beyond the bodies of the humans he could see more gray stone and a flight of steps cut into the rock. "I am capable of speaking in many different languages," he added. "I extend greetings to you."

They had drawn back into a tight, defensive cluster, and Data noted that they all had their hands on the butts of weapons that his memory identified as "phasers." His eyes took in their suddenly paled features and wide eyes.

"Ah!" he said. *"A typical human fear reaction! Please be assured that I mean you no harm. Would you please identify yourselves?"*

The first man swallowed. Data watched, fascinated, as his Adam's apple moved, and his throat muscles rippled. (I must try that! What would it feel like?) *"We're from the Starfleet vessel* Tripoli,*"* the light-skinned man said in a voice rather higher-pitched than he had used before. *"I'm Lieutenant Adams, this is Ensign Sait."* He indicated the dark-skinned woman. *"And this is Lieutenant Maginde."* He nodded at the other man, who had the darkest skin color of all.

"It is an honor to meet you," Data said as his memory banks supplied an appropriately polite response.

"How did you get here, uh . . . Data?" asked the woman.

The android gazed around him again. For some reason, his eyes were drawn to the rocky wall to his left, but he did not know why, and memory supplied no answer. *"I do not know,"* he said slowly. *"I sense that I was programmed to awaken here, in this manner, when I was discovered by sentient beings such as yourselves . . . but I do not know why."*

"Are there any people living on this world?" Maginde asked. *"We thought there was supposed to be a colony, but we can't find any traces of it."*

Again Data glanced at the rocky wall, but no memory awoke. *"I do not know that, either. I must have been placed here by* someone, *but whether that party is or was indigenous to this planet, I cannot say. It is equally possible, I suppose, that I was brought here from somewhere else."*

The humans glanced at each other.

"Listen, Data," Adams said, *"we're going to beam back up to our ship now and report to our captain . . . our superior officer. She'll decide what to do with you."*

"Will you return?" asked Data, suddenly wishing that they would not leave.

There must have been something in his voice that revealed his concern, because the woman smiled suddenly. "Don't worry, Data, I promise you that someone will come back."

Moments later, the three disappeared by means of what the android's memory banks identified as a standard Federation transporter beam.

Data inched his way over to the edge of the rock slab and sat so his legs dangled down it. He gazed down upon himself appraisingly. He was clothed in a plain gold coverall. Curiously, he unsealed it and regarded the fleshlike substance that covered his chest. Abnormally pale, it seemed to have a faintly golden, opalescent sheen. He touched his head, discovered hair, and wondered what color it was. He unsealed his jumpsuit further and discovered, as something in his programming had told him he would, that he possessed all the equipment necessary to perfectly simulate a human male.

His programming also told him that he was fully functional as a human sexual partner. His memory core contained extensive information on the subject.

Data resealed his coverall and slowly, tentatively, stood up. He took a step, wondering whether it was his first. Beneath his feet the ground was hard and slightly uneven. Cautiously, the android walked a few paces until he was outside the rock-walled niche where he had awakened. He gazed at the flight of stone steps.

Who made me? *he wondered.* And why? I have a consciousness . . . but it is an artificially generated one. I am not human. *He thought of Adams and Sait and Maginde.* They regarded me as an "it," a "thing." They did not see me as human, no matter how nearly I may resemble one.

Slowly the android climbed the rock steps, until he

was up on level ground. Effortlessly his memory provided names for what his eyes took in: trees, grass, bushes, fields, sky . . . until his view was halted by the mountains in the far distance. Data stepped onto the grass at the top of the stairs and walked until he reached a nearby tree. He gazed around him, noticing suddenly that the vegetation did not fall within the parameters of "healthy" as defined by his memory banks. This place is dead, *he thought, concerned that something was wrong with this world.* Why?

Moments later, he thought, I will live for thousands of years. I can be destroyed, but, barring injury, my mind and body will endure indefinitely, given proper replacement parts.

He thought of the humans again. But they will die. Another thing that sets us apart.

Data looked up at the sky, wondering where their ship was now. Would they keep their promise and return? Or would he be abandoned here, on a dead world, left to exist for centuries until some vital circuit failed and his consciousness was erased? The notion of that happening filled him with a fervent wish that it would be otherwise. He did not want to be left alone. He desired companionship. He knew that he had been made to be useful, not to exist in solitary idleness.

He spoke aloud, gazing up at the sky. "Do not leave me alone . . . please. I wish to go with you."

Thinking of the humans aboard their ship, talking, sharing companionship, duties, and a purpose in life, Data experienced for the first time the thought that would characterize and define his entire existence. I wish I could truly be one of them. I wish I could be human . . .

"Just one more tap on this loose connection . . . there! That should do it!" said a familiar voice. Data opened his eyes and found Geordi La Forge and Doctor Selar regarding him intently. "Data, can you hear me, buddy?" asked Geordi anxiously.

"I hear you, Geordi," Data said, and he watched La Forge's dark features break into a broad, relieved grin. Even Lieutenant Selar's normally expressionless face relaxed slightly.

"Great!" La Forge said. "Man, you had me worried there for a moment, Data! I thought we had you all put back together, but you still hadn't regained consciousness. Scared the pants off me, until Selar saw this one connection that wasn't quite touching."

The android ignored his friend's words as he realized something extraordinary. "Geordi," he said urgently, putting a hand on the engineer's arm, "I had a dream!"

"You *what?*" La Forge's mouth dropped open. "Is that possible?"

"It happened," Data said wonderingly, remembering. "I dreamt of when I first awakened on my home planet, where Doctor Soong made me. I relived the entire experience, just as it happened!"

"Do you think it was the artifact?" La Forge said, still struggling to comprehend the notion.

"More likely the loose connection," Selar opined. "It stimulated a specific location in your memory core, Data."

"However it happened," the android said, "it did happen. I shared the experience of the rest of the crew. This time"—he tightened his grip on La Forge's arm (careful, as always, not to exert too much pressure)—"I was not set apart. I shared the experience of so many humans aboard this ship. I reacted in a human fashion."

Geordi shrugged. "I guess you did. Tell me, Data, was it a good dream or a nightmare?"

"It was a very good dream," Data said with profound seriousness. "Dreaming it made me realize how far I have come in the twenty-eight years since then. Unlike most of the other beings on this ship, I must be grateful to the artifact for giving me this glimpse into the past."

Chapter Ten

THERE WAS DANGER, and it was all around him. The entity that in the outside world knew itself as William T. Riker was acutely aware of the danger, and the necessity of staying hidden, of remaining still, safe for the moment in this dark, secret place. He was not entirely sure where he was . . . all he knew was that the *things* that had driven him into this refuge, this hiding place, had not found him. For the moment, he was safe. But he also knew that if he tried to leave, the things would get him. They would devour him, swallow him whole, and he would be gone forever. Even though part of him chafed at hiding, because he was someone who had always been courageous and had faced danger head-on, the tiny rational part of him that remained told him that some threats are too overwhelming, too terrifying, to confront.

He had seen a map once, long ago, that had been copied from one made in the sixteenth century, when man sailed the oceans, not the stars. Channels, passages, and trade winds had been marked, the safe routes that the ships could use to travel to the New World. But there had been other areas left blank, uncharted. Those areas had been filled with fantastic creatures much like the beings of Berengaria Seven, scaled and studded with fangs and wings and forked tails. And the map had proclaimed, "Here Abide Monsters."

Riker decided that he was trapped in the middle of one of those unchartered regions, surrounded by things much worse than dragons. For the moment he was safe, but only so long as he didn't move, didn't attempt to come out. His memories supplied him with examples of times that he had reasoned his way through danger or, as a last resort, fought to protect himself. But these monsters were too strong. Only if he stayed hidden would he be safe.

So he crouched in his tiny, dark refuge, hiding.

He realized, in a dim, faraway fashion, that he couldn't stay here forever, but the small part of his mind that still maintained any reasoning ability argued that if the monsters didn't find him for a long, long time, they would go in search of other prey, and then he could emerge. But he would wait until he was positive they were gone.

Of course, there was no way to determine the passage of time here, but Riker didn't let himself think about that. All he could be sure of was that he was safe, just as long as he didn't move, didn't come out of hiding.

Suddenly he sensed some disturbance at the borders of his sanctuary. He grew alert, feeling panic again. The monsters had found him!

Will . . . Someone's voice echoed down the recesses of his mind. *Will Riker* . . .

The voice (or was it a thought? he could not be sure . . .) seemed familiar. But the monsters, some of them, had been clever. One of them could be trying to lure him out of safety with a ruse.

Riker did not respond. *Go away,* he thought, with as much of his reasoning mind as was available to him here.

Time passed . . . he had no idea how much. He began to relax again.

Then, abruptly, it was there again, and much closer! *Will! It's Deanna. Where are you? You must come out, it's safe now.*

Deanna? He had known a Deanna once. They had been lovers for a time, then, more recently, friends. He could trust Deanna . . . he'd always trusted Deanna . . .

But perhaps it was a monster, trying to lure him out. He stayed hidden.

Will! The summons was almost in his hiding place now! *Will, come out. You're safe now, come out. Contacting you is extremely difficult for me. Will, if I stay here much longer, I could lose myself! Will,* izmadi, *I need you, you must trust me!*

Only Deanna called him *izmadi.* No one else could know that secret endearment. That, and her pleading "I need you!" reached him as nothing else could have.

Deanna? he thought, moving a bit toward the presence in his mind. *Deanna, is it really you?*

Her response was filled with wild joy and relief. *Yes, Will, it's really me! Oh, God, I'm so glad I found you! Come with me!*

But there are monsters there, he said, childlike in his simplicity.

Not when we're together, there aren't, was her response. *When we're together, we're safe and happy, right?*

Yes . . . , he admitted.

Will, it's dangerous for us to stay here, she said.

Especially for me. If you don't want me to be hurt, you must come now!

He didn't want Deanna to be hurt. He loved Deanna, would always love Deanna, though that love had changed throughout the years, to the love of a dear and true friend rather than the romantic flame it had been in the beginning. There was no way he could let her be hurt because of him.

A phrase remembered from childhood filled his mind. *All right, ready or not, here I come!*

He launched himself toward the other presence.

Deanna was there with him, it was really Deanna. Her love surrounded him, keeping him safe, and, like Dante's Beatrice, she guided him, pulling him along, past the monsters, through the inferno, out of this private hell . . . and the monsters snarled and gibbered and howled but were impotent now that they were together.

The bleak landscape of his own private purgatory lightened, brightened, as he emerged back into the conscious world. His full reasoning ability returned to him, along with the sense of his own body, and all his knowledge.

He was whole again . . . healed.

Will Riker opened his eyes to see three faces staring anxiously down at him. Deanna Troi, Jean-Luc Picard, and Beverly Crusher. Deanna was holding his hand in a grip so tight it hurt—but he did not want her to let go, he needed the human comfort of her grasp. Will ran his tongue around a mouth that felt as dry as the sands of Velara Three.

"Hello," he whispered. He was confused. Hadn't he been going to beam out with the away team? How had he gotten *here*—wherever *here* was? "Where am I?"

"He's back!" Crusher said, sounding extremely relieved. "Deanna, you did it! Now it's back to bed for you . . ."

Two of the faces disappeared. Riker felt Troi's fingers unclasp. Feeling bereft, he tried to turn his head to follow their retreating figures with his eyes, but he was so stiff and sore, his neck would barely move.

But immediately another hand closed on his forearm in a tight, welcoming squeeze. "Will," Picard said warmly, a relieved smile lighting the captain's tense features. "Welcome back!"

Riker struggled to form words, and finally managed, "It's good to *be* back. Wherever that is." The last thing he remembered was passing out aboard the artifact. He rolled his eyes from side to side, and saw familiar surroundings. *I'm in sickbay,* he realized.

"You're in sickbay," Crusher said as her face appeared again. "Back aboard the *Enterprise.*"

"Where's Deanna?"

"I had to sedate her again," Crusher said. "Staying awake was too stressful for her."

"Can I sit up?" Riker asked, pushing gently at the diagnostic and treatment console that covered his torso. "And could I have something to drink?"

"Yes, you can sit up, as long as you take it easy," she replied, moving the unit off him. Picard helped him as he made the effort, and, moments later, he was sitting up on the couch and sipping gratefully at cool water.

"I hardly remember a thing," he confessed. "Except that I was somewhere . . . safe, and that I didn't want to come out . . ."

Memory expanded, and Will twisted around, looked over his shoulder, and saw the occupant of the next couch, now fast asleep. She appeared much as he'd seen her before the away team mission—except that now there seemed to be a faint smile on her lips.

"Deanna!" Riker exclaimed as memory surged back. "It was her voice, her mind, calling me back!"

"Yes." The doctor nodded. "She came out of her

own withdrawal long enough to contact you, then I had to sedate her again. But she saved you, Will. When she wakes up, you owe her a sizable thank you."

"Dinner at the best restaurant at the next starbase we dock at," Will agreed fervently. "And two dozen red roses." He thought for a moment. "Make that three dozen, *and* a box of her favorite chocolates."

Beverly Crusher smiled. "I'd say that's a start."

Picard sat in Crusher's small office, gazing around him at the resurrected away team. All of them were there, except for Worf, who was still asleep. The captain was only too happy to let him sleep off the artifact's effects—a Klingon in a battle rage was not something he wanted crashing around his ship. He now had a good idea of why the crew aboard the *PaKathen* had not survived long.

Will Riker still appeared pale beneath his beard, but his eyes had regained most of their usual twinkle. Geordi La Forge's features beneath the VISOR appeared rather haggard, but his grin was back. Data sat with his strange eyes fixed on a point somewhere over the captain's shoulder, as though he were ruminating about something intensely personal. Gavar seemed in the worst shape, perhaps not surprisingly. The Tellarite physician's features were hard to read, but her pose was one of near exhaustion, as she sat leaning her elbows heavily on the table, her arms folded before her.

Data's tricorder lay on the table, hooked into the briefing room's computer link. The recording and sensing instrument had been discovered clutched in the android's hands after the beam-over. Since the machine had fallen beneath his body and lay covered by it for most of the away team's mission, it had few visual images, and those were unviewable by a human except in a highly filtered state. The sounds it had recorded were not something Picard wanted to listen to again, either.

But the instrument's sensing apparatus had recorded a considerable amount of information about the artifact's gravity, atmosphere, energy sources, and interior structure. They now knew a great deal about the way the alien structure was configured. Picard had reviewed those findings, wondering all the while whether anything that he was seeing indicated the presence of defensive weaponry or energy field controls.

The captain cleared his throat. "Before we begin our discussions of the away team's abortive mission, I would like to extend my warmest appreciation to Doctor Gavar for her heroic actions in saving the lives of her crewmates. Lieutenant"—he fixed the Tellarite with a grave look—"I thank you, and intend to do everything in my power to see that your actions are suitably and formally recognized by Starfleet Command."

A dull wave of red spread over the nurse's fleshy features as she looked down shyly. "Thank you, Captain Picard."

Good Lord, Picard thought, amused. *She's blushing!*

The other officers immediately chimed in with their own personal thanks to the physician. After a moment of this, when poor Gavar was looking so embarrassed by all the attention that she seemed on the verge of bolting from the room, the captain raised a hand for quiet. "Now, to business," he said. "I would like each member of the away team to describe your experiences in as detailed and coherent a fashion as you can manage. Commander Riker?"

The briefing continued, with each officer giving his or her version of the events. Gavar's account, of course, was the longest, and Picard had saved it for last. When she finished, he gave a sigh.

"A most distressing experience all around," he commented. "Recommendations regarding our next move?"

Riker straightened, looking grim. "Captain, we can't afford to wait any longer. We must risk using our photon torpedoes in an attempt to destroy the artifact. We *must* break free! None of the tricorder's information suggests any sort of armament aboard that thing."

"Indicating that it is not a weapon at all?" Picard asked, raising an eyebrow.

"I didn't say that, sir," the second-in-command corrected. "I still believe that it is a weapon, and an extremely deadly one. It's just not a *physical* weapon, except in its secondary effects. It's a weapon designed to destroy minds, which I find even deadlier and crueler than any bomb or phaser ever invented."

"I agree, Captain," came a gravelly voice from the doorway. Lieutenant Worf stood there, braced against the bulkhead, looking as though he were staying upright only by force of will. The Klingon staggered into the briefing room and sank into a chair as though he was afraid his legs might buckle.

"Lieutenant—!" Picard began.

"I tried to stop him," Crusher said, following the Klingon into the room, her slim body taut with indignation and her red hair mussed as though she had been physically brushed aside by the security commander. "But he was determined to get out of bed!" She glared at the Klingon.

"Captain, it is my duty to be here," Worf said, in a tone that might almost have been pleading.

The captain waved at the ruffled, bristling physician. "Very well, Doctor Crusher, since he is here, let him stay. His insights may be valuable."

"Thank you, sir," said Worf. Beverly Crusher

turned away and marched back through the entrance, emitting an audible sniff of disgust.

"Lieutenant, we would like to hear your version of what happened aboard the artifact," Picard said.

Worf related his memory of what had happened, then finished with a diffident glance at Gavar. "And Doctor, they told me of your actions. I must in honor inform you that I was wrong when I judged you unfit to accompany us on our mission. You behaved today with all the courage of a true warrior. You acquitted yourself with honor."

"Thank you, Lieutenant," she murmured.

"Captain," the Klingon said, fixing Picard with a somber gaze beneath his extraordinary eyebrows, "I concur with Commander Riker's assessment. The artifact is a most deadly weapon, and we must make every effort to destroy it immediately!"

"But we don't know that photon torpedoes will get through the artifact's protective field," the captain pointed out. "And launching them at this close range would be extremely dangerous for the ship."

"That's true, sir," Riker said. "But I feel we must take that risk, whatever the cost."

Picard turned to Data. "What are your views, Commander?"

"I must point out, Captain, that I was not conscious long enough to have gained any impression of the artifact's interior. However, if the artifact is indeed malign, a weapon, why is it that some of the dreams and hallucinations experienced have been benign— even, by report, pleasant?"

"A good point," Picard said. "However, I don't believe that the purpose of the artifact's construction —as a weapon or not—is nearly as important as the effect it is having, which is overwhelmingly negative and dangerous. I am beginning to believe that taking whatever measures necessary to destroy it, whatever its original purpose, is our only course. Yes, there is considerable risk, but staying here means insanity and eventual death for all those aboard this vessel. Doctor Gavar, do you have anything to add?"

"No, Captain," she said. "I'll leave the tactics and decisions to you and the officers who are experienced in such matters. My main interest and duty, at this point, is returning to my patients."

"I understand." Picard nodded at her. "You are dismissed, Doctor."

"Thank you, Captain." Hastily, the Tellarite beat a retreat.

"Lieutenant La Forge, you are the only one we haven't heard from," Picard said. "What do you think our best course would be? From all your observations and readings, should we launch photon torpedoes at the artifact?"

The chief engineer sighed. "Yes, Captain . . . I believe that is probably our only choice, as things currently stand . . . although I have to say that my gut feeling is that they won't have any effect—at least on the artifact. The backlash of energy could have plenty of effect on *us*." His fists clenched on the tabletop before him. "But I must say that it's a damned shame to have to destroy such beauty."

Riker, Data, and Worf all turned in their seats to stare at La Forge incredulously. Riker was the first to say it. "*Beauty?* Geordi, did that thing get to you? It was terrible over there! How can you call it *beautiful?*"

"I agree that it was terrible over there," La Forge conceded. "It nearly drove me insane, too, remember!" His mouth tightened stubbornly. "But I know what I saw. The images on the walls, the flowing colors, the designs and patterns—they were the most beautiful things I've ever seen. I could have looked at them for hours."

Picard leaned forward intently. "Mister La Forge," he said, "I want you to describe as accurately as you can exactly *what* you saw over there."

Geordi gestured helplessly, then shrugged. "Captain, it was literally indescribable. There were images of things, and some of them were the same. They flowed, and moved at times, and some of them were still. The images were on the walls, and some on the ceilings. They were different colors from any I'd ever seen before, but they looked beautiful to me."

As if realizing how incoherent he sounded, he sighed again. "I'm guessing, of course, but I think the images that were repeated the most often were the artifact's builders. They had bodies, but not like anything I ever saw before. They were like . . . elongated triangles made from different kinds of crystals, or metals, because they were shiny. And they had these streamers coming off them, different for each one. Each one had individualized beautiful patterns. I don't know, of course, whether that was their equivalent of skin, or clothing."

Picard frowned in perplexity and glanced around the room. Riker looked skeptical, Data curious, Worf disturbed. Geordi shook his head. "You have to understand, Captain, that when I use a term like *triangle,* that's an approximation. All of what I'm saying is the best I can do at putting something that's not translatable in any human language into English."

"I understand," Picard said. "Go on."

"Anyway, these triangle things, there was a texture to them, to their patterns, smooth or rough or silky— all in addition to being shiny. And I'm not sure, but I think the sounds were tied in with them in some ways, too. But while my VISOR could translate the images so that I could make some sense out of them—as Commander Riker's and Lieutenant Worf's natural eyesight could not—my other senses, including my *ears,* are normal. So I heard those sounds as terrible noises, a cacophony that made me wish I were deaf. I could smell them, too, and taste them and feel them on my skin." He shuddered at the memory.

"Did you see anything besides this one place where we materialized?" Riker asked.

"No, I passed out too quickly. But I wish I had."

"Were there other things besides the triangles that you thought of as living beings?" Data asked.

"Yeah, but the triangles were the most prevalent. That's what made me think they were the image of the people who built the artifact."

Geordi began making shapes in the air as he continued. "There were these slithery things that looked sort of like snakes, only with fronds like willow trees. And big blocks of something lumpy that looked kind of like mountains seen through water—you know, with ripples running through." He shook his head. "That's just about all I remember. I was only conscious for a few seconds longer than Commander Riker."

Geordi fell silent as the captain seemed lost in thought. "You say it was beautiful," Picard murmured.

"It sure was!" Geordi said. "It was so beautiful that I'll remember it all my life."

"Beauty," the captain said, raising his head, his hazel eyes very serious, "is in the eye of the beholder."

"A common expression, often applied to the appreciation of art," Data volunteered helpfully.

Picard nodded. "Exactly."

"Art?" Geordi mumbled, then his face lit up, and he straightened abruptly. "Of course . . . *art!"*

Will Riker looked nonplussed for a second, then the light slowly dawned across his bearded features. His blue-gray eyes widened. "You're saying that the artifact is . . . a repository of alien *art?* Like an art gallery?"

"I believe so, Number One," the captain said. "What other type of place includes small rooms that contain a single object? What other type of place has corridors and rooms where the walls are filled with images?"

"An extraordinary idea," Data intoned. "That would indeed explain a great deal about the artifact. For example, it would tell us why there are many objects there, but no two are alike. They must be sculptures or other three-dimensional art objects."

"But why would the artifact prove so destructive?" Worf rumbled, still puzzled and skeptical. "It injures humanoids to look at it or exist near it."

"Because it was never intended for humanoids to appreciate," Geordi said eagerly. "Some other race built it, some race that I'll call, for want of a better term, the Artists. And these aliens had some kinds of art that were similar to human art forms—sculpture and music and painting and moving pictures—but their minds were so alien that their art makes humans sick to see or hear it, just as their architecture does!"

"Yes, and I believe there is another component," Picard said. "I believe that the Artists created an art form using emotions. They composed with emotions. Like telling a story where you never discover the plot but only feel what the protagonists felt. But their alien emotions are extremely distressing to human"—he nodded at Worf—"or humanoid minds."

"So the energy field that's surrounding us is trying to tell us something that would be comprehensible to the Artists, but our brains can't tolerate it." Geordi shook his head wonderingly. "No wonder the Klingons were all dead. The artifact's emanations awaken in them the urge to fight."

"It certainly had that effect on me," the Klingon officer said.

"I believe that we have indeed solved part of the

mystery," the captain said, "but discovering the true nature of the artifact, while very interesting, still does not help us with our problem. The artifact, even if it is not intentionally destructive, nevertheless poses a grave threat to this ship."

"And I suppose that we're still going to have to try and destroy it," Riker mused. "I wish we could find some way around that. The idea of blowing up an art gallery . . . well, I would have liked it better if I'd still been able to think of it as an abandoned doomsday weapon." He shifted restlessly in his seat. "At least we don't have to worry any longer about whether the place has an automatic defense system, I suppose."

"Not necessarily, Number One," Picard said. "Human galleries have security systems, remember. However, from these sensor readings"—he indicated the tricorder—"and our other information, I do not believe that the alien emplacement possesses defensive capabilities . . . except, of course, for the energy field that is able to absorb phaser blasts."

"Photon torpedoes are our most powerful weapons," Riker said. "And they employ a different kind of energy. Hopefully, an energy the artifact won't be able to absorb."

"Destroying the artifact might well mean that we would be destroying the last legacy of a now-extinct species, Captain," Data pointed out. "That would be most unfortunate."

"I know, Data. I agree." The captain sighed. "If there were any way we could get free of that tractor field, or shut it down somehow, then I'd be willing to try it. But there is not."

Geordi frowned. "Maybe I could go back with my ears plugged and search for the controls to the tractor field." The chief engineer leaned forward, his voice low and intense. "Dammit, there's *got* to be something we can do! I can't bear the thought of destroying such beauty forever! Captain, the artifact could prove a galactic treasure, if its works could be studied and translated into terms all humans could comprehend."

"You're forgetting the mental compositions," Riker reminded La Forge grimly. "Geordi, within sixty seconds you'd be a screaming wreck, and that wouldn't get us anywhere."

"Perhaps the Tellarite . . . ," Worf said, and Picard glanced at him, raising his eyebrows in surprise. Art appreciation was not something one expected from a Klingon.

Riker shook his head. "Doctor Gavar isn't a technician. Even if she could find her way around, blind and deaf as she'd have to be, she wouldn't stand a snowball's chance in hell of finding and shutting down tractor field controls."

"Yeah," agreed La Forge glumly. "The person who's best suited for that role would be Data, but his circuits aren't calibrated to handle that place."

There was a short, depressed silence, then Picard straightened his shoulders, stood up, and addressed the group. "I wish we did not have to do this, but the safety of this ship must remain paramount." He turned his attention to Worf. "Lieutenant, you will prepare to fire photon torpedoes on my command."

Worf rose to his feet, still a bit unsteady. "Yes, Captain."

"Captain," said Data suddenly. "Please wait. I believe that I may have a solution."

Picard sat back down, and Worf sank back into his seat a second later. "Go on, Mister Data," the captain said.

"Lieutenant La Forge is correct in saying that my circuitry and programming are not calibrated to endure and comprehend the environment aboard the artifact." The android's golden eyes were extremely serious. "But, sir . . . I am a machine. I can be reprogrammed, and my circuitry recalibrated . . . adjusted, so that I could withstand the artifact's effects." Data turned to La Forge. "You and Doctor Selar could make it possible for me to function aboard the artifact."

Everyone stared at the android. "Data, do you know what you're volunteering to do?" Picard said finally.

"Yes, sir," replied the android steadily. "I do. I would not have made the suggestion were I not willing to carry it through, Captain."

"But there's no guarantee that once we change your circuitry and programming we can return you to your present state, Data," La Forge said. "You could be volunteering for the equivalent of a . . ."—he shook his head warningly—"a suicide mission!"

"I am willing to take that risk, Geordi. I believe that you are correct in saying that the artifact constitutes a treasure. It may well be the last memorial to a vanished race of beings. We will never know who they were, or what happened to them, or if any of them survived, unless the artifact can be studied by Federation archeologists."

"But even if the tractor and emotional field surrounding the artifact were to be eliminated," Riker said, "the environment aboard the artifact is so . . . insane. Archeologists couldn't work over there. They couldn't stand it any more than we could."

"They might be able to do most of the preliminary work by robot probe," Picard said. "Presented with a tantalizing mystery from the past such as the artifact, I feel sure they would find a way. However, that is not our concern. Our concern is Commander Data's proposal." He stared steadily at the android. "Data, how long would you anticipate it would take for your programming and circuitry to be altered to be compatible with the artifact's environment?"

"At least an hour, Captain. Doctor Selar, Doctor Crusher, Wesley Crusher, and Geordi would be able to do much of it while I was turned off. I would not experience any distress or discomfort, sir. The only problem would be that once I was altered, and reactivated, I would then find the environment of the *Enterprise* extremely unsettling. I would have to be kept in very restricted, featureless surroundings until I could be beamed over."

"If we darkened the transporter room and kept it silent—" Geordi began, his mind already racing ahead.

Picard raised a hand, stared at all of them in turn. "Gentlemen, I am willing to authorize this experiment, because I believe that Commander Data's suggestion may prove feasible. However, whatever you need to do to him to accomplish this recalibration and reprogramming must be accomplished within the next ninety minutes. I cannot countenance waiting any longer than that. Remember that every hour more people experience the profound suffering the artifact can cause."

Sobered, they all gazed back at him. Then Geordi shook himself and bounded eagerly to his feet. "Come on, Data, we've got a deadline to meet. Let's shake a leg."

"Shake a leg . . . ," the android repeated, puzzled, as the two of them started for the door together. "Oh, I understand. You mean let us hurry, or quit dragging your . . ."

The android's precise tones faded into the distance. Riker was grinning, but then his expression sobered. "I hope we don't lose him because of this scheme, Captain."

"A feeling I most definitely share, Number One," Picard agreed soberly. "Let us cross our—"

A loud buzzing noise interrupted his words, and

both officers glanced at Worf. The sedative still in his system had finally triumphed over the Klingon's sense of duty, and he was fast asleep, slumped down on his spine, head tipped back. Extraordinary sounds emerged from his open mouth.

Riker winced theatrically. "I never heard a Klingon snore before," he said. "Thank God when I was serving as first officer aboard the *Pagh,* the officers had private cabins."

The captain was already on his feet. "Let us leave Sleeping Beauty to complete his interrupted nap, Number One."

Quietly—though Picard was privately convinced that they could have galloped out on horseback without arousing the somnolent lieutenant—the two humans left the room.

Chapter Eleven

LIEUTENANT COMMANDER DATA walked down the corridor with a calm, unhurried step, carrying a box under his arm. Reaching the entrance to sickbay, he went inside. With part of his attention, he noted the crowded condition of the medical facility—stifled moans, soft sobs, and quiet whimpers came from many of the beds, creating a pervasive, misery-filled undertone. Data decided that the sounds must be extremely unnerving for the doctors and nurses who had to listen to them constantly. He glanced quickly around the outer room, and his gaze stopped on a familiar face. La Forge was sitting at a computer link, intent on his work.

The chief engineer looked up as the android approached. "Hi, Data. We're almost ready to make those final changes to your programming so we can recalibrate your circuitry."

"Good," Data said. "I am ready, except for one request."

"What is it?"

"Since your final changes require that I be switched off, I would appreciate it if you would keep something safe for me." The android glanced around the busy sickbay and self-consciously lowered his voice. "That way, if anything were to happen to me . . . that is, if you find that you cannot return me to my normal . . ."—he hesitated—"personality, for want of a more precise term, then this will be safe."

Slowly, hesitantly, the android held out the box. La Forge took it, then glanced inside, noting the stack of computer flimsies filled with neat, closely spaced handwriting. "It's your novel."

"Yes."

"I'll take good care of it until you come back," the chief engineer promised. "And, Data, you *will* be okay. I swear to you, I won't rest until you're fully restored."

"I have every confidence in you, Geordi," the android said. "I know I am doing the right thing." He watched as La Forge absentmindedly riffled through the pages. "I know that you will be very busy, but if you have any extra time and wish to read it, please do so."

La Forge cleared his throat uncomfortably. "Uh . . . I *am* going to be pretty busy," he murmured.

"You will find that it has changed a great deal from when I first read you that scene," Data said, hoping that the engineer would find time to read his words. Stories were meant to be shared with readers. What other reason was there for writing them? "I changed the setting to a more romantic one, and the dialogue is, I believe, far wittier."

"Uh . . . yeah." La Forge glanced up, his expression suddenly troubled. "Data," he began, "are you scared? You can still change your mind, you know."

"I am not capable of experiencing fear," the android said evenly. "But even if I were, I feel sure that, in this case, curiosity would outweigh any apprehension I felt. I *am* capable of curiosity, and the artifact is a mystery that is intriguing in the extreme."

"You can say that again," Geordi said, placing the box of manuscript into a container and sealing it.

Obediently Data began. "I am not capable of experiencing fear—" He halted at La Forge's hasty headshake.

"No, I didn't mean it like that! I just meant that you had spoken the truth—'you can say that again' is another human colloquialism."

"A new one," Data exclaimed, pleased. "My memory now contains a great number of slang and colloquial terms."

"I know," La Forge agreed. He stood up with a sudden air of decision. "Selar ought to be finishing with those replacement microcircuits any time. Are you ready for us to make the final changes?"

"I am," Data said firmly.

"Okay, then, let's head for the transporter room. I'll have Selar meet us there, and we'll do the final changes onsite. Then we'll beam you directly over as soon as we're through."

The two officers walked through the corridors of the huge starship, not talking. *Geordi is worried that he will never see me again,* Data realized. *He is concerned that the changes they will make will mean my "death."*

The android tried to think of words that might ease La Forge's mind, but none would come. The situation was too serious, too uncertain. At such times, Data reflected silently, humans often cloaked or dissipated their tension with jokes. But he'd learned long ago that human humor was a complex and chancy exercise. Every time he'd intentionally tried to be funny, the effort had been wasted. And yet the humans were often amused by him, sometimes for reasons that Data himself could not fathom.

Data wished again that he could laugh the way they did. Only once had he experienced true laughter; it was now a cherished memory. Q was a quixotic and often dangerous being, but he had given the android a great gift on that one notable occasion when he made it possible for Data, however briefly, to laugh.

When they reached the transporter room, Geordi notified Selar of their location, and then the two officers stood waiting. Geordi seemed to find the minutes extremely taxing. He fidgeted and paced uneasily. Data stood patiently while Chief O'Brien fitted him with a transponder that he'd adapted especially for the android, so the transporter chief would be able to keep a constant fix on him, in order to beam him back at a moment's notice.

The doors to the transporter room slid open, and Wesley Crusher and Doctor Selar entered. "My adjustments are complete," Selar told Geordi. "Wesley helped me finish the last of them."

The teenager walked over to the android, his eyes troubled in his thin face. "Data, I want you to know that I think you're really brave to do this for all of us," he said quietly.

"My actions do not seem to me to require courage, Wesley," the android officer said. "Merely the desire to preserve ancient art treasures from being forever lost."

Wes shook his head. "I think that in just about anybody's book what you're doing would count as courage, Data."

Gravely, the boy held out his hand. After a moment, Data shook it, careful as always not to exert too much pressure. "Thala was tagging along on our way down to the transporter room," the young officer said. "When I told her you were going over to the artifact to try and free us, she said she wanted to tell you something. Would that be okay? She's waiting outside."

"That would be fine," Data said, wondering what the child wanted to see him for.

The acting ensign walked over to the door of the transporter room, opened it, then beckoned. "It's okay, you can come in."

A little hesitantly, the Andorian girl walked into the transporter room. "Hello, Thala," Data said.

"Hello, Data," she said, then she turned, evidently checking the readings given her by her sensory net. "Oh, hello, Chief O'Brien. Hello, Geordi."

The officers returned her greeting.

"Thala," Wesley reminded her, "the captain has given us a deadline. You'll have to hurry."

"Okay," she said, then walked up to Data. "Wesley told me that you're going to try and stop the artifact from giving all of us those terrible dreams, and that it's very risky for you. I wanted to say thank you, Data. I think you're very brave."

She held out her thin blue hand, but when the android bent over to take it, she impulsively flung her arms around his neck and kissed his cheek. Evidently embarrassed by her display of emotion, she turned and raced for the door. The automatic portal barely had time to get out of her way. With a final glittery sparkle from her sensory net, she was gone.

Data turned to Wesley. "When you see her again, tell her I said thank you for the kiss." The boy nodded. Slowly, deliberately, Data walked over to the portable antigravity unit Selar had set up in the corner, and stretched out on it.

The two humans and the Vulcan busied themselves with final checks on the replacement microcircuitry. Data lay listening to them, until Geordi straightened. "Okay. We're as ready as we'll ever be." The engineer walked over to stand beside the android. "It's time to turn you off, Data. Okay?"

"I am ready," Data said steadily. "Wish me luck, Geordi."

The chief engineer nodded. "All the luck in the universe, Data." He patted his friend's shoulder reassuringly. Then La Forge bent over, and Data felt the human's fingers moving beneath his left arm, searching for his "off" button. He experienced and repressed a sudden urge to change his mind. *Am I about to die?*

And then, he felt nothing.

Consciousness returned, and with it the knowledge that something was extremely wrong. His surroundings, dimly glimpsed as they were by the infrared portion of his vision, were disorienting in the extreme. The contours of the chamber, the angles—all of them were unsettlingly *wrong.*

Data remembered the reason for his disorientation, but that was of little help in dealing with the knowledge that the transporter room was just the same as it always had been—it was he who had suddenly, completely changed. He was no longer himself.

He heard sounds as he was moved, and he understood intellectually that they were voices, speaking English in undertones. His memory even assigned meanings to the words, but that meant little—the words and sentences would not correlate within his mind. He could no longer comprehend the context in which the words and sentences had meaning.

It was like being two people, like that ancient (and erroneous) term for schizophrenia—split personality. One small portion of his mind that he thought of as old Data remembered who and what he was, and why he was doing this. While all the while the other, larger, new Data portion of his mind was totally disoriented and confused.

He had to fight the urge to get up and bolt away from them. Their very presence created in him a vast discomfort. It was all he could do to remain still and silent.

New Data wanted to produce noises, this body's best approximation of the sounds it was now pro- grammed to find familiar, but the old Data portion of his brain insisted that he must be quiet, that to make noises would only distress the beings who surrounded him. New Data could not see the beings properly, his eyes could not follow their alien contours, but, even though their forms were strange, they were still famil- iar to the old Data portion of his mind.

He worried briefly about whether new Data would overwhelm old Data before the transporter could be activated, but then a sensation surrounded his body, and the old Data portion of his mind recognized it for a transporter beam. New Data wanted to struggle against it, not comprehending, but old Data managed to hold the body still until the sensation halted.

He was lying on the floor aboard the artifact. Slowly he rose to his feet. New Data was in control now, had to be in control, for this was the reason he had been created. New Data *was* Data, for the moment, at least. In the back of his consciousness, old Data was worried that new Data would be Data forever, but this was a small, far-off concern that he squelched effortlessly.

The android gazed around him with his altered vision, heard with his altered hearing, felt with his altered senses.

Geordi had been right. It *was* beautiful.

Data looked at the murals surrounding him, his eyes catching and appreciating every nuance of color, shade, texture, and shading. Some of the pictures were stills, but others were more like holographic recordings—they moved, going through a sequence of motions that were never quite the same.

And the sounds! Data played the violin and considered himself knowledgeable about music from many different worlds of the Federation, but he'd never heard anything to equal this. The scale was extraordinary, soaring both below and above the range of human hearing, with tonals and atonals threading and weaving their way through the notes, creating a tapestry of sound.

The sound accompanied the pictures, as La Forge had guessed. Each figure had its own theme, its individual *leitmotiv,* and its story was partly expressed in music, in song. The nearest comparison to any human art form that Data could arrive at was grand opera, except that the emotions the participants had felt were also a component to each story, changing from image to image and moment to moment.

Data could discern, but not feel, the emotional content. Here, too, he was handicapped by having been created a machine. He could sense and follow the emotional component of each story, but he could not experience the emotion itself. And that was, as always, a profound disappointment to the android.

All the figures had their own individual stories, and yet those stories interwove and touched to form one huge theme. A theme of hope and benevolence and courage in the face of death's inevitability. Art had been an inextricable part of these people's lives. They had truly lived to create, as some cultures lived to explore, or make money, or accrue power.

Data began to walk, gazing all around him, listening. All the while, of course, he was recording with his tricorder. Such beauty must not be lost!

He passed little rooms where sculptures rested, rare

and intricate, shining and flowing. Some of them moved also, and many changed in slow, fascinating ways—which was part of their message.

Each artwork had its accompanying emotional component and musical accompaniment.

Noticing that a small light was flashing on his tricorder, Data remembered suddenly that he had promised to report his progress to the *Enterprise* (the human word now felt so alien in his thoughts that it was difficult to think it). As he had previously arranged, he tapped a button on the tricorder, sending a signal to the ship that would indicate that he was unharmed and going about his mission. A different button would signal when he wished to be recalled.

Automatically memorizing the path he had traveled, Data went on, recording, savoring, but never forgetting that he was looking for the control center that must be somewhere in the artifact's labyrinthine structure.

He went on, eyes following the images and stories on the walls, ears straining to catch the sweet, elusive tones of their accompanying music.

Many of the chambers he passed were too physically small for him to enter; he was forced to content himself with stooping or kneeling to peer inside. He gained the impression that the Artists, whoever they had been, were small beings, perhaps no more than a meter or so tall.

Mapping, observing, recording, Data wandered on, aware that he was the first being in hundreds—or it could be thousands—of years to gaze upon these wonders.

Some of the stories struck him as intensely sad (though he could only recognize that sadness intellectually), others were happy, others he could not figure out the purpose of—they reminded him of the human poetry called *haiku,* where a single impression was the purpose of the image and sound. Most of these impressions were incomprehensible to him.

He checked his tricorder readings, tapped the button that would send another "all's well" message to the starship, and saw that he had covered barely a third of the monolithic structure.

The many small niches containing individual solid-form works meant that there was a great deal of room within the alien gallery. On impulse, remembering the way human systems were designed, Data bypassed a number of corridors and headed directly toward the center of the artifact.

And in this one thing, if not in any other, the designs of the Artists proved like those of humans. The central portion of the structure possessed several chambers where artificial devices vibrated softly, maintaining atmosphere, heat, lights, and, somewhere it must be, the field that surrounded the gallery. The field that had trapped and killed the crews of more than a hundred ships throughout an unknown span of time.

Data began checking the functioning of the machines. Of course, the Artists' language had been completely different from any human method of communication, but the Universal Translator that was a part of his positronic brain should be able to handle translations, if provided with a sufficiently large sample of their language.

Moments later, he found it—just as the Artists had left it, for whoever would come after them. One console, when touched, began projecting images. It was an interstellar Rosetta Stone that began with simple, universal concepts such as counting and numbers, terms such as *planet* and *star.* The images progressed gradually, logically, to more complex ideas and terms, such as *light-speed, spaceship,* and *disaster.*

Data's positronic brain functioned with the speed of electrons (the same as that of light), so he was only constrained by the physical speed at which his eyes could scan—and they could scan, comprehend, and memorize at a rate far faster than human eyes.

In a very short time, he had scanned their Rosetta Stone, learned their language, and absorbed the history of the artifact and its creators.

They had called their world Yla, and themselves Ylans. They had been a peaceful people, given to gentle, benevolent pastimes and amusements. Their vocabulary contained no word equivalents for *war* or *fighting*. The closest they could come was *disagreement*. Art had been their abiding passion, and almost all of their populace practiced some form of it, no matter what they did as an actual career. Not all Ylans were skilled artists; it was recognized that talent varied from one to the other. But all efforts were truly valued.

The Ylans had existed as a unified, civilized society, in harmony with each other, for at least fifteen thousand years when their fate came upon them, in the form of a deadly burst of solar radiation from their previously benevolent sun. The radiation had killed nearly a quarter of their population outright, a tragedy terrible enough to envision. But over the years, it became clear that the radiation had had an even more deadly effect. The males—*all* the males—were rendered sterile.

It was a death sentence for their race, of course, and they soon realized it. They were a long-lived people, so many of them set out to try and solve their problem scientifically. Their history chronicled their efforts, which had all failed.

Centuries before their sun's betrayal, the Ylans had developed space travel—more as a curiosity than as a means to any end. They were not possessed of humanity's driving need to explore, and trade had not been a motivation, for they had never discovered any other intelligent species than themselves in their remote sector of the galaxy. They had never had or needed colonies. Population control had been one of the earliest problems they had mastered as a civilized people.

As the older Ylans began dying off, unreplaced, their younger population also plummeted. Suicide rates soared because the people could have no children, and they felt that they had no more reason to live.

It was at this juncture that several of the Ylan leaders had conceived the idea of the artifact. Its design and construction gave the remaining people a reason to go on, the chance to make one final, creative effort. The artifact had been a planetwide project, and to build it had meant that the Ylans had to revive half-forgotten technologies and engineering abilities. Slowly, over the remaining lifetime of their people, they had built, in space, a structure to house their planet's art treasures.

They had built the artifact as a memorial to themselves and as a gesture of galactic goodwill to any intelligent species that would come after them. They had built it and set it moving on a trajectory designed to take it slowly through the Orion Arm of the Milky Way.

As near as Data could figure, the artifact had been drifting for at least a half a million years.

Drifting . . . and trapping. And killing.

Data was very glad that the gentle Ylans would never know what they had unwittingly unleashed on the cosmos, or how many hideous deaths they had caused.

After a moment to digest what he had learned, Data tapped the "all's well" signal on his tricorder again and began scanning more of the records. Interesting . . . most interesting. The Ylans had possessed, as Wesley had surmised, most original ways of looking at the universe. Much of their scientific knowledge was completely different from anything Data had seen before. For example, stored aboard the artifact were seeds that, when planted in fertile soil according to the instructions left, would grow into living art forms. Data knew that many horticulturalists on Earth regarded gardening as a type of art, but this was something different—genetically engineered plants that were designed to grow into living sculptures, somewhat like a preprogrammed *bonsai,* the android thought.

Would the seeds still be fertile after more than five hundred thousand years? It hardly seemed possible, but Data found himself considering taking some of them over to the *Enterprise* and experimenting with them in one of the botany labs.

Realizing that he'd been aboard the artifact for more than an hour, the android began sorting even more rapidly through the records, scanning quickly for any reference by the Ylans to the energy field surrounding their creation.

Finally, he found it—and knew that, once again, Wesley Crusher had demonstrated his own particular brand of genius. The boy had said that he felt instinctively that the field surrounding the artifact had not been intended to be harmful.

Wesley was right. The tractor field effect was an unexpected by-product of the artifact's alien type of energy—it would have never reacted in this manner to ships engineered in the way Ylans had discovered to cross interstellar distances—which was, as Wesley had said, by going *around* space. But on ships engineered to enter and leave space warps, the energy field had behaved in the same manner as a tractor field.

The Ylans had designed the energy field surrounding the artifact to serve as a signpost, an invitation, "Come one, come all, to see our art gallery!" Basically, it was a form of advertising.

Data glanced through the references, scanning as rapidly as his android eyes would function, until he found the section he wanted. Then he went over to the farthest console and squatted down so he was on a level with the controls.

He touched a red disk inset into the top of the console, then, when the blue lights flashed, tapped them in a prescribed sequence. After a half-million years of steady and faithful operation, the machine's barely felt vibrations ceased, and its lights darkened.

The energy field shut down, and with it the destructive emotional emissions. The space Sargasso was no more. The *Enterprise* was free.

"I've got it," exclaimed Chief O'Brien excitedly. "The recall signal!"

"And I've got something else!" cried La Forge, who was keeping the transporter chief company while they waited for Data's return. "He turned off the energy field! The artifact isn't emitting anything anymore . . . so we can lower our shields!"

O'Brien's broad features relaxed. "Then we're free, thank God," he said softly.

Geordi's communicator signaled. The chief engineer tapped it. "La Forge here."

"I assume you are monitoring, Mister La Forge?" Picard's voice emerged.

"I sure am, Captain! He did it!"

"Yes, Mister La Forge, he certainly did." On Geordi's tactical schematic the ship's shields went down, one by one. "Has Commander Data signaled for recall?" Picard asked.

"Yes, sir. We're bringing him back now."

"Keep me informed about his status."

"Yes, sir."

"Picard out."

Geordi tapped his communicator. "Lieutenant Selar?"

"Selar here."

"We're bringing Data back."

"I am on my way."

O'Brien carefully dimmed the lights, then he operated the controls, and the characteristic sound of the transporter emerged. A dark form appeared in the beam, solidified . . .

Data appeared, swayed on the platform. "Data, are you okay?" Geordi said, starting toward him. His friend shrank back, away from him, arms up to cover his eyes. Noises emerged from the android's throat that bore no resemblance to any human language or sounds the engineer had ever heard.

"What's wrong with him?" O'Brien demanded. "It looks like he's scared."

"No, this isn't an emotional reaction," La Forge said, studying his android friend closely. "It appears to me as though he spent so much time over there aboard the artifact, that now he's having trouble making the switch from his alien-calibrated sensory input to his normal functioning modes."

"Why is he covering his eyes and ears?"

Data crouched farther away from the sound of human speech, and Geordi lowered his voice. "His audio and visual sensors are giving him contradictory input, which is disorienting and impeding the functioning of his positronic brain."

"Why didn't he just shut down the way he did before?" O'Brien asked, frowning worriedly.

"I'm not sure, but I suspect it's because he at least is

basically familiar with this environment, where he wasn't familiar with the environment aboard the artifact—at least the first time. But now he's spent enough time aboard the artifact that his brain has adjusted to coping with its environment." He sighed. "You see, to do this, Data had to divide his brain . . . in a manner of speaking. Now his alien-calibrated and his normal-calibrated sides are in conflict."

"So what do we do now?"

La Forge stared bleakly at the android. "I don't know. If I could shut him off, I could effect the switchover for him."

Slowly, he began to move forward. "Steady, Data," he said, as he would have soothed a strange dog. "Take it easy . . . it's Geordi. You're going to have to let me turn you off, so we can work at fixing you so you can function aboard the *Enterprise* again."

He took another step, and the android staggered back until he was crouched against the far wall, eyes wide and wild, those terrible coloratura and basso profundo and everything-in-between sounds still shrilling and booming from his throat. When Geordi stepped forward again, the android flailed at him, making pushing and striking motions in the air, growing ever more agitated.

"Oh, hell," La Forge muttered, and he cast a despairing glance at O'Brien. "He's stronger than a squad of Klingons. If he won't let me near enough to turn him off, there's no way I can force him!"

"Can you use a phaser to stun him?" O'Brien asked.

"He's an android, not a man. His positronic brain wouldn't be affected by a stun-force beam. And if I used a stronger setting, I might injure him seriously!"

Data shrank back farther, and Geordi laid a finger to his lips. "When we talk it seems to disorient him worse," he whispered.

O'Brien nodded and shut up.

Suddenly the door to the transporter room slid open, and Selar stepped through. She glanced at La Forge in the dim lighting, then from him to Data's crouching form. It was obvious that she'd quickly assessed the situation. She turned back to the humans, her eyebrow rising in a "What now?" inquiry.

Geordi shook his head and shrugged.

The chief engineer's communicator beeped, and everyone—most of all Data—jumped. "Mister La Forge, how is it going?" Picard asked.

Geordi tapped his communicator. "Not very well, sir," he whispered. "The altered portion of his mind seems to have taken over. We can't get near him. He's obviously extremely disoriented and defensive."

"Commander Riker and I will be down immediately."

While they waited for the captain, Selar, O'Brien, and La Forge stepped outside so they could discuss the situation in normal tones—after first locking the transporter against use.

"If we call in a squad of security guards . . . ," O'Brien began, only to have Geordi shake his head.

"Somebody would get hurt. Data's *strong,* I tell you! I've seen him force open a solid metal door, or pick up a boulder weighing five hundred kilos."

"They wouldn't have to restrain him for long," Selar said. "Just a second, until one of us could reach his off switch."

"It's too dangerous," La Forge maintained. "If only there was some drug or something . . . but Data wouldn't be affected by tranquilizers, would he?"

Now it was Selar's turn to shake her head.

"The only thing to do," Geordi decided, "is for both of us to beam back to the artifact together. Once he's not so disoriented, he'll recover, and I can turn him off over there, and both of us will beam right back."

"From what I have heard about conditions aboard the alien structure, that would present a serious risk to your sanity," Selar said.

"It's no fun over there, I agree, but I could hang on for the few seconds it would take. At least I think I could . . ." Geordi trailed off.

Footsteps approached, and the three officers looked up to see Commander Riker and Captain Picard approaching. La Forge quickly summarized the situation for them, including his suggestion of beaming over to the artifact.

"I've lost enough crew to that thing," Picard said grimly. "I won't take a chance on losing another." He frowned, thinking. "Where exactly is Commander Data's off switch?"

"On his left side, sir," Riker said. "Toward the small of his back."

Picard gestured at the door. "Open it, Chief O'Brien. I want to assess the situation for myself."

Riker stepped forward. "Sir, you're not planning to approach him, are you?"

Picard did not respond, only motioned to O'Brien. The transporter chief quickly released the lock, and the portal slid aside. Riker made a move as if to block the captain, then, as Picard shook his head warningly, with a "Don't argue with me, Number One" look in his eye, he reluctantly stepped aside.

The captain walked quietly into the room, then stopped a few steps past the threshold to stare at the crouching figure that was his android third-in-command. "Commander Data," he said quietly.

A soprano screech filled the room, and Data thrashed awkwardly, trying unsuccessfully to squirm away.

Picard took a step toward the android.

"Sir," whispered Riker urgently, "let me. The risk should be mine."

Picard ignored him. "Data," said the commanding officer quietly, "this is the captain. You know who I am."

The android rumbled in a warning tone and flailed his arms defensively. Picard took another step. "Sir," said Riker urgently, "don't you think it would be better to—"

"No, Number One, I don't," Picard interrupted, not turning his head. "Commander Data is inside there, even if his normal mind is not the dominant one at the moment. He will not hurt me, I know it. I trust him, and I trust Doctor Soong's programming. Data is incapable of harming a human being, no matter what his provocation."

"Doctor Soong programmed Lore, too, sir," Riker reminded the captain. "And Lore was only too willing to cause the deaths of all of us."

"Data is . . . Data, Commander. I trust him." He took another slow, easy step.

"Enough to stake your life, sir?" Riker whispered tensely. "Remember how strong he is."

"Data will not hurt me, Number One." Picard eased forward again. By now he'd nearly reached the transporter platform, where the keening, rumbling android still thrashed and jerked convulsively.

He continued to move forward, talking softly, soothingly. Data crouched lower, drawing into a ball, still flailing occasionally, but mostly seeming to withdraw. The sounds he made grew softer.

Geordi held his breath as the captain stepped slowly up onto the transporter platform, then across it. Data screeched and moved, making pushing motions with his hands, but he never touched the captain.

"Steady now, Data," Picard whispered as he leaned over, his hand going out to brush past the android's side.

A second later, Data slumped bonelessly.

La Forge let out his breath in a long sigh of relief.

An hour later, the chief engineer turned to Beverly Crusher within the crowded sickbay. "Tell Selar that I'm ready if she is."

Moments later, the two completed their final systems checks. Geordi tapped his communicator. "La Forge here. You asked me to let you know when we were ready to make the attempt, Captain."

"I am on my way," replied the captain.

By the time Picard and Riker arrived, accompanied by Wesley Crusher, Geordi's hands were sweating. Gazing down at his friend's slack features, he prayed silently that soon they would be animated again with that air of innocent wonder that was uniquely Data's. *If anything goes wrong,* he silently promised his friend, *I swear to you that I'll see that your book gets published, if it takes me two years' pay to convince somebody to do it, Data. But I sure hope that won't be necessary.*

Picard nodded at him. "Go ahead, Mister La Forge."

Behind his back, Geordi crossed the fingers of his left hand, and inside his boots he crossed his toes. Then, with a right hand that shook slightly no matter how he tried to steady it, he reached over and tapped the switch.

Data's golden eyes flew open. Slowly he looked around him at the circle of faces: Doctor Crusher, Selar, Riker, Picard, Wesley, and finally Geordi himself. "Geordi," he said distinctly, "you were right. It was beautiful."

"Data!" La Forge exclaimed jubilantly. He threw an

arm around Wesley Crusher's shoulders and hugged the younger man, who was grinning like a fool. After a few moments of muted but sincere celebration (mindful of the crowded sickbay), the group quieted down as Data sat up, then swung his legs off the stretcher and stood up, looking quite his old self.

Slowly, formally, Jean-Luc Picard put both hands on the android officer's shoulders. "Data," he said, "there is an old saying on Earth, 'Greater love hath no man than he give up his life for his friends.' It seems to me that a willingness to give up one's life counts just as much as the actual sacrifice. We are truly in your debt."

"But, Captain," Data protested, "I am not a man, I am an android."

"You are yourself, Data, unique," Picard corrected firmly. "And we are all very lucky to have you as a friend."

"You can say that again, Captain," Geordi said, grinning.

Chapter Twelve

"THALA?"

The Andorian girl jerked awake, wondering who had called her. After a moment, the voice spoke again. "Thala, are you there?" With a feeling of relief, she recognized the voice and realized it was coming from her cabin intercom.

Hastily she sprang out of bed and activated her computer link. "Wesley, I'm here."

"Where were you?"

"I was asleep, but it's all right. What's going on?"

"You asked me to let you know when we were getting ready to dock. We'll be docking at Starbase 127 in about ten minutes."

The child felt a mixture of emotions wash over her—excitement, sadness, apprehension, determination. "Oh," she said. "Thank you for remembering, Wesley. I really appreciate it."

"No problem," he replied cheerfully. "I'll see you later."

"Uh . . . yeah. Thanks again."

So, the moment she had dreaded for so long had

come. It was time to leave the *Enterprise* forever. Thala swallowed hard. It had been a long journey back from the artifact, but now it was ending, and her own journey would begin.

Following Commander Data's successful attempt to turn off the force field that had held the starship captive, the *Enterprise* had used its phasers to destroy the *PaKathen*, in accordance with the Klingon High Command's request. Then, with the *Marco Polo* in tow, the ship had headed back for Thonolan Four to deliver the overdue seed grain to the Andorian colony.

Thala had been in a quiet state of panic the entire time they orbited the Andorian colony, for fear the authorities there would change their minds and decide to accept her, but they evidently had not.

In the past days, the child had stayed quietly in her quarters. Because of the overcrowded conditions in sickbay, Selar had been too busy to visit, but the Vulcan had managed a few moments each day to call and ask after her young friend. Yesterday, the doctor had asked Thala to join her for dinner, saying that she had something important to discuss.

I'm sorry, Selar, Thala thought sadly. *I wish I could leave you a message apologizing for missing dinner, but I can't afford to leave any clues behind.* Moving over to the Andorian statue, she quickly twisted it open, then removed the jewelry. For a moment, she wished that she could take the statue with her, but it was too heavy, and she couldn't afford to burden herself with extra weight. She might have to move fast today.

Quickly, the Andorian girl moved around her cabin, forcing herself to eat something (she had no idea how long it would be before the opportunity came again), taking a sonic shower, then laying out her clothing. Before dressing, she used a piece of surgical pseudo-skin she'd purloined from sickbay to fasten the antennae webs to her ribcage. Then she pulled on several layers of clothing before slipping on her best sensory mesh. She had no way to pack anything, it would make her look suspicious.

Last of all, she wadded a cloak of Altairian spider silk into one of her father's belt pouches, and, in the small space that remained, she stuffed a meager lunch. The spider silk's insulating properties would keep her body heat from registering on the ship's sensing devices.

When she checked her chrono, Thala discovered that the entire process had taken less than an hour. She sighed. It would take far more time than that for the starship's medical personnel to supervise the transport of all the patients to the starbase's medical facility. She sat down tensely to wait.

Fortunately, there weren't as many patients as Selar and Beverly Crusher had worried there might be. Once the artifact's malign field had been turned off, many of the depression and withdrawal cases had begun to recover spontaneously.

But Counselor Troi still had her hands full, counseling them, since the artifact-inspired dreams had awakened issues and events many would have preferred to have kept buried. However, lately she had seemed encouraged by her patients' progress. Thala had overheard her saying to Beverly Crusher that there were only one or two cases that still had her concerned about their full recovery.

Many of the patients being transferred to the starbase's medical facility were scheduled for trans-shipment to the Vulcan Science Academy, where the telepathic healers could gently help them to repair their damaged psyches.

Finally, after waiting a full two hours since the *Enterprise* had docked, Thala rose from her seat, took one last "look" around her home, then left the cabin.

She walked out into the corridor and headed left, toward the nearest turbolift, her destination the transporter room.

As she went, she said a silent farewell to all that she had known. She refused to let herself think of Selar. Her steps were quick and unhesitating, and she did not look back.

"Counselor, are you busy?"

Deanna Troi sat at her favorite table in Ten-Forward, eating one of Guinan's exquisite hot fudge sundaes lavishly sprinkled with chocolate chips. She swallowed thickly and looked up at the diffident hail. "Oh, Data!" she exclaimed. "No, I'm just indulging one of my favorite vices. Sit down, won't you?"

"Thank you," the android said, and did so. Troi noticed that he was carrying a box with him. She delicately licked chocolate from the corners of her mouth, then patted her lips with a napkin. "How are you?" she asked. "Entirely recovered from having your circuitry recalibrated?"

"I am completely recovered," Data assured her. "And you, Counselor?"

"Data, we're relaxing here. Call me Deanna, please." She smiled warmly at him. "I am also fine, thank you. At the moment, I am rewarding myself for all the hard work on the trip back. My patients are all recovering nicely." She took a final bite of the sundae, let the exquisite taste fill her mouth, then swallowed and sighed. "Wonderful stuff, chocolate. Poetry for the palate, as well as the soul."

Data's golden eyes gleamed. "Speaking of literary matters, Deanna . . . ," he said, and he placed the box on the table beside him.

She glanced at it curiously. "What have you got there?"

The android hesitated, then said, "I would like your

225

honest opinion on a manuscript I have written. Would you please read this scene and tell me what you think?"

"A manuscript?" She stared at him in surprise. "You mean that you've written a *book?*"

"Yes. A novel. It is a romantic adventure set in the earliest days of space travel, about the relationship between one of the first starship captains and the woman he loves." He paused, then continued, in a rush, "I have asked the opinion of several people aboard the ship, but Doctor Crusher suggested that I get an additional woman's opinion, so I thought of you."

The counselor shrugged. "Okay, I'll read it, but I want you to know that one of my best friends back on Betazed is a well-known author. Kathella used to ask me to read her stories, because she valued the fact that I am a tough critic. She told me once that her books would not have been half as well written if I hadn't given her astute literary criticism and advice."

"That is what I want," Data said firmly. "Here is the same scene I had Doctor Crusher read, except that I have rewritten it since she perused it." He handed over a small sheaf of pages.

Deanna settled herself in her seat, licked the last traces of chocolate off her lower lip, and read:

Scarcely had Margaret returned to the botanical garden to resume her interrupted stroll before she caught sight of Mr. Rodriguez, who was walking toward her with a most singular purpose etched across every feature. In the Earthlight streaming down from the dome overhead she could see his dark head and his piercing eyes fix on her with such a steadfast gaze that she colored and the civil greeting she had intended to offer him died unspoken on her lips. Striding directly up to her, he fixed his remarkable gaze upon her, and began.

"My dear Lady Margaret, since I must embark on the morrow on a voyage of perilous and uncertain conclusion, I am driven at last to confess my deepest regard for you. I admire you, but that is but the half of it." Seizing her unwilling hand in both his own, he continued in a most agitated manner, "To be frank, my dearest Lady Margaret, I love you!"

Margaret's confusion and utter astonishment at hearing such sentiments from the lips of the proud, high-born Rodriguez can easily be imagined; she stared at him in silence, wondering if he had lost his wits—or she hers.

As she struggled to summon words, he dropped to his knees before her on the path of the botanical garden, and, with a sudden movement, pressed her hand to his lips, not once, but several times, groaning ardently all the while, "I love you, I love you!"

Margaret in vain attempted to regain possession of her hand; she struggled to the utmost to address him with composure. "Pray relinquish my hand, Mister Rodriguez," she cried, in an agony of embarrassment lest some solitary stroller invade their privacy at such a moment. "I must tell you that I had not known you for a fortnight before I realized that you were quite the sort of man I had been looking for all my life. If only our stations in life were more comparable! If only—"

Unable to keep a straight face any longer, Deanna Troi stopped reading and dissolved into a fit of giggles. "Oh, Data, this is hilarious!"

The android's expression was one of pleased satisfaction. "I am relieved that you like it. I worked very hard to make the dialogue sophisticated and witty."

"I adore it!" She giggled, turning over another page. "This is one of the best-done parodies of Jane Austen —or is it Charlotte Brontë?—that I've read recently! It's hysterically funny!"

Data's pale features suddenly froze. "It is not intended," he said slowly, "as a parody."

Deanna immediately stopped laughing. "It's not?"

"No."

"Oh, Data . . ." She swallowed. "I'm sorry. I thought you'd intended to parody that old-fashioned style in order to be funny."

"I was attempting to write in a more sophisticated, mannered style, in emulation of Miss Austen's. But this novel is intended, basically, as a serious work." He gazed at her, his yellow eyes very intent. "As a serious work, what is your honest opinion of what I have written, Deanna?"

Troi took a deep breath. "My honest opinion is that you're never going to get anywhere as a writer until you find your own voice, Data. It's a well-known fact that writers write best when they write what they know. That doesn't preclude the use of imagination, by any means—but it means that a person who has no children and detests them shouldn't try to write for them." She took a deep breath. "And it means that a person who has never been in love is not well advised to attempt an intense, passionate love story."

"So you do not believe that my story is good."

She shook her head, determined to give the android the honest opinion he'd requested. "No, Data, I don't."

He slowly picked up the pages and placed them back in the box. "I believe, upon reflection, that your opinion was shared by all of my other critics . . . but they were not as honest as you were in expressing themselves. I would like to thank you, Deanna. I needed to hear what you have just told me."

She put out a hand toward him, feeling as though she'd just committed a minor murder of some sort. "Data, I can help you try and improve," she offered.

"Thank you, Deanna," he replied gravely. "I will take your offer under consideration."

He nodded at her, rose, then walked out of the lounge. Troi stared glumly at her dish, then beckoned to Guinan. "I'll have another of these," she said to the hostess, indicating the melting remains of the sundae. "Now *I'm* depressed."

The dark-skinned woman nodded. "I heard the whole thing. But you were right to tell him, Deanna."

"You think so?"

"I know so. It's like they say, the truth always hurts—but, except in the cases of fashions and hairstyles, honesty is the best policy."

"Thanks, Guinan," Troi said, with a warm smile at the hostess. "Sometimes even the counselor needs a little counsel. Especially if it's as wise as yours."

The hostess picked up the dish and started away. "Another sundae, coming right up."

Selar did not often come to Ten-Forward alone, but after overseeing the transfer of all those patients, she felt the need for a quiet moment to reflect. Besides, she had forgotten to eat today, and she was hungry.

Entering through the double wood doors, she walked into the lounge and sat down at the bar. Guinan gave her a welcoming smile and asked, "What will it be, Lieutenant?"

Selar considered for a moment. "Does your selection include *plomeek* soup?"

"The best you'll find outside of Vulcan," the hostess promised. "Coming right up."

When the soup arrived, Selar's nostrils twitched at the aroma, and her stomach tightened hungrily. She began eating, pausing only when the bowl was empty.

Without being asked, Guinan pushed a bowl of celery sticks and carrots with a tofu dip across the bar, and a glass of sparkling water. "Rough mission," the hostess said, her dark eyes observant, missing nothing.

Selar dipped a carrot into the seasoned dip and took a bite. She nodded silent agreement as she chewed. Then, when she had swallowed, she said, half surprised at herself for feeling the urge to confide in the hostess, "It may be my last mission with the *Enterprise,* Guinan."

The dark-skinned woman raised one nearly hairless eyebrow. "Really? Where are you going? Have you been transferred?"

"Not precisely. Starfleet has placed me on an indefinite leave of absence so that I may take the offer of a position with the Vulcan Science Academy," the doctor said. "I will be head of bioelectronic research."

Guinan looked suitably impressed. "When will you be leaving?"

"When the *Enterprise* departs tomorrow, I will not be on her," the lieutenant said. "I will remain at the starbase to care for the patients, and when some of them are transshipped to Vulcan next week, I will accompany them there."

"Oh, you're really short-timing it, aren't you?"

Selar nodded.

"I guess after this last mission, it'll be a relief to have peace and quiet to do research," the hostess said, polishing the glowing bar with a cloth. "In other words, you won't miss us much."

"I will miss the *Enterprise,*" Selar admitted. "But at least the person I will miss most will be on the same world with me, so I will be able to visit her occasionally."

"Who is that?"

"Thala, the little Andorian girl who lost her father

recently." Selar took a celery stick, dipped it slowly and thoroughly into the tofu, then began to munch.

"I know Thala. You've brought her in here several times, and so has Wesley. So she's going to Vulcan? With you?"

"Not exactly. I will be traveling aboard a Starfleet medical ship. But I have purchased a ticket for Thala aboard a passenger liner that is leaving at almost the same time as the *Lancet*, my ship. We will arrive on Vulcan within a day of each other."

"What will happen to Thala then?"

"I intend to see that she is placed in an excellent medical and teaching facility, so she can receive a proper education and the best treatment for her blindness. I believe that ultimately she will be able to receive prosthetic eyes that will enable her to do anything she wishes in life. Developing prosthetics for Andorians will be one of my first priorities."

"That's commendable of you," Guinan said, beginning to polish again. Selar was about to mention to the other that she had already done that section of the bar when the hostess observed blandly, "It's nice that the little girl will be in a really good institution, too . . . but I'm not sure that any institution can take the place of a real home."

"I know that," Selar said, uncomfortably aware that the alien woman had hit upon a thought that had been simmering quietly in the back of her own mind for days now. "But the child is an orphan . . ."

Guinan gave the Vulcan a knowing, sideways glance. "There's no law says she has to *stay* an orphan."

Selar had raised her glass to her lips. Now, slowly, she put it down without drinking. "What do you mean?"

"She could be adopted," the hostess said. "If someone cared enough about her."

"I doubt that many Vulcan couples would wish to adopt a child of such a passionate, emotional people as the Andorians," Selar said.

"Probably not," Guinan admitted. "But it doesn't necessarily take a mother *and* a father to make a family. Many people are highly successful single parents, you know." She gave the Vulcan another of those knowing glances. "Thala would be better off with one parent than with none, don't you think? I mean"— she smiled—"that seems only logical to me."

Selar raised her glass and took a sip, her mind racing. "You are suggesting that *I* should adopt Thala?"

Guinan shrugged. "Why not?"

The doctor stared at the hostess for nearly a minute in silence. "Why not, indeed?" she said finally. "There is a certain elegant logic to your suggested solution."

Guinan smiled enigmatically. "There is, isn't there?"

"If I were to adopt Thala, I could oversee her medical care and schooling myself. I would not have to trust her to the competence of others. I could ensure that she lacked for nothing."

"Yes, you could," agreed Guinan quietly. "And from an emotional standpoint, you're used to Thala, so you'd be able to get along with her better than other Vulcans." She gave the doctor a knowing look. "Who knows? You might even come to . . . enjoy her company."

"I already do," Selar said flatly. "Thala's happiness and welfare are very important to me."

"Does she like you as much as you like her?"

"Yes, I believe she does."

Guinan spread both hands in a "There you have it" gesture. "Well, what more could you ask for?"

Selar's eyebrow rose, and her mouth quirked. "Your logic is impeccable, Guinan." Resolutely, the doctor tapped her communicator. "Selar here," she said. "Doctor Crusher, I have decided to—"

Beverly Crusher's anxious voice interrupted her. "Selar, I was just about to call you! Thala has run away!"

Selar forced calmness. "What happened? Where was she last seen?"

"She talked La Forge into taking her over to the starbase, and then, when he turned his head for a moment, she must have slipped away. He looked and shouted, but he couldn't see her. She'd completely disappeared."

"Kidnapped?"

"No. Geordi says it had to be deliberate on her part. They were crossing through the park, and there wasn't another soul around, because the starbase is currently on its night cycle. When he couldn't find her after a minute or so, he notified the starbase's security people, and they threw up a sensor net around the park, but so far nothing."

"Then the logical conclusion is that the child is still in the park."

"Yes, but where could she be? Geordi scanned for her with his VISOR, but no luck. Even if she were hidden from normal vision, he should have been able to pick her up on infrared."

"Do not forget that Thala is also blind. If any child could think of a way to escape La Forge's unique vision, Thala could."

"So you also think that she's run away and is hiding out? Why would she do such a thing? Some kind of prank?"

The Vulcan remembered the little girl's study of the starbase layout. "It was no prank, but an intentional effort to escape from the *Enterprise,* I am certain," she said. "Now that I think of it, I believe that Thala has been planning this for some time."

"We'll have to go look for her. I'll call *Enterprise* security."

"Let me try first, alone," the Vulcan requested. "I have something I want to say to Thala. I have decided to adopt her . . . if she wishes me to."

"Oh, Selar, that would be wonderful!" Crusher's voice was warm with enthusiasm. "Of course she will. She's very fond of you!"

"I believe that it would be better to ask her in private. So let me try to find her myself first. I will call you within thirty minutes."

"Okay. I'll be standing by."

"Selar out."

The Vulcan rose from her seat and gave Guinan a long look. "Thank you," she said. "For helping me arrive at the only logical solution."

Guinan smiled. "Where will you look?"

"Obviously, I will start with the park. If I cannot find her there, I will continue until I do find her."

The hostess nodded. "Good luck."

Thala crouched beneath the Altairian spider-silk cloak, huddled into a tiny space beneath the huge roots of a large *flinan* tree from Deneb Four. The *flinan*'s root structure left small, cavelike openings beneath them, something that most people did not know but Thev had once shown her during a shore leave visit. With the cloak shielding her thermal readings, she was virtually undetectable, except by the most sophisticated of sensing devices.

With a sigh, she wriggled a little, trying to get comfortable, and checked the chrono built into her sensory net. Only a little more than an hour had passed since she had slipped away from Geordi. She'd hated to do that; La Forge was her friend, and she had felt terrible hearing the worry in his voice as he'd called, searching for her. But her resolution had stayed firm, and she'd stayed hidden.

She wondered whether the people from the *Enterprise* would bother to look for her. They might; she'd have to be prepared to move in case they did. Summoning to mind the layout of the starbase, she pinpointed her closest alternative hiding place, in a storage room of a nearby computer center.

How long would the *Enterprise* stay docked? How long before she'd be able to move about freely, visit the jewelry stores to see which one would give her the best price? She'd been afraid to ask Wesley how long they were supposed to remain at Starbase 127. She hadn't wanted to seem too curious.

Suddenly her blood seemed to congeal in her veins. A familiar voice was calling her name. "Thala! Thala! *Thala,* where are you?"

Selar. The child clamped her hands over her ears, not wanting to hear the Vulcan doctor's voice. She had to get away, she just had to! She couldn't let herself be swayed from her purpose. If she gave in, Thala knew, she'd end up on one of the colony worlds as a useless burden or a breeding slave in a hive harem. That wasn't going to happen to her!

Cautiously, she took her fingers out of her ears, listening. "Thala!" Selar was shouting, louder and closer than ever. "Thala, this park is only a tenth of a kilometer wide, so I know that, with your Andorian hearing, you can hear me! Listen well, and know that I am telling the truth. I swear it on my honor as a Vulcan . . . you will *not* be sent back to any Andorian world."

Thala's mouth dropped open in wonder as she listened to her Vulcan friend shouting a personal message in a public park at the top of her lungs. Even if it was the middle of the "night" here, there was a good chance that she'd be overheard. And, at the moment, the normally imperturbable Selar sounded anything but calm and logical.

"Thala, I am asking you to come with me back to Vulcan. I wish for us to be together." Selar cried. "Logically, it is the only thing to do." She coughed, then resumed, her voice growing raspy, "Thala, can you hear me? Please come out! I am becoming distinctly hoarse from shouting."

With a gasp, the child flung off the cloak and scrambled up out of her hiding place. Scarcely noticing the readings from her sensory net in her excitement, she darted around the trunk, toward the Vulcan officer's voice. "Selar!" she shouted.

As she dashed forward, her toe caught on the end of the tree's root, and she tripped and fell hard, twisting her ankle. The child hardly felt the pain. Her mind was racing. *Is Selar telling the truth?* she wondered incredulously. *Vulcans don't lie, so she must be!*

"Selar!" she shouted, and scrambled up. "Selar?"

She heard running footsteps, perceived a fast-moving blur from her sensory net, then hands grabbed her shoulders, held her hard. "Thala!"

"Did you mean it?" the child gasped. "Did you mean it? That I can come to Vulcan with you?"

"Certainly I meant it," Selar said, kneeling before her and also sounding breathless. "We will go home together. Thala, if you would like it, I want to adopt you. I want you to be my daughter."

The Andorian girl could only gape at her friend. Finally, dumbly, she nodded then managed to whisper, "That would be wonderful!"

"Good, that is settled," the doctor said, and she got up. "Come, we must go back to the *Enterprise.* Everyone is worried about you."

"They are?" Thala tried a halting step, and she winced as her wrenched ankle hurt her.

"What is it?" the Vulcan demanded, kneeling back down, her expert fingers probing gently at the child's injury.

"I twisted my ankle," Thala said, trying to rest her weight on it. The pain was ebbing gradually. "It's all right."

Strong hands clamped onto her sides, and she was picked up, clasped, as though she were a much younger child. "Put your arms around my neck," Selar directed.

"I can walk," Thala said, obeying nevertheless. It felt so good to be held—almost as good as it felt to know that she would now have a real home!

"I would prefer to carry you," Selar said, striding forward. "Logically, it is the fastest, most efficient way to reach our destination."

Thala gave a happy sigh. "I guess I'll be doing everything very logically from now on."

"That," said Selar firmly, "constitutes a most logical deduction."

"What shall I call you now?" the child asked timidly. "Will I really be your daughter?"

"You will," Selar said. "And you may call me whatever you would find most comfortable."

"I'll think about it," Thala promised.

Geordi La Forge was dreaming about the artifact, seeing in the eyes of his memory the beauty of its walls, when his intercom sounded, jerking him out of sleep. With a muttered imprecation, the chief engineer rolled out of bed and called aloud, "La Forge here."

"Geordi," said Data's voice, "I would like you to assist me with a personal task. Can you come to my quarters?"

La Forge swallowed a yawn. "Sure, Data. I'll be right there."

Bracing himself, he reached over and picked up his VISOR, slid it into place, felt the familiar ache bite into his temples. He sighed. *Dammit, I wish I didn't have to put up with this pain . . .*

The images in his dream flooded back to him then, and he smiled as he thought of the beauty of the artifact. Geordi ran a caressing finger along the edge of his VISOR. *If it weren't for this—and my ability to use it correctly—all of that beauty might have been lost forever,* he thought. A slow, faint smile touched his mouth. "Guess it all kind of evens out, doesn't it?" he muttered aloud. "Maybe that old Vulcan proverb about treasuring the differences as well as the similarities is right . . ."

He thought of Data, waiting for him, then began to hurry. Whistling cheerfully, he dressed, then made his way down to Data's quarters. There he found the android arranging pages into two neat stacks. "Can you carry one of these, Geordi?" he asked.

"I could always get a floater from the loading dock," La Forge said, eyeing the stack dubiously.

"No," said Data firmly. "That will not be necessary."

"Okay," Geordi agreed, recognizing that this was not an issue open to discussion. He scooped up one of the stacks without further argument.

"Where're we going?" he asked as they walked down the corridor, each juggling a massive pile of manuscript.

"You will see," said Data enigmatically.

They wound up in the transporter room. Data waved O'Brien aside, then the android laid his stack on the transporter platform and motioned La Forge to do likewise. "But, Data, this is your *book,*" the chief engineer started to protest, but his friend determinedly shook his head.

"No, Geordi," he said quietly. "This is something I must do."

When the piles of manuscript were deposited on the platform, the android adjusted the controls to wide-beam dispersal, then pressed the switch.

All the various incarnations of the android's novel shimmered, then vanished.

La Forge scratched his head, baffled. "What the hell did you do *that* for, Data?" he asked finally.

"Because it was poor," the android said quietly. "Worse than poor, it was *bad.* Counselor Troi finally told me the truth, which is that writers must write what they know in order to write well. I am not human, therefore I have no business trying to write from a human point of view."

"Data . . ." La Forge felt extremely awkward, wanting to comfort, but not knowing how. "God, I'm sorry. Maybe you could try writing what you know."

"I thought of that," Data said, and he held out a data cassette. "But I discovered that it has already been done."

He handed the cassette to La Forge, who read the label with a sinking heart: *I, Robot.*

"I wish there was something I could say," La Forge said miserably. "Dammit, Data, you're *not* a robot."

"But I am not human, either," Data said. "And it is time to stop pretending."

"I'm sorry," La Forge muttered. "What you just did took guts. Maybe we should have talked it over before you just . . . vaporized . . . all that work."

"I appreciate your concern, Geordi," Data said, his expression impassive, "but it was my decision to make."

La Forge shrugged. "You're right, it was your decision. I know it was a hard one."

The two friends left the transporter room and the

obviously puzzled Chief O'Brien, then headed down the corridor. "Want to go down to Ten-Forward?" Geordi asked hopefully.

"All right," Data said, without enthusiasm.

When they reached the lounge, a familiar voice reached them. "Data! Just the person I wanted to speak to!"

The officers made their way across the nearly empty room to join Picard and Riker, who were, since the *Enterprise* was safely docked, enjoying a rare drink together. "Sit down, join us," the captain said jovially. Picard was obviously in an excellent mood.

After a hesitant glance at Data, La Forge took the indicated seat. "Hello, Captain," he said. "Hello, Commander."

Both senior officers returned the greeting.

Beside La Forge, Data paused for a moment, as though he were considering declining the invitation. Guinan materialized as if by magic and placed drinks before the newcomers. Seemingly decided by the presence of the drink waiting for him, the android sat, too, and nodded politely to his superior officers. "You said you wanted to see me, Captain?" he asked.

"Yes indeed, Mister Data!" Picard smiled, a rare, face-lighting grin. "I've just been talking to Professor Jonas, the head of the Federation archeological team on Castor Three, and he was almost incoherent with excitement after reading our report on the artifact, particularly your report on the Ylans and their art forms."

Data nodded silently.

"He asked me if he could borrow you for the next couple of weeks to assist the preliminary archeological team they're dispatching to study the Ylans and the artifact. He says that the artifact represents the most valuable archeological find of this century!"

240

Riker whistled softly with admiration. "That's really something, Captain. There have been a lot of significant discoveries made in the last fifty years."

"Ah, but the artifact . . . Professor Jonas believes that the artifact will top them all by the time it has been thoroughly studied."

"This Professor Jonas . . . he was impressed by my report?" Data asked slowly. La Forge was relieved to see the android's expression brighten a little.

"He most certainly was! He says that you could make a unique contribution to the expedition if you will consent to join them during their preliminary investigation."

"I have been working on my programming, smoothing the transition from old Data to new Data, so that the transition will be completely under my volitional control," Data said thoughtfully. He brightened still further. "How do you think I would look in a pith helmet?"

"I think it would give you an air of rakish distinction," Picard said, smiling gently. "Does that mean I should request Starfleet Command to place you on detached duty for the next few weeks?"

The android nodded. "Yes, Captain, I believe I would like that."

La Forge sighed. "I was just dreaming of those murals aboard the artifact. It's a pity you and Commander Riker couldn't have seen them, Captain."

"I regret that, Mister La Forge," Picard said. "I have a great deal of interest in art. I've even, from time to time, dabbled a bit with painting myself." He glanced at Data and smiled wryly.

"If only there were a way that the Ylans' art—their whole history, images, music, literature, everything—could be translated into terms that human minds could comprehend," Geordi mused. "Then everyone could know their story, the way they intended when they set out to create the artifact."

"I'm afraid that's impossible," Riker said regretfully. "No one can see or hear their art without going crazy."

"*I* can," Data corrected solemnly.

"That's true, you can," Riker conceded.

There was a long silence. Geordi felt a slow smile start across his face, and he turned to Data, who was looking extremely thoughtful. "Data!" he said urgently. "This is it! This is your chance! Something *only* you can do—something only you can *know.* Your chance to give a gift of great art to the universe!"

"I was just thinking the same thing," Data said. His strange eyes were bright with curiosity and excitement. "It would be a truly unique gift, would it not?"

"Something no one else could give," Geordi said earnestly. "Truly unique."

"I could record the entire structure and the material stored in its computer banks, then work on it when I am off duty," the android said thoughtfully, then added, "The project would take years."

"The greatest art, the greatest literature, often does," the captain pointed out. He smiled. "I can't think of a bigger challenge. The story of an entire species, from beginning to end—a project of heroic proportion. Are you going to tackle it, Commander?"

Data nodded. His impassive features filled with a new resolve. "I will do it," he said, and the simple declaration took on the ring of a solemn oath.

Jean-Luc Picard raised his glass, and La Forge and Riker quickly followed suit. "A toast," the captain said. "To Data and his new venture!"

Data's golden eyes were bright as the three officers solemnly drained their glasses together in a formal salute. Their moving images were silhouetted against the windows in Ten-Forward, surrounding android and humans alike with the unwinking glory of the distant stars.

STAR TREK®
PRIME
DIRECTIVE

JUDITH AND GARFIELD
REEVES-STEVENS

Starfleet's highest law has been broken. Its most honored captain is in disgrace, its most celebrated starship in pieces, and the crew of that ship scattered among the thousand worlds of the Federation . . .

Thus begins *PRIME DIRECTIVE,* an epic tale of the STAR TREK universe. Following in the tradition of *SPOCK'S WORLD* and *THE LOST YEARS,* both month-long *New York Times* bestsellers, Garfield and Judith Reeves-Stevens have crafted a thrilling tale of mystery and wonder, a novel that takes the STAR TREK characters from the depths of despair into an electrifying new adventure that spans the galaxy.

"YOU HAVE BROKEN OUR MOST SACRED COMMANDMENT, JAMES T. KIRK—AND IN DOING SO, DESTROYED A WORLD . . ."

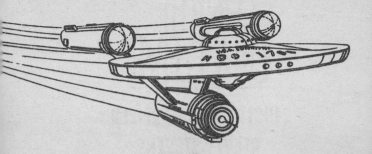

A mission gone horribly wrong—the *Enterprise* is nearly destroyed as an entire planet is ravaged by nuclear annihilation. Captain James T. Kirk is blamed and drummed out of Starfleet for breaking the Federation's highest law: the Prime Directive. Kirk and his crew must then risk their freedom and their lives in a confrontation that will either clear their names or lead to the loss of a thousand worlds.

In the third blockbuster Pocket Books STAR TREK hardcover, Judith and Garfield Reeves-Stevens have created the biggest, most exciting STAR TREK novel yet . . .

Watch for a Pocket Books September 1990 Hardcover Release:

PRIME DIRECTIVE